"Your fiancé's getting rich the quick and easy way."

Logan's jaw tightened. "A few forged checks, and a little matter of a thousand sheep trucked off at night and later sold up-country." The gravelly tones were low and intimidating. "There won't be any charges laid, though. Your dad's too wrapped up in his only daughter to let that happen."

Fleur had turned very pale. She pushed away the shadow of doubt his words evoked and sprang to Bart's defense. "There's been some awful mistake. Bart wouldn't—he couldn't— you've made it all up!"

"Why would I do that?" His voice hardened. "Unlike Bart, I have no need to pretend a romantic interest in the boss's daughter!"

These books may be available at your local bookseller.

Don't miss any of our special offers. Write to us at the following address for information on our newest releases.

Harlequin Reader Service
P.O. Box 52040, Phoenix, AZ 85072-2040
Canadian address: P.O. Box 2800, Postal Station A,
5170 Yonge St., Willowdale, Ont. M2N 6J3

Southern Sunshine

Gloria Bevan

Harlequin Books

TORONTO • NEW YORK • LONDON
AMSTERDAM • PARIS • SYDNEY • HAMBURG
STOCKHOLM • ATHENS • TOKYO • MILAN

Original hardcover edition published in 1985
by Mills & Boon Limited

ISBN 0-373-02713-3

Harlequin Romance first edition September 1985

CHAPTER ONE

FLEUR first saw him as she stepped down from the plane at the country airport. Tall, lithe, broad-shouldered, how could she help but notice him? During the year spent away from her own country she had forgotten the special breed of the young New Zealand sheep farmer. With that deep mahogany tan, he just *had* to be a sheep farmer! At that moment his glance meshed with hers and for a dizzying moment she had a heady awareness of the dark-haired man with the strong face and at the same time, the oddest impression that somehow the clear warm sunshine had suddenly become a-dazzle. She wrenched her glance aside. Ridiculous to be feeling this way about a stranger, even such an attractive one!

Anyway, she reminded herself as she went down the steps from the plane, she should be looking to see Bart. He was the man she was in love with. Now that she had returned after completing her stint as a World Vision nurse in one of Thailand's most crowded refugee camps, there would be nothing to stand in the way of their marriage.

Together with groups of passengers from the plane she moved along the path leading to the sunny reception lounge where friends and relatives waited to greet the new arrivals at Wanganui. A fresh breeze blowing from the green paddocks surrounding the airport tugged at Fleur's topknot and whipped coppery strands across her eyes. She brushed them aside and went on thinking about Bart, her excited gaze raking the groups of people lining the barrier. Even though she carefully avoided letting her gaze linger on the face of the tall man standing alone at the barrier, she was nevertheless disconcertingly aware of his silent scrutiny, but she willed herself to think only of Barton. Even though she couldn't see him standing among the waiting groups of casually dressed people she knew he would be here at any moment to welcome her. Nothing, but nothing would prevent his getting here today, not after those long months of separation. He would be over the moon with delight at seeing her again—his ardent love letters left her no doubt on that score. He couldn't wait for their reunion, he had written, he was marking off each passing day on the calendar, living for her return.

And yet . . . a shiver of apprehension feathered down her spine. What could have happened to delay him? The plane had arrived at its destination bang on time and she had written letting him know the day of her arrival here and the flight number of the plane she would take following her arrival at Auckland's International Airport. She quelled suddenly rising panic. Foolish to let herself get in a state because Bart wasn't yet here. He'd be a little late maybe, but what of it? As manager of her father's vast acreage at Te Haruru station he could have a hundred emergencies to delay his arrival at the airport. Didn't she know it? He'd be along at any minute now, she assured herself, of course he would. She had only to wait and pretty soon he'd be hurrying towards her, begging her forgiveness for his delay in arrival, talking fast and excitedly in his emotional way, his thin dark face alight with love for her.

She had reached the barrier now and her anxious gaze scanned the sea of faces, her glance sliding over the grim unsmiling face of the tall stranger. For some inexplicable reason he seemed to have the power to affect her. Could it be the sardonic twist of well-cut lips or the hard compelling expression in hazel eyes veiled by thick dark lashes? Thank heaven, the thought ran through her mind, that I'm not the passenger he's waiting for! She brought her thoughts up with a jerk. It's Barton I'm looking for, and there won't be the slightest doubt about *his* welcome for me!

She hurried into the lounge, threading her way through laughing, chattering groups, and all the time the niggle of apprehension deepened. 'Excuse me! Excuse me, please!' As she pushed her way through the crowd, appreciative glances followed the girl with the sweet, square-jawed face and gleaming coppery topknot, but Fleur was intent on her quest and did not notice.

'Miss Kennedy?' Startled by the masculine tones, she swung around to meet the deep compelling gaze of the man she had noticed as she stepped down from the plane.

'That's me.'

'Logan's the name—Logan Page.'

Seeing him at close quarters the thought shot through her mind that he was even more devastatingly attractive than she had imagined. He was hard and good-looking in a tough suntanned way and there was something about him, an impression of strength and authority. It was there in the strongly moulded chin, the direct expression in his eyes, and you could almost *feel* the sense of masculine magnetism he emanated.

All at once she became aware of his cool, assessing appraisal. 'Seems I had the right description of who to look for!'

She stared up at him, puzzled. 'How do you mean?'

'My instructions were to keep a look out for a pint-sized girl with red hair!' She caught a glint of amusement in the depths of his hazel eyes.

Her soft lips tightened. 'And freckles,' she put in tersely, 'don't forget the freckles!' She was prickling at his description of herself that was light years away from the reaction she had come to expect from newly met male acquaintances. It seemed they just couldn't help commenting on her attention-getting hair, a shimmer of flame in sunlight, glinting copper in the shade. Nor did they appear unappreciative of her smooth pale skin and petite figure.

His impassive gaze went to the dusting of freckles on the bridge of her short nose. He appeared almost uninterested, so why did she get an impression of leashed power and sinewy strength? 'Now that you come to mention it——' came the deep gravelly tones.

Fervently Fleur wished now that she hadn't. The way in which he was studying her flushed face was disconcerting—very. The deep masculine tones broke across her thoughts. 'Let's get cracking, shall we? Luckily your plane came in bang on time and if we hit the highway now we'll be home before you know it!'

'Home?' she echoed, staring up at him in bewilderment. 'I don't understand . . . you don't need to take me home.'

'I do, you know!' His gaze, deep and compelling, held hers. Before she could argue the matter further, he ran on, 'They're unloading the luggage. What have you got, one bag or two?'

'One, but——'

'Right, Fox! You wait here and I'll go and collect it and we can get on our way. I——' At the sight of her outraged expression he broke off. '*Now* what's the matter? That is your name, isn't it? I haven't picked up the wrong Kennedy girl?'

'My name's Fleur,' she told him stiffly. 'F-L-E-U-R,' she spelled. 'Got it?' A glint of amusement in his eyes sparked her to a fierce spurt of anger. 'And please don't forget!' The next moment she realised with horror that she was shouting at him. Oh, he made her so mad! With an effort she forced her tones to a low tense note. 'Just a stupid childish nickname.'

His laconic glance swept her flushed face, then lifted to the coppery-reddish hair. 'Actually,' came the deep rumbling tones, 'I would have thought it suited you fine.'

'Well, I don't!' Fleur snapped. Anger sparkled in her green eyes. 'No one ever calls me by that ridiculous name nowadays!'

He regarded her with his deceptively bland stare. 'Your father does,' he observed, and before she could think up a sufficiently crushing retort he had turned away. 'Don't go away,' he threw over his shoulder.

'Just a moment!' she called after him, but it was too late. Already his purposeful strides were taking him in the direction of the area where baggage from the plane was being claimed by passengers.

She stared after him resentfully. 'Pint-sized . . . red hair.' Come to think of it, the bold unflattering description of herself was one that her father might well have used. As was the nickname 'Fox', a leftover from childhood and a father's affectionate pet name for a little daughter with a mop of red-gold curls. But what could this authoritative stranger have to do with her dad? To hell with him! she thought hotly. He can collect my bag if he likes, but if he imagines I'm going off with him he's got another think coming! For some reason he seems to have this crazy notion that he has to collect me and take me home. The nerve of him! A fresh thought struck her. Who was he anyway? His easy air of authority, the aura of substance he generated, made her think he must be a run-holder new in the sheep-farming district of fertile green acres. Somehow she couldn't see him as taking orders from another man—not him!

'Right!' The gravelly tones broke in on her musing and she realised he was looking down at her expectantly, her battered suitcase held in his hand. 'The old bus is over in the car park.' All at once his voice was tinged with impatience. 'Let's get cracking, shall we?'

She glanced up at him, small danger lights flickering in her green eyes. 'Go home with you, you mean?'

'That's the big idea.' All at once he grinned, a flash of strong white teeth in a deeply bronzed face. It was a smile so unexpectedly heart-knocking that it took Fleur a moment or so to recover from the impact. What was he saying?

'That's the story!'

'I'm sorry,' she forced a brisk no-nonsense note into her soft tones, 'but I'm not coming.' Belatedly she realised she owed him some explanation, seeing he seemed to have taken time and trouble in coming especially to pick her up at the airport. 'Thanks all the same, but,' she put on her brightest, most carefree smile, 'I'm expecting someone to meet me here. He must have been delayed, but I'm not worried about waiting a while longer, he'll be sure to come along at any moment now.'

He stood motionless and the authoritative note was back in the rumbling voice. 'Your dad asked me to call and pick you up and bring you home. He'll be getting a bit restive if you don't turn up. Maybe even,' he regarded her with his hard implacable look, 'concerned, shall we say?'

'My dad asked you that?' She stared up at him in bewilderment. 'I don't get it. Why on earth would he send you to pick me up here? I told him in my last letter not to bother coming to the airport, that I was being met.'

For a long moment his compelling gaze held hers and you could tell by the hard light in his eyes, Fleur thought, that he was a man who would give nothing away. 'You can sort that out with your dad when you get home. He'll put you in the picture about it all—ready?'

'No, I'm not!' she threw at him. She lifted her small square chin defiantly. 'My—friend will be along at any minute now and he'd be disappointed if I'd let him down and taken off just because he'd been unavoidably delayed for a short while.'

His mouth hardened. 'If it's Barton Howard you're hanging around for,' he told her harshly, 'you're wasting your time.'

She drew a deep breath of apprehension. 'He's all right, isn't he? He's not ill or anything?'

The hateful stranger shrugged powerful shoulders beneath his cotton shirt. 'How would I know? Like I said, your dad's waiting,' he reminded her, and pinned her with his implacable hazel-eyed glance.

Fleur raised her eyes heavenwards. 'I keep telling you and telling you,' she protested fiercely, 'that I'm not leaving with you. *You're* the one who's wasting your time waiting around here!' She eyed him defiantly. 'Barton will be along any moment now, I know he will. I wrote letting him know the day I was due to arrive at Auckland airport and the plane I was booked on down here today, flight number and all, and I know that he'd never let me down!'

His lips curved in the sardonic twist that was beginning to become familiar to her. 'You reckon?'

The bright flush of anger deepened in Fleur's cheeks. How dared this arrogant stranger criticise Bart! In the angry silence he surveyed her through narrowed eyes and for a crazy moment she imagined him to be capable of carrying her off with him. Then to her relief his shoulders lifted in a shrug. 'Right!' The deep tones were steely. 'If that's the way you want it——?'

'It is! Definitely!'

He turned on his heel and she watched him move away through the crowd, a tall man who moved with a light athletic tread. All at once a thought occurred to her. The way he was acting she got the idea that he knew something of the reason for Bart's delayed arrival here. But with those set lips and forbidding expression in his eyes, trust him not to give anything away! The thoughts tumbled wildly through her mind. What had he said? Something about her father having asked him to collect her at the airport? If only she'd queried him, found out more about him—but he had made her so furious that everything except putting this interfering stranger firmly in his place had fled her mind. 'Wait!' she called, and began to push her way through the thinning groups. Soon, however, he had vanished through the wide doorway. She hurried after him, but he was moving in the direction of the parking lot, and before she could reach him he had started the engine of his station waggon, swung the vehicle around and shot out on to the open road.

Fleur tossed her head in a defiant gesture. What did she care? He was nothing to her, nothing. Just a man who had a knack of annoying her so intensely she could feel her hackles rising at the mere thought of him. She was glad, glad, glad that she had refused his offer of a ride to her home. As she went back into the reception lounge she reflected that Bart would be along at any moment now, of course he would. Bart with his caressing voice and disarming grin that made you forgive him just about anything, even arriving late to meet her after a whole year's separation!

As the minutes ticked by and the big reception room emptied she tried to rally her sinking spirits. After a time she dropped down at one of the small yellow tables and a friendly girl brought her coffee. At least it would be something to do to while away the time and made her feel less conspicuous in the room. When an hour had gone by she rose to her feet and went into the nearby phone booth. Why hadn't she thought of ringing through to home before? As he was manager of her father's station, Bart's movements must be known to others there. Surely someone must know what had happened to delay his arrival at the airport on this most important of days. There was no answer, however, to the call. Not that that meant a great deal, Fleur told herself as she replaced the reciever in its cradle, more than likely Daphne the housekeeper would be in another part of the homestead and everyone else, including her father, would be out of doors.

She turned dispiritedly away, to find herself facing a hateful masculine face that was becoming all too familiar.

'No luck?' She caught a gleam of triumph in his eyes.

'No, there's not!' she said shortly.

'They'll be all outside by now, lined up for the welcome committee,' came the derisive tones.

She ignored that, saying stiffly, 'I thought you'd gone ages ago.'

'You're in luck.' He eyed her with cool detachment. 'I had to pick up a sheepdog out on a farm a few miles out, so I decided to call back here on the way and give you another chance. But I'm warning you, Fox——'

'Don't call me by that name!'

He ignored her sibilant whisper, the rumbly tones with their hidden barb running on, 'This is definitely my final offer. Unless you want to hitchhike a ride all the way to Te Haruru—and I wouldn't give much for your chances, with everyone away at the Show in town today.'

'I'm waiting for Barton.' Even to her own ears her voice held a betraying wobble.

'If you're putting your trust in your boy-friend——'

'He happens to be my fiancé,' she broke in, tight-lipped.

He ignored the interruption. 'You're in for a mighty long wait. A week, a month, more than that, I'd say at a guess.'

All the frustration and disappointment and anger gathered in a ball inside her and she faced him, eyes sparkling with resentment. 'I don't believe you.'

'Too bad.' The hard lines of his mouth were anything but inviting. 'Are you coming back with me?'

'No, no, no!' She spat the words out.

He threw her a cool, ironic glance. 'Too bad. Like I said, you're in for a hell of a long wait! I'll tell you something else,' the deep voice rasped along her taut nerves, 'your father's waiting for you, it won't hurt you to turn up, and whether you like it or not, I'm taking you along with me!'

'Don't be ridiculous!' she threw at him—and realised the next moment that the girl behind the cafeteria counter was following the little drama with interest. 'You can't make me go,' she hissed vindictively. Then, on an incredulous breath, 'You couldn't, you wouldn't——'

'Can't I.' At his threatening tone involuntarily Fleur stepped back.

'Don't tempt me!' he gritted, and advanced purposefully towards her. 'Right, you've asked for it!'

'All right, then.' Almost without her own volition she heard her voice saying quickly. 'I've changed my mind.' As she hurried along trying to keep up with his long strides, she added breathlessly, defensively, 'But not because of you, because of me!'

It was useless trying to explain, she realised the next moment, he wasn't even listening.

When they reached the dust-smeared Land Rover standing in the parking area, he threw open the passenger door and she climbed up the high step. He flung the door shut, and as he seated himself at her side she could feel her cheeks burning. A disadvantage of her hair-colouring, she thought wryly, was that one had to put up with the pale transparent complexion that was such a giveaway at times like this. Pray he wouldn't notice her heightened colour. As they moved away from the airport she took a quick sideways glance. His bronze face was aloof and forbidding, and clearly, her appearance was the last thing on his mind. A woman-hater? Scarcely, not with his devastating good looks and undeniable male magnetism that even she couldn't help but be aware of, God help her! Could it be something about herself that got under his skin, for the sight of her appeared to fill him with irrational resentment. Maybe he had something against redheads, and that included copperheads like herself.

Her thoughts ran on. Why had her father sent this strange man to meet her at the airport? It must mean that Barton was no longer at the station. The questions to which there were no answers continued to plague her. Who was this Logan Page anyway? Maybe he was a guest staying at the homestead. So many strangers arrived out of the blue at the isolated homestead in the hills—duck shooters in the season, hikers and trampers who had lost their way, wild-life students studying the breeding habits of seabirds nesting on the rugged coast, hunters and possum trappers. They were all welcomed at Te Haruru, given food and shelter and later sent on their way with warm invitations to return at any time.

Soon they were passing through wide streets where Colonial homes of an earlier era were set amid spreading lawns and towering trees made pools of shadow on the lush grass. Then they were approaching a modern housing area where timber bungalows painted in soft pastel tonings of primrose, pink, green and blue were bordered with bright flower gardens and arches and gateways were festooned with roses in full bloom. They moved through the attractive town where women wearing colourful summer frocks and men in shirts, work-shorts, knee-length socks and leather sandals strolled the pavements with their cool verandahs. Fleur, however, took in the passing scene with only half of her mind, aware only of Logan Page. Maybe, she mused, if she sounded him out without letting her too easily aroused temper get the better of her, she might be able to find out what she wanted to know. Carefully she steadied her voice to a light conversational note.

'I just can't make out why you had to come to the airport to collect me and why Dad didn't come himself. For that matter,' she was speaking her thoughts aloud, 'how did Dad know that Bart wouldn't be on time to meet me?'

Logan didn't answer for a moment, his attention apparently centred on a great stock transporter and trailer closely packed with sheep he was manoeuvring his way past. 'Your dad couldn't make it and I happened to be on the spot at the time. Bart? Well, you'll have to ask your dad about that one.'

She eyed him suspiciously. In a way he'd answered her questions, but somehow his words had made her wonder all the more. Clearly he was giving nothing away. If only she could catch him out and discover just what was happening at home! Maybe, she acknowledged reluctantly, she had some explaining to do herself.

'It's having been away for a whole year,' she told him. 'I mean, so much can happen, and where I've been——' She broke off. 'Did Dad tell you I was offered a chance of working overseas with a World Vision team? Of course I grabbed it, even though it meant that Bart and I would have to postpone our wedding for a while.' Her lips curved in a rueful smile. 'I think he understood—eventually. Trouble was, I was so far away and I was moving around a lot and mail didn't always catch up with me.' All at once a cold hand clutched her heart. 'Dad! He's not ill, is he? That isn't the reason he couldn't come to meet me today?'

'He's okay.' His voice was deadpan. 'Gets his good and bad days—up and down. But you'd know all about that—or wouldn't you?' He flicked her a sideways glance and she was piercingly aware of the cool disapproval in his tone that said all too clearly, 'Or didn't you take the trouble to find out? Too wrapped up in your own concerns to bother to care about what was happening at home.'

She said very low, 'What's wrong with Dad?' In the silence her thoughts were rioting. She might have known Logan was a man who would give nothing away, she'd felt that from the beginning. So why for heaven's sake had she given him the chance of putting her down, an opportunity he would be sure to pounce on? He did.

'That's something you'll have to talk over with his doctor. I'm practically a stranger.'

Fleur pressed her lips together and her green eyes sparkled angrily. 'For a stranger,' she flung at him, 'you seem to know an awful lot that you're keeping to yourself! What's the matter? Don't you trust me? The way you're treating me I might be a silly little teenager instead of a grown-up woman of twenty-one!'

'Really?' The bland amazement in his tone was like a slap in the face. So that was what he really did think of her . . . but why, why?

She lapsed into silence, gazing around her at a world where sheep-dotted paddocks stretched around them and farmhouses were taking the place of suburban bungalows. Far ahead was the hazy blue of distant hills. She had forgotten, in the heat and turmoil and distress of her work on the other side of the world, the warmth and clarity of the air here, the sheer shimmering quality of the atmosphere. A wonderful day, the sort of day on which things happened—unexpected, exciting things! Oh, things were happening all right, she flashed a resentful glance towards her driver, but not at all in the way she had planned. In place of Bart Howard, whom she loved, she was being taken home by this hateful enigmatic stranger who took a perverse delight in needling her, pushing her around, refusing to answer the most simple question concerning himself. The maddening thing about it, she admitted reluctantly, was the way in which he was affecting her. He had no need to speak to get it across to her that in his view she rated in importance on a par with the black-and-white sheepdog at this moment curled up asleep amidst a clutter of dog nuts, gumboots, boxes of horseshoe nails and coils of wire in the back of the vehicle.

All at once her soft lips firmed. She would force him to be a bit more human, she vowed silently. At least give him a chance to be agreeable, put it that way. So she lifted her small rounded chin and said brightly, 'While I've been overseas I've lost touch with things at home. A year's a long time, but I'm glad that I went, it's so satisfying doing something that you know is really worthwhile. You see, I've been away in Thailand, working in refugee camps,' and waited for the reaction of interest that, during her brief time back in her own country, she had come to expect from listeners.

Logan didn't even bother to lift his eyes from the curve of roadway ahead. His laconic, 'So I believe,' couldn't have been more off-putting. Her cheeks did a slow burn. She must have been out of her skull, she thought hotly, to have attempted to be friendly with him. What an idiot she had been to make a mistake like that! Never again! Right! She settled back in her seat, hoping he wouldn't choose this moment to glance around to catch the heightened colour in her cheeks. If that was the way he wanted to play it, that was fine with her.

The next moment they swung around a hairpin bend and she was thrown violently against him as the vehicle swerved to avoid a pile of rocks that had slipped down from the crumbling cliff face high above. Involuntarily she clutched his arm. What was the matter with her today? she scolded herself as she jerked herself away. Heaven knew she was used to the sharp bends and rock falls from the precipitous cliffs above the road. After all, the many notices along the route—BEWARE FALLING DEBRIS—weren't put there for nothing. But how about her driver?

She glanced across at the strong masculine profile at her side. She had to admit that he drove fast but skilfully, with a somewhat contemptuous nonchalance for the tortuous curves. At that moment he began to roll a cigarette with one hand, and she held her breath. Country men, she knew, still carried 'the makings' in their pocket and she wouldn't put it past him to lift both hands from the wheel. In this, however, she found she was mistaken, for with a dexterous twist of sun-bronzed fingers he had completed his task and flicked a lighter to the flimsy roll of paper. He was well accustomed to the road, no doubt of that. Fleur longed to know where his property was situated. Everything about him pointed to an assumption that he owned land somewhere in this district, but pride forbade her making any further attempt to gain his confidence. Besides, deep down something told her that he wouldn't give anything away—and especially not to her!

The wind rushing through open windows of the Land Rover tore the coppery-red strands from her coiled topknot and tossed a veil across her eyes. She pushed them away and tried not to think about the man beside her, he just wasn't worth it.

They were sweeping down a slope when she realised that Logan was slowing speed, waiting until a great stock trailer closely packed with sheep thundered past them, then turning off the road into a clearing in the bush. It was a cool fragrant spot that Fleur knew well, where sunlight filtered down through towering native trees and the long grass underfoot was green and lush. Already she caught the soft gurgle of creek water running over stones in the gully below.

She threw him an enquiring glance. 'Comfort stop?'

'If you like.' He was jumping down from the vehicle to the shadowed grass. 'Actually I was thinking of Duke. It's thirsty weather.'

'Duke?' The next moment she realised he was referring to the sheepdog. He would! Oh, she might have known that her welfare wouldn't be of the slightest concern to her. As he reached to the back of the Land Rover for a tin dish, some imp of nastiness made her say, 'I suppose he's a valuable dog? You've just bought him today?'

'That's right.' He was letting the sheepdog loose. 'I was coming into town today anyway to pick him up from a farm a few miles out.' Turning away, he began to push his way through the thickly growing bushes covering the slope leading down to the creek in the gully.

Fleur was seething with anger. He couldn't have made it more plain that picking her up at the airport had been for him a time-consuming, unpleasant duty— but a duty to whom? Could it be that he was still annoyed with her because she had turned down his offer to drive her home? Surely a grown man couldn't behave so childishly?

In a few minutes' time he had returned, a panful of water in his hand. 'There you are, mate!' He set the dish down on the grass and the sheepdog, after one greedy gulp, upset the dish, spilling the water out on the grass. Fleur heard a muttered oath, then Logan was once more hurrying down the slope.

'But don't you worry,' she told the dog whom she found at her side, peering anxiously down the bushy slope. 'You'll be all right. He'll look after you, no matter what! He's like that, darn him! I'll tell you one thing,' she wiped a hand across a dust-smeared forehead, 'he might be your boss, but he's not mine—thank heaven!'

All at once she realised that Logan had returned and was once again giving the sheepdog a drink. Fleur's green eyes sparkled with annoyance. He might have enquired first as to whether she were thirsty, which she was—very. If only she had bought a pack of fruit drink at the airport cafeteria and brought it with her, now it was too late. One thing's for sure, she told herself grimly, he'll never offer me anything!

'What would you like to drink?' the rich tones cut across her thoughts. 'Orange, mango, pineapple, a cold beer?'

'Oh——' it took her a moment or two to collect her thoughts. 'Orange will be fine. You seem to have quite an assortment.'

He had gone to the vehicle, returning with a chilli bin in his hand, and as Fleur caught sight of packets of wrapped sandwiches and packs of chilled drinks and cans of beer, she couldn't help the expression of relief that showed in her face.

Carelessly Logan tossed a sandwich to the sheepdog. He *would* think of the dog first! Fleur thought indignantly. He dropped down to the grass and placed the chilli bin between them. 'Help yourself.' Once again she felt the impact of the smile that transformed his sun-darkened face. A force, unseen but powerful, flashed between them, and to stifle the moment of awareness, she wrenched her glance aside and said quickly, 'Super sandwiches—cold meat and home-made pickle and all. You must have a very caring...' For some reason the last word stuck in her throat and the moment of silence pinpointed her stupid hesitancy, 'wife.'

'The housekeeper takes care of the culinary department,' he returned carelessly, and Fleur would have given anything to have taken the words back. She could kick herself now for that involuntary betrayal of interest in his personal life. And yet ... did he have a wife or didn't he? Somehow the matter seemed terribly important to her. Thirtyish, maybe a bit more, he was fairly certain to be married. Poor unfortunate girl, Fleur didn't envy her one little bit.

'Are you sure?' jeered the goblin deep in her mind.

'Of course I'm sure!' she threw back, 'I can't stand the man! Though come to think of it,' a wry smile twitched the corners of her lips, and a deep verticle dimple ran down the side of one cheek, 'it might be rather fun to tame him, to *make* him change his ideas about me!'

A sandwich and a fruit drink later, Fleur got to her feet and Logan rose to stand beside her. All at once she was very much aware of his appraisal, and the thought crossed her mind that maybe, just maybe, he didn't find her unattractive after all.

'Here, take this,' he was fishing a spotless white handkerchief from the pocket of well-cut jeans. 'Your face is all over dust.'

'I'm okay.' Huffily she gave her face a quick swipe with the handkerchief, wondering why such a simple statement of fact should make her so angry. 'Thanks,' she handed it back to him, 'you'll be needing it yourself!' As she turned aside, she was unaware that to the man's eyes she looked young and vulnerable, tiny silver earrings in her ears and coppery topknot all over the place.

Because she couldn't stand being with him one minute longer, she hurried towards the bushy incline, throwing over her shoulder, 'I'm off to dangle my feet in the creek.'

'Good idea!'

She was ahead of him, running down a narrow path cut between the overhanging tea-tree that she knew well. Before he could catch up with her she had tossed her jandals on the bank and was plunging bare feet in the creek, letting the delicious coolness of the clear running water play on her wrists.

On the steep upward climb she hurried ahead once again. She knew every inch of this track—Or did she? The thought shot through her mind the next minute as in her haste she stumbled over a fallen tree trunk lying in her path and would have fallen headlong had not strong arms caught her and broken her fall.

For a moment Logan held her close, surely no more than the space of a heartbeat, yet Fleur's senses were in a riot of emotion. She must have a touch of the sun, she thought wildly, for this man's touch to affect her this way. The thoughts ran dizzily through her mind, then she had wrenched herself free and was pulling herself upwards with the help of a tree branch. 'I only hope this holds,' she said tremulously, and shot up the slope so fast that she was breathless when she reached the flat grassy area above.

Soon she was seated once more in the Land Rover and Logan was swinging back on to the dusty metal road. Now there were only the sheep-threaded slopes with their barbed wire fences, and at lengthy intervals, fleeting glimpses of rambling red-roofed farmhouses with their shelterbelts of tall native trees, the tea-tree loading ramps at the side of the road. In the gullies between sun-dried slopes, luxuriant native bush formed a backdrop for the lighter green of the softly moving fronds of lacy tree ferns. Then they were swinging into a back road, riding the corrugations in the metal and throwing up clouds of dust. It was fiercely hot, the sun blazing down from the cloudless blue bowl of the sky. The road twisted and turned and the drumming of stones thrown on the underside of the vehicle made conversation difficult.

Not that she cared, Fleur told herself, not after the disastrous effort at polite conversation she had made a while ago. She must have been crazy to have handed him such a chance to put her down.

All at once they turned a hairpin bend to come on a flock of sheep being driven across the road by a stockman with his dogs. 'Ben!' Logan slowed the vehicle to a crawl and as the woolly mass milled around them, Fleur leaned from the open window, waving wildly to the stockman on horseback.

The lined face of the small wiry man split in a delighted grin. 'G'day! You home again, Fleur?'

'I'm on my way, Ben!' She turned to wave farewell as the Land Rover left the milling sheep behind. For a moment, charmed by the sight of a familiar face, she forgot the hard profile of the man at her side and cried happily, 'I've known Ben all my life. He used to work at Te Haruru once. A sort of "do everything" man, you know?'

Logan nodded, his gaze fixed on the hairpin bend they were negotiating, and they swept on.

'He's not worth talking to!' she told herself hotly. Staring ahead, she let her thoughts wander. Back to last summer when her father's indifferent health had forced him into an early retirement and he had decided to employ a manager for the property. Barton Howard had applied for the position, and although young and lacking experience in management, he had had excellent references, and these, together with his charm of manner, had earned him the job. Fleur, home for the holidays from her work in a Wellington hospital, had applauded her father's choice of manager. She and Barton had fallen in love with each other almost at first sight and planned to marry immediately. 'Sort of keeping it in the family,' Fleur had told her father happily, when they had announced their plans for a wedding in a few weeks' time. Then, due to the influence of a friend of her father's, had come the opportunity of working with World Vision, using her nursing qualifications to join a team of dedicated workers giving their talents to help underprivileged people overseas. Fleur hadn't hesitated for a moment in taking advantage of the offer that had come her way. Of course, Bart would approve of her decision, she knew, of doing something really worthwhile, even though it would mean the postponement of their marriage plans.

But Bart, when she had put the matter to him, hadn't seen things her way at all. Tense and angry, he had refused to listen to her side of the argument. 'Marry me before you go, then,' he had pleaded at last. 'We don't need to wait! Please, please, girl, do this for me!' His passionate kisses and despairing tones had all but shattered her resolution to leave him, but in the end he had given in to her wishes, albeit with a bad grace.

'Don't look like that,' she had chided him, touched by the intensity of his low husky voice. 'I'll be back before you have time to miss me!'

'Promise—promise you'll come back to me!' he had whispered brokenly. Then, on a groan, 'If only you'd let me buy you a ring, to show that you belong to me!'

She had stirred in his arms, whispered, 'As if I need a ring to remember!'

She could still feel the poignancy of his goodbye kiss, the warm pressure of his lips on hers as they parted at the airport. It was a long time before she could banish from her mind her last glimpse of Bart's thin dark face, despairing, set, sullen. But that was only because he loved her, truly loved her, she told herself, just as she loved him.

It was a long hot drive, the dust rising behind them as they made the long haul up hills where native bush threw long shadows across the metal roads. Being with Logan made the route seem twice the length, Fleur mused resentfully. Apparently unaware of her deliberate lack of communication, his gaze was intent on the winding road ahead that climbed up to meet the blue of the sky. She couldn't understand this enigmatic stranger who seemed so attractive at first glance but when you were stuck with him on a long and tedious journey, turned out to be anything but entertaining company.

Once again she lapsed into an angry silence, and to prevent herself from becoming even more perturbed by Logan's off-putting attitude, she occupied herself in watching for the sight of various homesteads set high on the hills they were passing. The names of properties and sheep stations were familiar to her, although they were situated at long distances from one another. As a child she had gone away to boarding school in town with other children living in the remote area. In later years she had hunted with them over the hills, joined them in sporting events at the annual agricultural shows and yelled herself hoarse with excitement at local race meetings when a familiar mount had come galloping in to victory. Oh, it was good to be on familiar land once again, to breathe in the clean fresh air with its tangy smell of the bush.

Lost in her thoughts, the dull boom of breakers on the beach below scarcely registered with her until, glancing up, she caught sight of a faded timber signpost all but obscured by overhanging bush. Te Haruru Station. Fleur leaned forward excitedly, forgetting even her taciturn driver as they swept over a rise and plunged down the curving track cutting between sheep-dotted slopes.

It was a scene she had been familiar with for most of her life, yet now it struck her as if seeing it for the first time. The sun-dried station land tumbled down to meet the cool blue Pacific Ocean below. On the beach sunlight danced over black sand, making it glitter like a myriad diamonds. High cliffs dropped steeply down to sea level and the curves of sandy bays stretched away to the shimmering horizon. Directly below, so close to the sand that it made no difference, was the rambling old white-painted homestead facing the sea with its backdrop of towering native trees affording protection from the winds sweeping in from the ocean.

From this height the scene resembled a miniature village, she thought, her gaze taking in the karaka trees behind the mellow red of the big woolshed, the stables, garages, a small building that long ago had served as a place of worship for earlier dwellers at Te Haruru. There too were the two cottages occupied by married shepherds and their families. All that space and air and sunshine! How fortunate New Zealanders were in their surroundings, she mused, and how wonderful this homecoming today would be for her if only . . .

They were nearing the homestead grounds now, dust rising behind them in a cloud. As they sped by a paddock where horses were grazing Fleur craned her head to glance backwards. 'I don't see Sally anywhere,' she was speaking her thoughts aloud. 'My mare,' she explained on a breath. 'I can't *wait* to ride her again! She's got a great heart and she's the best show-jumper for miles around—at least I think so! Dad bred her for me and I trained her myself.' A worried frown creased her hot forehead. 'No one's mentioned her in any letters I got from home lately. I do hope nothing's happened to her——'

'Don't worry, she's okay.' Logan's interested tone took her by surprise and she stared across at him in bewilderment.

'How do *you* know?'

'Should do!' He threw her a mocking sideways glance. 'I've been exercising her.'

Just like that, she thought, incensed. Aloud she cried incredulously, 'You?'

'That's right!' came the cool masculine tones.

Fleur was about to explode in a storm of protest when her first words were drowned by wild yahoos as two young stockmen urged their stock horses down a steep slope. Waving their stetsons wildly in the air, they made welcoming noises as they approached the Land Rover. 'Hey, Fleur! Welcome home! How was Thailand?'

'Not so good as here!'

Logan slowed the vehicle to a crawl and the stockmen drew rein beside Fleur, their young voices echoing around her. 'Thought you'd taken off for good! Glad to be back?'

She smiled, wrinkling her nose at them. 'What do *you* think?' As Logan drove on, her spirits lightened. The friendliness of the eager boyish faces had warmed her heart. She couldn't imagine why she had allowed Logan to spoil the day for her. Of course everything was all right now, the waiting and uncertainty forgotten. In a few minutes' time Bart's absence from the airport would be explained away quite simply and she would be laughing at herself for even thinking there could be anything to worry about.

Even before the vehicle had fully come to a halt on the wide curving driveway, Fleur was leaping to the ground. Flinging open the small gate leading to the homestead, she hurried up the winding path bordered with flowers, took the steps two at a time and hurled herself into the arms of the tall, frail-looking man who had come to stand on the sunny verandah.

CHAPTER TWO

'DAD!' All at once she was overcome with emotion, her eyes misty. 'It's so *good* to see you!'

She felt his arms tighten around her. 'Great to have you back, Fox! Thought for a while today that you'd missed your plane.'

'I know, I know!' The thoughts were racing through her mind. He was as erect as ever, but he looked thinner, a cold hand seemed to close around her heart, and he was pale beneath the tan. The anxious words fell from her lips before she could stop them. 'You're feeling all right, Dad? It's been so long.' All at once she became aware of Logan. He was standing motionless, her suitcase in his hand, blocking out the sunshine, looking, just looking ... and listening. 'I haven't had any news from home for ages, it seems like forever. I guess the mails let us down and I was moving around a lot ...' The words fell into a trail-away silence as she glanced up to meet Logan's ironic glance. It was a look that said quite plainly, 'Liar!' With an effort she wrenched her mind back to her father's quiet tones.

'I'm right as rain! Better than ever now that you're back——' his gaze moved to Logan. 'Guess you two have got acquainted by now. You know Logan——?'

Fleur nodded. Logan's mocking glance was somehow unnerving, and she turned with relief as a tall angular woman with snapping brown eyes hurried into the room. 'So you turned up after all——' Her voice held more than a tinge of disapproval. 'Thought I was wasting my time cooking dinner for you tonight. Just as well you showed up, or the meal wouldn't be fit to eat!'

Fleur, however, was accustomed to the grumbling tones and took no notice. Daphne had been housekeeper for her father for many years and to Fleur it seemed like forever. 'I know it will be super. Anything would be delicious after the food I've been used to this past year. And now, that succulent New Zealand lamb, plus your cooking!'

'If it's not ruined with being kept so long,' Daphne muttered darkly, and vanished into the kitchen.

'Dad——' At last, Fleur thought with relief, she could rid herself of the niggling doubts that had assailed her throughout the long journey today. 'Where's Bart? He wasn't at the airport to meet me and I wrote him letting him know I was arriving today——' She broke off, puzzled by something evasive in her father's expression. 'He did get my letter?'

'It's on the mantel waiting——'

'Then Bart's not here? Is that it? Then where is he?'

He didn't answer for a moment. 'He's gone,' he said at last, and she caught a shuttered expression in his eyes. 'Took off from here over a month ago.'

'A month ago?' she echoed, aghast. 'But—surely you have his new address?'

Her father shook his head. 'He said something about moving around the country a bit.'

Bewilderedly Fleur stared at him. 'Didn't he leave a message for me? A letter? Anything at all?'

In the silence her mystified gaze moved from her father's embarrassed face to Logan, and hurriedly she averted her glance. Something in his enigmatic expression gave her a feeling that he knew a lot more about Bart's movements than he had let on to her, and she was fairly certain that it wouldn't be good news.

'He shot through in a bit of a hurry,' her father vouchsafed at last.

'What do you mean? There's been some trouble between you, hasn't there?' she demanded tersely.

'Something's happened to Bart and you're shielding me from knowing what it was. But you don't need to,' the words tumbled wildly from her lips. 'He knows I wouldn't let him down even if he's lost his job as manager here—That's it, isn't it?' She faced him with accusing eyes. 'I can tell by your face! If you've got something against Bart, why don't you come right out with it and tell me? What did he do, for heaven's sake, to make himself so unpopular around here all of a sudden?'

'Nothing . . . that I know of.'

'But you suspect him of something!' she flashed back. 'You're putting blame on him for something you're not even certain about! Anyway, what is this dark deed he's supposed to have got away with? Like sheep-stealing, back in the good old days?' She saw something leap in the faded blue eyes, then it was gone.

'Look, Fox, we'll go into it later. No use ruining your homecoming dinner. Daphne would never forgive me if you didn't do justice to her cooking! Tell you what, you have a brush-up after the trip and later we can fill you in on the news.'

'We?' She threw Logan a suspicious glance. 'What's that supposed to mean?'

'Oh, don't mind Logan,' said her father with a rueful grin. 'He's in on all this too.'

'I'll bet he is,' muttered Fleur angrily, 'up to his neck!' The furious glance she tossed him was met by a flint-eyed stare. The next moment she wrenched her mind back to the older man's quiet tones. 'No need to get so het up,' he chided her. 'Barton's okay, or he was the last I heard of him. You know him, he's quite capable of taking care of himself.' Did she detect a tinge of irony in the words? she wondered.

'But he's not manager here any longer, he's gone——' She stopped short, aware of Logan's attentive expression. But she wouldn't, she decided, give him the satisfaction of listening in on a private family discussion. So she gathered herself together, summoned up her brightest smile and laying a hand on her father's thin bare arm said: 'It's all right, Dad, you don't have to tone things down for me! I'm not a child now, you know, I can take it! I'll tell you one thing, though, whatever it is that's happened to Bart, he knows that I'll stand right by him.' Encountering Logan's sardonic look, she finished defiantly, 'All the way! I'll have a quick wash and a change and after dinner,' she promised her father, 'you can fill me in with what's been happening around here—*in private*,' she added significantly.

As a put-down, however, it failed miserably, for Logan merely shrugged powerful shoulders. 'Just waiting for you, Fox,' came the gravelly voice. 'Where do you want your suitcase?'

She only hoped the look she darted him would leave him in no doubt as to exactly where she wanted him, but she forced her voice to a fairly normal note. 'The bedroom at the end of the passage, please.'

'Right!' He strode from the room and when she reached her bedroom he was placing her battered suitcase on a low table.

'Thanks,' she said shortly, watching him as he moved towards the door. If only, she mused, this Logan creature hadn't gained such an influence over her father. But she was home again now, her soft lips firmed in determination, and she would soon sort Logan out, put him in his place.

'If you can!' jeered a goblin deep in her mind, but she thrust it aside and forced herself to think of the present. How fresh and welcoming was her room, with the long french windows letting in the sea breeze and perfume that wafted in from the blossoming bushes outside.

Her toilet necessities were in the capacious embroidered bag she carried with her, and swiftly she ran a comb through tangled hair and secured her wind-tossed topknot with a tortoiseshell comb. In the bathroom next door she ran soft rainwater from the tap, splashing hands and face and washing away the dust of the journey. In a few minutes she was back in her room, slipping out of jeans and T-shirt and tying a batik-printed skirt in muted tonings of russets and browns around her slim waist. Then she pulled on a blouse of cool creamy muslin.

'Not,' she told herself, 'that I care what Logan thinks of me,' she paused for a glance in the long mirror, 'it's just that I feel more comfortable this way and it will please Dad if I look as if I've taken trouble to look nice for him tonight.' Surprisingly her mirrored reflection left no doubt that for a girl with a lot on her mind she appeared to be astonishingly carefree. There was no sign of jet-lag either. Indeed, tonight there was about her a sparkle, an animation that she couldn't help but be aware of. Even her eyes—Put it down to light of battle, she told herself, and went down the long hall.

In the big shadowy dining room with its massive sideboard and faded carpet, the long kauri table was set for five. The next moment Fleur was pleased to see Rusty, the head shepherd, rising from a deep wing-chair to greet her. The rangy red-haired man of middle age with a sun-weathered face was an old hand on the station and had always had a soft spot in his heart for Fleur. His handshake, so firm as to be almost crippling, left no doubt as to his delight in seeing her once again.

As the meal progressed Fleur tried to appear bright and entertaining as she recounted happenings that had occurred during the months she had spent travelling in foreign places. She went on to describe the poverty and misery of refugees arriving at the camps where she had worked. All the time she was disconcertingly aware of Logan, who was seated opposite her. What was it about him that made her feel so—so *aware* of him? she wondered wildly. With an effort she concentrated her attention on Rusty, endeavouring to draw him out on the endlessly fascinating subject of life on the remote sheep station. Tonight, however, Rusty, who as a rule was a prolific talker, seemed evasive and ill at ease. What was it they were all hiding from her? she asked herself.

Conscious of Daphne's watchful eyes, she forced herself to eat the delectable meal that had been served to her. Not for all and sundry, she knew, would the housekeeper set the long table with the second best lace tablecloth, polish the silver, arrange a centrepiece of pink Queen Elizabeth roses. Indeed, although Daphne was apt to describe herself as a 'plain cook', the meal tonight was a tribute to her culinary skills. The local wine was slightly chilled, the lamb chops with their accompanying minted pear halves grilled to perfection, the sweet a mouthwatering confection of silver-green kiwi fruit topped with a fluffy meringue. It should have been a memorable meal, Fleur thought on a sigh, then catching Daphne's glance, she endeavoured to look as though she was enjoying the food she was forcing herself to eat.

To Fleur the meal seemed to last for ever, but at last Daphne carried a tray of steaming coffee mugs into the comfortable old lounge room where long picture windows showed a vista of a sunset-painted sky and darkening sea. After a time Rusty put down his whisky-laced drink. 'See you around, Fleur.'

''Night, Rusty.' Out of a corner of her eye she was aware of Logan rising to his feet.

'I'll say goodnight——'

'Don't go, Logan!' The older man raised a detaining hand. A smile crinkled the sun-lined face. 'I promised Fleur I'd let her in on a few things that have been happening around here while she's been away. Guess you two got a few things sorted out on the way here, hmm?'

Fleur said tightly, 'Not really.'

'Logan didn't put you in the picture about the new set-up here, then?'

'Over to you,' came Logan's gravelly tones.

Fleur's bewildered gaze moved from her father's thin face to the forceful dark-haired man standing apparently relaxed, not saying a word, yet somehow she got the feeling that his presence filled the room. 'Since you went away,' her father was saying, 'there've been a few changes at Te Haruru. A couple of months ago I decided the place was too big, getting a bit beyond me, so I got the idea of splitting the property and selling off half the place. I had a word with the lawyer in town and we chewed things over between us. Thing is, Logan here is now part owner, equal shares for both of us, and he's agreed to take on the job of manager for the lot.' The glance he threw the younger man was bright with confidence. Confidence in *him*? Fleur thought, appalled. News such as this was just too horrific to take in.

'You!' She raised horror-stricken eyes to his impassive face. 'I can't believe it! You actually own a half share in Te Haruru!'

The thought raced through her mind that the contempt and loathing she had managed to put into her tone would have sparked any other man into a defensive flood of explanations plus a glowing account of his qualifications. Not so Logan. He merely regarded her with his mocking hazel-eyed glance. 'You'll get used to the idea,' he said coolly, 'after a while.'

'Never!' She tossed him a scornful look. The man in command, she thought angrily. The man who, just because he had money and possessions, had somehow talked her father into letting him own half of Te Haruru. It wasn't fair!

The next moment another thought drove everything else from her mind. Painful, inescapable, the truth hit her like a blow. 'So that was why Bart lost his job here,' she said slowly, and flung around to face Logan. Her eyes sparkled dangerously. 'You drove him out! It's your fault too!' she accused her father. 'Just because you divided up the property it didn't mean you had to put someone else in as manager. As if there wouldn't have been work still for Bart—did you ask him about it?'

'No need,' came Logan's deep forceful tones, 'I would never have had him around the place.'

'Not that it ever came to that,' her father put in placatingly. 'As soon as Bart got the word about the change of ownership he took off. He wanted it that way—Now, Fox, don't take on——' For her face had flushed with anger and her green eyes were shooting sparks.

'Do you expect me to believe that? You drove him away,' she said in a low voice throbbing with emotion. 'You didn't give him a chance. What were you thinking of, Dad?' Her eyes blazed. 'Why didn't you tell me?'

'Listen to me, Fox,' Logan's quiet tones cut across

her rioting emotions. 'You're making a big mistake——'

'There's no mistake,' she cried fiercely, 'and don't call me Fox!'

Her thoughts were whirling in a frenzy of shock and anger and disappointment. Between them, Logan and her father had driven Bart away from here. 'If only you'd written to me——' she eyed her father exasperatedly.

'Didn't want to worry you.' At something in the drawn look of his face, her anger died away.

'I guess you thought you were acting for the best,' she conceded, 'but if only I'd known what was happening back here——'

'Bart didn't let you in on it, then?' Logan cut in tersely, and she saw an odd unreadable glance pass between the two men.

'Of course he wrote to me!' she protested indignantly. 'It's just that I didn't get his letter. The mails over in Thailand were very chancy, there must have been heaps of letters that never caught up with me. But he would have told me everything, he always does!'

The older man dropped down into a deep chair and it struck her once again how frail he looked. There was a look of strain about his features, or could it be something more than that, a sensation of weakness? A wave of remorse surged over her and she said softly, contritely, 'Dad, I'm sorry—throwing a wobbly like that! I got such a shock. When Bart didn't turn up to meet me at the airport I had a feeling something was wrong, but I didn't dream that things had changed as much as they have.' Suddenly there rushed into her mind Logan's veiled references to her father's state of health. 'No more mysteries, Dad,' she dropped down to kneel beside his chair and took his work-roughened hand in her own. 'How have you been feeling lately? And don't tell me, like your precious partner did,' she threw a resentful glance towards Logan, 'to have a word with the doctor. I want *you* to tell me,' she smiled up into his face. 'Agreed?'

'Right, Fox! Doc says I'm fine. The old ticker's been playing up a bit, but——'

She snatched at the words. 'How do you mean?' She caught her breath. 'Are you telling me that you had a heart attack while I've been away?'

'Something like that,' he answered evasively, 'but the doc's fixed me up now, tells me I'll be as good as gold with his medication. A few reservations, of course—I've got to live quietly, no shocks, no worry, take things easy from now on.'

'I see.' Compassion and regret mingled in her glance. 'And you didn't let on about that in your letters to me either?'

He evaded her questioning eyes. 'No sense in worrying everyone else when there was no need. Anyway, things are going along fine now. Logan here is my right-hand man, and now that I've got this business about Bart off my chest, told you the bad news——'

Fleur said very low, 'But you've no proof against him, nothing!'

'Did I say anything about his not keeping in line?'

'Not in so many words,' she conceded, 'but all the same I know there's something you're keeping from me! I suppose it was a matter of Bart's word against Logan's, and of course you'd believe Logan, just because,' she muttered bitterly, 'he's got that charisma and he's so damned good-looking!' The next minute she could have bitten out her tongue for letting her thoughts surface. The tell-tale pink deepened in her cheeks. How could she have forgotten even for an instant that Logan was standing right here at her side, listening, getting the wrong impression of things she said? His bland expression of interest did nothing to ease her confusion. 'Well,' she said lamely, 'I guess that's what some folk would get taken in by.'

He surveyed her with his mocking stare. 'But not you?'

She flung him a defiant glance. 'What do *you* think?'

'Just as a matter of interest,' he was perched on a chair arm swinging a long jean-clad leg, 'what makes you think your boy-friend is way beyond criticism?'

She flung around to face his cool gaze. 'He's not here to defend himself, so someone has to do it . . . all those lies and insinuations——'

Her father raised a protesting hand. 'Easy now, Fox, you don't know they're lies——'

'Neither do you!' she sparked back. 'The way things look, it seems to me——' She stopped short, groping for words.

Logan was regarding her with polite interest, his eyes deep and intent. 'Yes? Go on.'

Somehow it was difficult to put into words the monstrous thought that had come to her. She drew a deep breath and twisting a strand of hair round and round her finger, spun around to face her father. 'I just can't understand you, Dad——' Her heart smote her as once again she was aware of his pale drawn appearance, but there were things that must be said. 'Why couldn't you wait until I got home and talk things over with Bart and me? Okay, I know your health made you think of sitting back a bit at this stage of your life, letting someone else take a share of the place and the responsibility, but you only had to let things ride for a month or two, then Bart and I would be married and he would have taken all the worry from your shoulders! You know how good he is at running Te Haruru. It would have been the ideal set-up, Bart and you and I, and you could sit back and take things easy. But all this mad rush to make changes, everything happening in a hurry, *before I got back*. And now Bart has gone from here, no one seems to know where, and another man has his job!' She tossed Logan a resentful glance. 'A stranger you don't know a thing about, yet you trust *him!*'

Logan put on what she termed was a horrible smirk. 'It's my fatal charm,' he pointed out, 'you said so yourself!'

Fleur turned on him with blazing eyes. 'Stop trying to put me off!' After a moment she added angrily, 'You're both keeping something from me, I know you are. I'm surprised at you, Dad.' Half to herself she muttered, 'You don't seem to care about Bart.'

The heavy silence that followed underlined the truth of the words and she eyed the older man accusingly. 'Well, do you?'

He said levelly, 'Not particularly.' The faded blue eyes beamed an unmistakable message. 'And you can make what you like out of that!' In a milder tone, he added, 'There's a cricket match being shown live on TV tonight, Fox, so if you don't mind——'

'You go ahead and watch it, Dad. See you in the morning.' She stared after him as he left the room, thinking: He's just avoiding any more questions I might put to him about Bart. Oh well, she consoled herself, at least now I can say what I want without regard to Dad's state of health. All at once she became aware that Logan was rising to his feet. How was it, she found herself wondering, that so big a man could move so fluidly? 'Look,' she gazed up into his face, 'what's been going on around here while I've been away? I know . . .' Her voice trailed into silence, for the strangest thing was happening. Something like an electric current was shooting through her, wild and sweet and dangerous. Logan was drawing her close to him, and as delight seemed to melt her bones, his firm lips found her mouth. In the pulsing excitement surging through her there was nothing in the world but his closeness, the tough-sweetness of him against which she seemed to have no defence. At last, shaken and breathless, she drew away. 'What,' she asked tremulously, 'did you do that for?'

He made no answer, and because she couldn't sustain the intensity of his gaze, she turned her face aside. She was unaware of the picture she presented or the effect it was having on him. Strands of glimmering copper had escaped from her topknot and the nape of her neck looked young and slender and very vulnerable. 'I suppose,' she said very low, 'it was your way of getting my mind off awkward questions?'

'It worked, didn't it?' She caught a maddening note of amusement in the deep tones. Before she could argue the matter he had turned aside. 'Sorry, I've got to go. Rusty's outside making "come-out-here" noises. I'd better go and find out what he wants.'

It's just an excuse, Fleur thought resentfully, but glancing through the window, she caught sight of Rusty waiting beneath the outside light. A moment later Logan came to join him and as she watched the two men talking together, the angry thoughts sped through her mind. The man in authority! How soon Logan had succeeded in getting everyone here on his side, so to speak. Her father, the station staff, even Daphne. They seemed to have forgotten all about Bart. You too? The thought came unbidden, and all at once it came to her how close she herself had come a few minutes ago to belonging to the same category, weakly letting herself succumb to Logan's male magnetism. But only because I was taken by surprise, she rationalised with herself. I won't ever fall into that trap again! Deep in her mind a small voice jeered, 'You can't afford to! Not when his nearness, his kiss, went straight to your head, made you lose sight of all the really important things, like the answers to the questions that you still don't know!'

CHAPTER THREE

FLEUR awoke very early in the morning to the sound of dogs barking, shepherds whistling and all the activity of the annual routine that had been established on the station for as long as she could remember. Just another muster, held on a clear summer's day when the sheep that had been grazing for months out to the far boundaries would be driven up steep slopes and down into gullies to join up with the main bunch. In the half light before dawn, stock horses would have been caught and saddled, and in the cookhouse Barney would have served a meal of colossal proportions to shepherds and musterers.

Dropping from the bed, she hurried to the window and pulling aside the curtains, peered towards a stockman who was riding up the slopes. Even from this distance sounds of shouting reached her on the clear air as one of the shepherds threatened his dog with dismemberment. Fleur, however, took no notice. She was accustomed to the colourful language used by the shepherds towards the team of dogs that were almost an extension of themselves.

In spite of herself her gaze roved the sun-dried hills and she was just in time to catch a glimpse of Logan as he rode his black stallion up an almost perpendicular slope. At the summit, horse and rider were silhouetted against the flaming sun-glow fanning over the eastern horizon, then they had vanished down the hillside.

For a long time that morning Fleur watched from the verandah as sheep came stringing around high slopes and along ridges, forming a woolly mass by the creek, to spill through the window and splash out on the opposite bank. Overhead a helicopter gave the head shepherd an opportunity of flying over rough country where sheep were hidden, cutting down the work by horseback.

When at last she went into the dining room she found her father seated at the long table while Daphne cleared away plates from an earlier meal she had served.

'Hi, Dad. Morning, Daph,' Fleur greeted the housekeeper. Helping herself to stewed tamarillos from a glass bowl, she poured coffee for herself and her father and slid bread into the toaster. 'Who was at the first sitting?' she enquired of Daphne.

'The helicopter pilot for one——'

'And an aerial photographer,' Fleur's father added.

'That's fantastic!' Fleur said happily. 'At last we'll have a really up-to-date picture of the whole station. We can hang it up over the fireplace in the lounge in place of that faded old photo that's as old as the hills and way out of date anyway.'

Her father opened his mouth to answer, then seemed to decide against it, and swiftly Daphne changed the subject. 'Are you going riding today, Fleur?'

'Am I ever?' All at once her face was alive with enthusiasm. 'I've been out of the saddle for so long it isn't funny!' Her face fell. 'I'll have to wait a while, though. I'm expecting a ... telephone call ... just a friend.'

When the meal was over the older man glanced up to

the big schoolroom clock hanging on the wall. 'Time I was off to give the others a hand.'

'I'll come down to the stables with you, Dad——' She paused thoughtfully. 'Tell me something—why did you give this Logan guy permission to ride my mare?'

Her father pulled at his ear, a twinkle in his eyes. 'That's an easy one to answer! I'm not riding much these days and that Sally of yours was getting fat and lazy. Logan offered to give her some exercise and I knew you'd be pleased as punch to come back and find her in good nick.' He eyed her with a teasing grin. 'Don't tell me you're not?'

'Of course I'm pleased about her being ridden. But,' she added crossly, 'why did it have to be *him*?'

'Logan?' Stan Kennedy looked surprised. 'You couldn't have a better man for the job. He's a crack rider ... plays polo, South Island show-jumping champion. Oh, he knows how to handle horses,' another teasing glance, 'women too, I wouldn't wonder.'

Fleur wrinkled her nose at him in disbelief. 'I only hope you're right—about the horses, I mean,' she amended hastily. 'I don't know a thing about the man. Neither do you, so far as I can see. A month or so doesn't seem long to put your trust in a man like Logan. You too, Daph——'

'Oh, Logan's okay,' Fleur's father said with a grin that made him look years younger. 'Get to know him a bit and you'll feel the same way about him. He's full value, Logan.'

'So *you* say,' said Fleur under her breath, and looked up to catch Daphne's smug smile. 'And you're as bad!' she flung at the housekeeper. 'You all seem besotted with the man, for some reason. Yet with Bart——'

Her words died away. It was weird, she thought, the way in which mention of Bart's name put a damper on any conversation with her family. It was as if everyone was suddenly on the defensive, wary, the air thick with something she couldn't put a finger on. 'For heaven's sake,' she cried into the heavy silence, 'what's he done to make you all change like this? Nothing you can tell me, that's for sure, so it can't be anything but horrible rumours! Both of you would believe what someone's told you about Bart without even bothering to hear his side of the story.' She swung around to face Daphne accusingly. 'That's it, isn't it?' she demanded hotly.

Instead of the heated denial she expected there was only the odd silence. The next moment she intercepted a significant glance that passed between the other two. Suddenly anger flared in her. 'All right, then,' she cried, 'don't tell me! It would be all lies anyway! Some wild story someone has dreamed up just to discredit Bart.'

'What makes you so sure,' her father said quietly, 'that it's all a matter of lies?'

'What makes you?' she flung back at him. He made no reply and she found herself regretting the outburst of temper. Why did I hurt him like that? she asked herself. But I had to stick up for Bart. There's no one else to do it. Aloud she said very low, 'Anyway, I trust him, no matter what's happened!' As her father rose to his feet she said quickly, 'I'll come down to the stables with you, Dad.'

In silence they made their way out of the room and presently Fleur was helping him to saddle up the stock horse waiting in the stables. He climbed up into the saddle and gathering up the reins, looked down at her, a twinkle in his eyes. 'I can still keep an eye on things, you know,' he told her, forestalling her unspoken query as to the wisdom of his riding out alone in the hills.

'Of course you can!' Indeed, she thought, this morning he appeared fitter, happier. One good thing, she mused, about her having come home. She opened the wide gate and closed it behind horse and rider.

The bad news was Bart. Restlessly she wandered back to the house, passing the line of empty sheepdog kennels and scarcely aware of the wide garden borders where the vibrant scarlet of exotic poinsettia rose above fragrant English cottage flowers. Today she was bound to the house, within call of the peal of the telephone bell. All the time she was unpacking her suitcase, placing frocks and shirts on hangers in the old-fashioned wardrobe and storing away underwear in bureau drawers, the thought niggled in her mind that at any moment Bart might telephone her. For he must have a rough idea of the date of her arrival home, and if she were lucky . . .

Presently she went down the long hall and into the spacious airy kitchen where one wall was lined with gleaming white deep-freeze cabinet, refrigerator and electric range. Daphne, who scorned all attempts by her employer to install a dishwasher, had evidently been delayed in performing her usual household chores, Fleur thought, for the housekeeper was starting to wash the breakfast dishes, and without even thinking, Fleur picked up the tea-towel from the rod.

'You know something, Daph,' she was watching the thin sun-browned hands plucking dishes from a froth of detergent, 'everything seems just the same, as if I'd never been away. Well,' she dried a cup absently and her face sobered, 'some things are a bit different.' She ran on in a rush of words, 'I keep wondering about Dad. He'll be all right, won't he, Daph? I couldn't bear to think he might be really desperately ill.'

No one could dispute the integrity of Daphne's lively brown eyes, and knowing her straightforward nature Fleur had no doubt of the honesty of the housekeeper's reply. 'I know exactly how he is,' she stated bluntly. 'The doctor had a chat with me about him, and your dad will be fine now. So long,' she added darkly, 'as he hasn't got things to worry him.'

Fleur wrinkled her nose at her. 'Like me?' It wouldn't be the first time, she mused, that Daphne had felt the need to do what she termed 'putting young Fleur in her place!'

The housekeeper shook out the dish mop. 'Could be, if you're not careful!' All at once she looked Fleur full in the eyes. 'Why don't you forget about Barton?'

Swiftly Fleur endeavoured to change a dangerous subject. 'Tell me something, Daph. Dad let on to me that he didn't want me to know about that setback in health he had a while ago. He didn't want to worry me, he said. But I can't help wondering if you did write me at the time and I didn't ever get the letter.'

'I certainly did!' Daphne said stoutly. 'I said to myself, "Someone should write to Fleur and tell her to come home right away." So I sat down at the desk that very night and told you all about it. But when I didn't hear a word from you in the next week and you didn't put a phone call through to us, I told the doctor you didn't seem to be coming home in a hurry. So he arranged for a trained nurse to come here for a month, and after that time, there was no need——'

Fleur exclaimed, appalled, 'As bad as that? Oh, Daph, if only I'd known! If only I'd received your letter——' She broke off, raising anxious eyes to the older woman's sun-dried face. 'You *do* believe me?'

Daphne didn't hesitate for a moment. 'I believe you, thousands wouldn't!'

Fleur breathed a sigh of relief. 'Thank heaven for that!' She added, 'And that wasn't the only letter that never arrived. Apparently Bart sent me one—Daphne, tell me, do *you* know what it is about Bart? Why everyone has it in for him?'

A shutter seemed to come down over Daphne's face. 'I only know what everyone else does.'

'I don't even know that,' said Fleur on a note of desperation. 'Tell me, Daph, why *did* Bart leave here?'

'How would I know?' The older woman evaded her eyes. 'Why does any man leave a job? I suppose he got the offer of a better one somewhere else. All I know is that he didn't even wait for a reference from your dad. He just took off the day after Logan arrived here.'

Fleur said thoughtfully, 'Did Bart look angry when he left here, or disappointed, or what?'

'I only saw him for a moment and he looked pretty mad to me. He drove away in his car very early one morning. Didn't say goodbye to me or to anyone else, for that matter. One of the shepherds was riding along the road and he told me he had a narrow miss from being collected by Bart's car. Seems he was driving like a bat out of hell!'

'Bart was always a fast driver,' Fleur said defensively. She was biting her thumbnail. 'It all seems so odd. You know Bart, Daph. Oh, I know he's a charmer, but he'd never let me down like this if he could help it!' She raised clear eyes to the older woman's dark orbs. 'You must know something about this that you're not letting on——'

Daphne looked away evasively. 'I never listen to gossip,' she said repressively. Then, on a note of relief, 'Listen—there's the phone ringing. Weren't you expecting a call this morning?'

Already, however, Fleur had dropped to the floor and was running out into the hallway, lifting the handpiece of the instrument. 'Hello! Hello!' Her heart dropped when a feminine voice said, 'Te Haruru Station?'

'Yes, yes!'

The next minute Bart's familiar tones took over. 'Fleur?'

'It's you, Bart! It's really you!' Relief and excitement and a sudden happiness were all mixed up in her tone. 'Where are you? When can I see you?'

'That's what I'm ringing you about. Look,' his voice had a taut, wary inflection, 'are you alone? Can you speak privately?'

'No problem. Daphne's the only one at home, all the men are away today at the muster.'

'Hell!' The word echoed explosively in her ears. 'What's that you said?' All at once his tone was terse and apprehensive, almost fearful.

'The muster,' said Fleur bewilderedly, 'Why? What's wrong with that?'

'Everything!' Suddenly the line was a jumble of voices.

'Bart? Are you still there?'

'Right here, darling!' The line had cleared and his voice was so normal that she decided she must have imagined a note of shock and horror in his tones. 'Look, I can't tell you now, it's a long story, but they've got it in for me at Te Haruru——'

'I know, I know . . . but what happened, Bart——'

'Tell you when I see you. That is,' all at once his voice sharpened, 'if you *want* to see me?'

'Don't say such stupid things! I'm just longing to see you. At the airport——'

'Never mind that,' he broke in, 'it's now that matters. Listen, I've got one day in Auckland before I catch my plane for Australia. I didn't think, after all those rumours that are flying about, that you'd want to see me again, but if you do——'

'Of course I do!'

'Well, here's the gen. Could you meet me in Auckland on Friday morning at the ferry buildings and we can get things straightened out. Maybe,' his tone was happy, caressing, Bart's voice as she had known it a year ago, 'we could make a fresh start, hmm? Everything the way we planned it?' All at once the low persuasive tones were threaded with excitement. 'I'll book you a seat on the plane and we can take off for Queensland together. All it takes is for you to believe in me. Trust me, my darling.' As always, the caressing magic of his low vibrant tone did things to her heart and wiped everything else from her mind.

'But I do trust you! It's just that I can't make out what's happening.'

'Pack of rumours, that's all!' The confidence and gaiety was back in his tone and so was the charm. 'Nothing we can't sort out between us. Once we're away in Australia——'

Fleur's thoughts were rioting on confusion. 'Why there? Is it a holiday, or what?'

'Better than that, my sweet. A honeymoon, you and me. Remember how we planned a honeymoon on the Queensland coast or one of the Pacific islands? What does it matter, so long as I can take you with me. Can't *wait* to see you,' the throbbing intensity of his tone touched her.

'But I—Where are you staying in Auckland? What if I can't find you on the wharf, if something happens——'

'Nothing's going to happen. Happenings are all in the future, like the special marriage licence I'm going to fix up. Marriage, a honeymoon in the most fantastic place you can think of, the lot!' All at once his tone was hard and taut. 'You won't let me down?'

'Let you down? What's the matter with you, Bart?'

Laughter and disbelief threaded her light tones. 'You know me better than that!'

'Great! We've been parted for too long already, my sweet,' the low caressing note was back in his tones, 'you know that! We're not going to let anything come between us ever again.' Suddenly his voice was threaded with bitterness. 'They've got their knife into me at Te Haruru, you can blame your precious new manager for that! So this little chat's got to be just between you and me. You'll keep it to yourself?'

'I'll have to,' she laughed lightly, 'if we're going to go it alone! Though how I'm going to explain away taking off for a day's trip to town carrying a suitcase with me——'

'Don't give it another thought!' Suddenly his voice rang with confidence. 'I've got swags of funds, so you can get all the gear you want in the shops here before we take off at five for the airport. Anyway,' came the intimate tones, 'why bother? I prefer you without, and I'm the guy who counts in your life from now on!' Before she could answer he ran on tersely, 'It's on, then? Friday at two at the ferry buildings on the Auckland wharf? You'll be there? I've got to know for sure.'

The thoughts whirled through her mind as surprise and relief mingled with a heady sense of excitement. She wanted to marry Bart, didn't she? Just as he longed to marry her, and a runaway wedding would be the solution to all of their problems. So why was she hesitating? Why this odd sense of misgiving?

'I'm coming with you!' There, she thought, the words were out, the decision made. The excitement running through her veins was mounting, and it was a moment before she became aware of Bart's voice over the wire.

'I knew you wouldn't let me down!'

'Bart——' all at once a thought struck her, 'you haven't told me where I can get in touch with you if anything goes wrong——'

'Nothing in the world could stop me from meeting you!' he cut in, 'You're mine, remember? My girl, my sweetheart, my—wife!' The low tones throbbed with emotion as if, she thought, what he was telling her mattered terribly to him. 'This is it! Our chance to thumb our noses at the world and make a go of things together. Our *only* chance!'

'How do you mean?' she said bewilderedly, 'There'll be other days——'

'No!' Roughly Bart cut across her soft accents. 'I'll make your air booking today, but there's something you should know. If you don't show up on time I can't wait for you, so don't let me down, honey. You'll come?'

'I will—I will! You can count on me!'

'That's my girl! Look, love, do something for me, will you?'

'Anything——'

'Just—all that rubbish people tell you, you won't hold it against me? You'll know that it's all a put-up job, nothing but lies?'

'Trust me——'

'Sorry, darling, there's an overseas call coming through, I've got to go. Love you!'

'You, too. 'Bye—Oh, Bart, wait——'

It was no use, he had gone. Slowly, like a girl in a dream, Fleur replaced the receiver on its cradle. She should be feeling so happy, she was really only . . . The niggling thoughts that had lain at the back of her mind, smothered by the excitement of hearing Bart's voice and the thrilling anticipation of the runaway wedding, now surfaced to prick her conscience. Her father. He would be hurt, surprised, deeply shocked at finding her gone from the house so soon after her arrival home. Rather than become involved in a family quarrel that she knew would ensue at mention of Bart's name, she would invent some story to account for her absence from home for a few days, then write later explaining all that had happened. Not, she mused on a sigh, that that would be of any help. On the contrary. The dark goblin in her mind raised his jeering head. Suppose your father's health suffered because of you? A shock such as that you're proposing to give him could do dreadful damage. You'd never forgive yourself if anything happened to him.

But he has recovered from his illness, she comforted herself. He'll be quite all right if he doesn't overtax himself physically and gives up heavy work on the station, the doctor told him. In a few weeks' time Bart and I will come back to Te Haruru and Dad will get over this stupid antagonism he has for Bart and everything will be forgotten.

'You reckon?' She thrust away the tiny voice of the goblin deep in her mind.

Of course it will be made up, their quarrel. This is the nineteen-eighties, not Victorian times. Dad will get over it, of course he will. A small loving smile quirked her lips. He's much too fond of his 'Fox', as he still calls me, to let anyone, not even Bart, really come between us.

Still the niggle of anxiety persisted. If only Bart had given her some details of his own life—where he was living in Auckland, what he was doing there. He wasn't short of funds, he had told her, so he must be working in town. But of course, she reminded herself, during the year she had been overseas he would have saved madly for their approaching marriage. Somehow, though, it was difficult to imagine Bart saving madly. He had discerning, expensive tastes and liked to have the best of everything, entertainment, clothing, wines. And why not? she scolded herself. A thought ran through her mind. Probably he'd had an outsized win at the races. He was a man who betted heavily in the hopes of collecting a huge dividend and by the law of averages he was bound to be lucky one of these days. Once he was married, of course, he would settle down ... she would soon change his ideas in that direction.

When she went back to the kitchen she found Daphne tidying a stack of cupboards. 'That was Barton Howard, I suppose?' said the housekeeper disapprovingly.

'That's right.' Fleur perched herself on the bench and reached out a hand to pick up an apple from the overflowing bucket at her feet. As she bit into the sun-ripened fruit she reminded herself that she must have forgotten the futility of trying to keep anything from

Daphne. The housekeeper had the sharpest ears in the district, although to give her her due, she never divulged anything of family affairs to outsiders.

'I thought as much!' Daphne banged a jar of nectarine preserves down on a shelf. 'If you want my advice——' she threw over her shoulder.

'I don't, you know!' All at once Fleur was lifted high on a wave of excitement. Why hadn't she noticed before the tender blue of the sky, the softness of the sea breeze blowing in at the open window! She brought her mind back to Daphne's demanding tones.

'What does *he* want?'

'Nothing much.' Fleur forced her voice to a careless note and hoped that Daphne wouldn't turn at that moment to take in her flushed cheeks and shining eyes, betraying an inner excitement. 'Everything's going to be all right,' she spoke unthinkingly, 'Bart will explain it all——'

'*What?*' Daphne's brown eyes were wide and incredulous. 'He's not coming back here, not after the muster?'

'For heaven's sake,' Fleur cried exasperatedly, 'what's the muster got to do with it? Don't be nosey, Daph. He rang to tell me he loves me, and that,' she threw the housekeeper a teasing grin, 'is really all that matters!' Ignoring Daphne's expressive sniff, she went out of the room.

Friday, she was thinking, the day after tomorrow. Probably the local plane will be fully booked with schoolchildren returning home after the holidays. I could take a hire car. It would cost the earth, but who cares when it happens to be the most important journey of my whole life! She would invent an excuse to her father to explain her hurried departure to town—maybe a sick woman friend who needed her help urgently in a nursing capacity for a day or so.

Then before long she would write home from her new address in Australia, explaining everything that had happened. Unconsciously she twisted a strand of bright hair round and round her finger in a worried gesture. Her father might possibly accept her fabricated story at its face value, but Logan would immediately see through the lie. Swiftly she pulled herself up. What did it matter what Logan thought of her? Hadn't he already made it perfectly plain that nothing she could do would further disillusion him on that score?—and she wondered why the thought should matter so much.

Back in her room she had the oddest impression that she had never been away. All she needed to complete the illusion was Bart. Excitement swept her anew at the thought of how soon they would be together again, with no more partings, the bewildering questions that had plagued her since her return home disposed of. Meantime, it was a champagne day, and up in the horse paddock, Sally was waiting to be ridden. Fleur's riding boots were still in the wardrobe and her thin cotton shirt and worn denim jeans would be fine for a gallop over the hills. Gathering her hair together, she fashioned it into a roll, securing it firmly at the back of her head. Presently she was running down the verandah steps, making her way between borders of flowers on either side of the winding path. Delphiniums, carnations, petunias, asters, all flourished thanks to Daphne's loving care. This morning the swimming pool with its overhanging bushes was shot with diamond points of sunlight and trees and bushes seemed to be a-glitter in the clear morning air.

Soon she was through the small gate and taking a dusty path leading to the stables. The garages and outbuildings appeared to be deserted, but as she approached the cookhouse a stocky middle-aged man with sun-browned face and twinkling blue eyes emerged from the open door.

'How are you, Barney?' She had always liked the cook, who had been at Te Haruru for many years.

'Hello yourself!' The weather-roughened face split in a grin. 'Good to have you back here again! How was your stint over on the Mekong River with that World Vision outfit you joined up with?'

'I wouldn't have missed it for the world!' Her green eyes were alight with enthusiasm. 'I got really first-hand experience over there of the plight of the refugees, and sometimes it was awfully frustrating trying to help them. They just didn't understand what things like immunisation against tetanus was all about. You needed lots of patience and a bit of knowledge of languages and the local culture, but it was worth all the effort, and they were so grateful for what we did. Would you believe, Barney, that I arrived back in New Zealand with lots of white strings tied around my right wrist as a thank-you gesture from the tribespeople.' All at once her eyes were dreamy. 'I'm hoping to go back there some day, but that's a long-term project. Right now, it's great to be home again and everything seems just the same, except for Barton——' She broke off at the sudden look of interest that had leaped into his eyes.

'You still planning to marry Barton?'

'Of course I am, Barney! We've been engaged to each other for over a year now,' the long dimple ran down her cheek, 'and I reckon that's long enough for anyone! Some folks,' she added lightly, 'would say it was too long,' and waited for his reaction to the words. The next moment she realised that if she had hoped to learn anything of Bart's movements from the cook, she was due for a disappointment, for all at once he appeared to have lost interest in her love-life.

'Depends,' he grunted noncommittally. ''Scuse me— I've left some tack on the stove and it's boiling over. I can smell it from here!'

'You've got a better nose than I have, Barney——' but he had already left her and was hurrying back towards the cookhouse.

Oh well, Fleur shrugged her shoulders as she went on down the winding path towards the stables, she might have known that no one here would give a thing away, not when it came to Bart's affairs. All at once she was swept by a surge of fierce loyalty. No wonder Bart had been surprised—well, he'd sounded that way when he'd spoken to her on the phone—at her loyalty and devotion. Around here she seemed to be the only one to believe in his integrity. But she would change all that, she promised herself. Before long they would all see how stupidly mistaken they had been in losing faith in Bart.

Presently she reached the deserted stables and soon, a bridle jingling from her hand, she was making her way up the sandy track to the slopes where the mare grazed. Up in the horse paddock, Sally gave a soft whinny at her approach, and Fleur's tumultuous reflections gave way to surprise and pleasure. For the white mare looked to be in peak condition, her snowy coat silkier than ever, the flowing tail and mane well groomed. As always, Sally was easy to catch. Indeed, as Fleur neared her, the mare nickered softly, then moved towards her mistress, standing quietly while Fleur fitted the bit into her mouth. Springing lightly on to the mare's back, Fleur guided her mount towards the wide Taranaki gate, and Sally waited obediently while Fleur closed the gate behind her.

She rode the mare down to the stables, then threw a sheepskin over the white back, followed by the saddle. She was tightening the girthband when a shadow fell across the opening and she looked up to find her father beside her. He had dismounted from his horse and was watching her approvingly. 'I've kept your gear well oiled while you've been away. I knew you'd be keen to get in the saddle once again once you were home.'

'Thanks, Dad.' She put a foot on his hand and jumped into the saddle. 'I'm off for a look-see up in the hills.'

He was removing the saddle from his own mount. 'Good idea—Oh, if you happen to run into Logan between here and there, give him a message from me, will you? Tell him to pick up a couple of horses at Martin's Gully. Dave wants to meet him there about three. You might come across him——'

'Not if I can help it!' Fleur made the observation silently, scarcely taking in the import of the message.

Soon she was taking a track up a grassy hill as she made her way towards the airstrip on the ridge above, for on the long mown stretch of flat land she could let Sally out into a full gallop. The airstrip had been made for the use of the crop-dusting planes that skimmed the high peaks as they dropped fertiliser dust over inaccessible slopes. Today, however, there was a difference, for a small red-and-white painted plane stood in a hangar. Logan's, of course! Who else? Not that it was unusual for a station owner in the hilly district to own a private plane, but certainly it was unusual for Te Haruru. Fleur refused to waste time thinking of Logan, she told herself, and urged her mount to a fast canter and then into a gallop. And indeed, in the exhilaration of the ride with the salt wind singing past her ears and the only sound the soft pounding of hooves on turf, she forgot everything else. All too soon they reached a hillside and she pulled the mare to a walk as Sally picked her way down the steep slope.

On and on ... Fleur lost count of time as she rode on, urging her mount to a canter on ridges, dropping down into gullies and climbing the steep slopes. Everywhere were sheep ... moving in single file over narrow ridges, milling together on the flats. Around her the barking of sheepdogs mingled with the shouts of drovers and the cries of sheep.

All at once from over the next rise, a horseman came galloping towards her. Logan, she thought, it would be! An instinct she couldn't define—defiance? anger?—impelled her to turn and urge her mount up a stony slope, sheer and slippery, where loose earth had already crumbled down the cliff-face.

The mare's hooves were scraping as she tried to find a foothold on the crumbling rockface. At last, finding smooth footholds, she gathered strength and lunged up the slope, her sides running with sweat.

'Take it easy!' She became aware of a male voice shouting behind her, and a swift glance over her shoulder showed her that Logan was gaining on her, the great black stallion almost perpendicular on the cliffside as he took the slope at a full trot.

'Grab a hunk of mane!' warned the voice behind her.

She turned an indignant face. 'I won't fall!'

'Horses do!' She caught the nervy thrust in his tones. 'Slip your feet out of the stirrups, lie along her back!'

Fleur took not the slightest notice. For one thing, she was already grabbing the hunk of white mane, and for another, she was determined to sit as straight as she could, which was difficult.

'Do as I tell you!'

For answer she tossed her head. Halfway up the stony slope she pulled in to give Sally a chance to catch her breath, and behind her Logan too reined in.

'Why didn't you do as I told you?' She was aware of his threatening tones.

She brushed away the beads of moisture from her forehead. 'Why should I?'

'Ask yourself! It's a steep one, this. I'd rather be out of the way if your horse fell.'

'Oh? It's yourself you're worrying about?' she threw over her shoulder.

'And you.' She sensed he was controlling himself with an effort. 'Best not to be between your mount and the rock if your horse takes a tumble.'

'Do you think,' she demanded scornfully, 'that I don't know that? I've been riding over these hills since I was seven years old!'

'You should know better than to take chances then!'

'Oh, you——' she cried exasperatedly, then as she caught sight of a few sheep, their backs heavy with wool, on the summit of the hill, her voice changed. 'Look, there are some stragglers up there!' The next moment she was urging Sally up the steep ascent once again and the mare scrambled up the rocky slope and, with a last plunge, reached the summit. Soon Fleur and Logan were heading the sheep along the ridge and down into the valley where they merged into the main flock.

Fleur was about to ride away when just in time she recalled the message she had promised to deliver to Logan, *if she met him.* The gully where she was waiting was cool and fragrant, the native bush with leafy green trees and thickly growing vines making it a place of sunlight and shadow. Somewhere in the branches of a tree high above a bellbird was chiming its magical notes.

At last he reached her, his face impassive, and she watched as he dropped down from the saddle and tethered his mount. 'Why are you stopping here?' Fleur demanded.

For answer he glanced up at the sun, a burning disc almost directly overhead in the blue bowl of the sky, then he shrugged broad sinewy shoulders. 'I'm ready for lunch,' he threw an ironic glance towards her mutinous, suspicious face, 'even if you're not.'

'I didn't say so——' she began, then realised too late that she had fallen into a trap. The heat and dust of the mountainous tracks had parched her throat and she could swear he was deliberately taking a Thermos of tea from his pack to tantalise her. 'There's swags of tea,' he threw off the statement offhandedly, 'so please yourself.'

Fleur weakened, she couldn't help it. If only she had got Daphne to put her up some lunch, if only she'd known she would be so long away, but time had slipped by and now it was too late.

'Well,' he was saying offhandedly, 'it's up to you.' He was anything but welcoming. She hesitated. It was the sight of Daphne's sandwiches that made up her mind. She had forgotten, in all the months of living on foreign foods, the goodness of Daphne's crusty homebaked wholemeal bread spread with yellow farm butter and filled with tomatoes freshly picked from the garden, crisp lettuce, cold mutton. It was all too much to cope with. Anyway, she told herself as she slipped down from the saddle and tethered her mare, I don't have to like him just because I happen to be thirsty—and hungry. She dropped down to the long sweet-smelling grass, taking care to sit as far away from him as possible. The two sheepdogs lay nearby.

Logan was filling the extra plastic cup on the flask with hot tea. 'No milk—I don't take it.'

'I prefer it this way,' lied Fleur. The next minute she discovered that it wasn't a lie at all, for never had she known tea to be so refreshing and thirst-quenching.

'Sandwich?' He was extending a foil-wrapped package and Fleur tried not to look too eager. 'All right, then.' The next moment she realised that any attempt at nonchalance was wasted on him, because he saw right through her pretence of non-caring. He would. You could tell by the ironic twist of his lips and the amused gleam in his hazel eyes. Beast! Aloud she murmured, 'I didn't expect to be away so long,' and hated herself for the note of apology in her voice. Why on earth was she bothering to explain to him? He wouldn't be deceived by anything she said anyway! He knew all too well that she was practically dying of thirst as well as being downright hungry. And that being so, she told herself, she might as well help herself to another sandwich.

When the picnic meal was over Fleur leaned back against a tree-trunk, hands crossed around her knees. In the tree above, the bellbird was still singing his heart out, and the salt breeze was cool on her face. Her glance went to Logan as he leaned back on one elbow. With his sombrero pushed to the back of his head, his black hair unruly, he looked younger, more carefree than she had yet seen him, she mused. His gaze was fixed on the white woolly mass flowing like cream over a green slope and he appeared to have forgotten her. Anyway, why would he want to talk to her? He had made no secret of his irrational intense dislike of the boss's daughter. And that, she told herself with a tightening of soft lips, makes two of us! He was insufferable, rude, arrogant, critical. Imagine telling her how to ride her mare up a dangerous slope, on her own territory! All at once a horrifying thought crossed her mind. What if he should imagine she had followed him up here for reasons of her own? Hurriedly she tried to explain. 'I wanted to see you——'

She broke off as an ironic grin lightened the sun-bronzed face and his thickly marked eyebrows rose. 'Already?' The word packed a power of meaning and Fleur's cheeks did a slow burn at the implications of the drawling voice. Frantically she pushed clinging tendrils of hair back from her damp forehead. 'To tell you,' she said thickly, 'that I——' Then it happened. A wild sweet excitement pulsed through her veins and she was

aware only of his eyes, deep pools of light in which she
felt as though she were drowning, making her forget
everything else in the world, even Bart. Bart ... the
name broke the insidious spell that held her and with an
effort she wrenched her glance aside, groping in her
mind for the words she had been about to say.

'My dad,' she said breathlessly—why was she
trembling?—'he wanted me to tell you to—to meet
Dave at Martin's Gully at three to pick up—a couple of
horses.'

'Can do.' All at once Logan appeared to have lost
interest in the matter. The silence lengthened, and
becoming aware of his mocking gaze, Fleur forced her
voice to a casual note. 'I came here by way of the
airstrip. Is that your plane on the runway? You've got a
pilot's licence?'

His glance was ironic. 'The Cessna goes better when
you know which lever to pull.'

Sarcastic brute! She flashed him a resentful look.
Before she could think up a sufficiently crushing retort
he was saying, 'I found the plane was a terrific time-
saver on the place I was running down South, so when I
took over here——'

'Half-share, wasn't it?' she cut in coolly.

'And manager,' he corrected her blandly, 'or didn't
your dad tell you?'

Blast him! she fumed silently. He wouldn't let her off
anything, and she brought her mind back to his deep
gravelly tones. 'The old crate saves a hell of a lot of
time and comes in mighty handy on occasions. Like
tomorrow, I'm due to meet someone in Auckland, just
a few hours' trip by air, and once the muster's out of
the way——'

Fleur had taken in only part of what he had told her.
'You mean,' she could scarcely contain her excitement,
'that you're going to Auckland? Tomorrow?'

'That's the idea.' His voice was deadpan. 'Want a lift?
I'd better warn you, though, it's just a quick run there
and back.'

'Oh, that doesn't matter!' Fleur forgot all her
resolutions to be remote and distant and condescending.

'I'd just love to come with you—it would suit me fine.
What time are you planning to leave?'

'Round about midday, the trip won't take that long.
The way you're looking,' he observed dispassionately,
'anyone would think I'd invited you along for a spin
over to Paris and back.'

She sent him a challenging look. 'Would you?'

'Not a chance!' He was eyeing her with his merciless
stare.

'I didn't think you would! But it doesn't matter.' She
couldn't hide her elation. 'Auckland is as far as I want
to go on Friday. Just to get there!' All at once she
realised that her intense excitement at his offer of a lift
to town might strike him as a little odd. He had that
observant way with him and she had an uneasy feeling
that he might read her thoughts. 'It will save me the
trouble of booking a trip by road,' she ran on in a rush
of words. 'I could get a plane seat maybe, but it's
chancy, with school holidays finishing this week——'

'Why?' She didn't trust his narrowed stare one little
bit. 'Is it so important for you to get to town all of a
sudden?'

'Oh, it is! It is——!' There, she thought in dismay,
she had said the wrong thing once again, giving him the
impression that something more than a shopping
excursion was on her mind. Hurriedly she gathered her
wits together. 'There's someone I want to see, a friend
in town. She isn't very well and I thought——' She
broke off, aware that he was eyeing her narrowly.
'Why,' she demanded, 'are you looking at me like that?
What's so odd,' she added defensively, 'about a girl
meeting a friend in the city? There's nothing unusual
about it, is there?' Even to her own ears her laugh had a
brittle sound.

'Nothing at all,' Logan agreed smoothly.

Fleur had never been skilful when it came to lies and
evasions, and the words fell from her lips before she
could stop them. 'I don't know why you're looking at
me that way—as if you don't believe me?'

'Oh, I believe you all right.' He was hatefully bland,
and inwardly she braced herself for what was coming,

for whatever it was she knew it wouldn't be to her advantage. 'I just wondered why you didn't ask when I planned on leaving the city.' His voice, offhand and pleasant, reached her with its damning implications. 'Or didn't you plan on coming back?'

It took her a moment or two to recover from the impact. 'Don't be silly! Why on earth wouldn't I?'

He shrugged wide shoulders, his eyes not leaving her face. 'You tell me!'

To divert a conversation that was coming perilously close to the truth, Fleur turned her face aside and looked around her. 'Goodness,' she cried, 'there's smoke coming out of the chimney of the old house on the hill! I suppose,' she nattered on wildly, 'you could call it our nearest neighbour, though no one has lived there for ever so long. I remember when we were coming back from the airport we passed the place and it looked just the same as when I went away—decrepit old house crying out for paint, deserted outbuildings.' She scarcely realised what she was saying as she ran on. 'Only the pink roses climbing everywhere looked the same. But someone must have bought it.'

'True.' Logan's cool uninterested manner was puzzling, especially when he was eyeing her so intently.

'And there's not much land left nowadays,' she ran on, 'only a few acres. Just enough to run a few sheep, wouldn't you say?'

'Seems like it.' He was laughing at her, she thought crossly. It was in the dryness of his tone, the way in which he was looking at her. But she wasn't going to give in now. 'Of course, if that's what you want——'

'That's exactly what I want,' he sent her an unreadable look, 'among other things. A house and sufficient land to run a few black sheep. That's why I bought it.'

'You?' The next minute she rallied herself. 'Funny, my dad thinks you're a top man when it comes to sheep-farming. It doesn't sound like that to me——'

'You'll have to wait and see, won't you?' All at once his tone was low and cutting. 'Could be you'll find you've been dead wrong about a lot of things around here, just like you are about your boy-friend——'

Fleur sprang to her feet, the hot colour flooding her face. 'If you're getting at Bart again, I don't believe you! You—and Dad's as bad—always hinting at something he's done wrong. It makes me so mad when he's not here to defend himself! Well, I'm not going to listen to lies about him——' She stopped short and regarded him with eyes glittering with anger. 'Tell me, did you ever meet Bart?'

Lazily Logan gazed up at her, and his twisted grin said it all. 'Briefly.'

'And you can judge him,' she grasped the opportunity he had handed her, 'just like that!' All at once she felt she could defend Bart against the whole world and win out. 'If,' she challenged him hotly, 'you had one scrap of proof to show me for all this smear campaign——'

He was replacing the Thermos in his saddlebag. 'Stick around for a day or two,' his voice was expressionless, 'and you might be surprised!'

'I doubt it!' She was throwing the reins over her mare's head. Lightly she sprang up into the saddle and without another word, still smarting from the hot anger that seemed to flare up in her whenever she found herself alone with this overbearing stranger, she dug her heels into the mare's flanks and cantered away.

CHAPTER FOUR

THAT night the talk echoing around the dinner table was all of the muster. Everyone agreed that it had been an unqualified success. The sunny weather had held and there had been no casualties among the stock, not even when the sheep had been driven across the river.

Bruce, the young helicopter pilot, a slim, alert-looking man with bright brown eyes, was seated opposite Fleur at the old kauri table, and he tried hard to capture her attention.

'You weren't around when I was here three months ago, spraying the gorse out on the far boundary,' his appreciative gaze lingered on Fleur's upswept coppery hair and vulnerable face. 'I sure would have noticed!'

'No.' For some absurd reason, awareness of Logan's cool stare was making her feel tongue-tied. She drew a deep breath and tried to ignore the watchful gaze of the big man seated next to the pilot. 'Would you believe? I've been away for a year nursing overseas with the World Vision Health Care programme at the Ban Vinai camp on the Thai side of the Mekong River. It all seems like a dream now that I'm back home again where everything's so different. There's so much space everywhere,' laughingly her gaze swept the heaped plates around the table, 'and such a lot of food about!'

The dark-eyed young man grinned, his mind clearly concerned more with Fleur's face with its changing expressions than with the words that fell from her lips. 'You enjoyed the experience, then?'

'Did I ever!' Her tones rang with enthusiasm. 'Though it could be very frustrating at times, and we had to overcome a lot of resistance to get results. Do you know, I don't think those sick refugees had ever heard of a doctor! But boy, did they know about their *sharman*—that's their medicine man—and we just had to co-operate with him. Oh, I wouldn't have missed that year away for the world!' Still discomfitingly aware of Logan's hard stare, some devil sparked her to say, 'I get the idea, though, that Logan doesn't approve.' She threw him a defiant glance. 'But of course,' she tried to speak nonchalantly, but her heightened colour gave her away, 'it's nothing to do with him! We're practically strangers,' she tossed him a bright smile, 'that's right, isn't it, Logan?'

Across the table their glances met and held. Then his powerful shoulders lifted in a shrug. 'That's right,' he agreed, and resumed his conversation with the aerial photographer, a serious-eyed young man with a quiet manner of speech.

All at once Fleur became aware of the pilot's eager persuasive tones. 'You'll have to come up for a spin with me. I'm booked in here for another day, so how about tomorrow? Come on, say you will?'

'Love to——' all at once she caught Logan's eye, 'but I'm off tomorrow for an air trip to town, hitching a ride with Logan in his Cessna.'

The boyish face fell. The next minute his expression brightened. 'Next time I'm over this way, then? I'll give you a buzz.' His eyes said, 'And I'll make sure that I am over this way very soon.'

'That would be great.' She dropped her gaze for fear the words hadn't rung true, especially to Logan's ears. What was it about him that disturbed her so? Even when he was apparently involved in a conversation with others, the aerial photographer, her father, Rusty, the head shepherd, still she had an uneasy feeling that Logan was nevertheless alert to every word she said. Alert, and suspicious of her motives. She shook the absurd impression aside. He couldn't possibly guess the real purpose of her journey to town tomorrow. Or could he?

She brought her mind back to the present. 'You'd be so lucky,' the aerial photographer, newly-married, was saying to his co-worker with a teasing grin. 'I got the word on the grapevine that Fleur's already spoken for. Some guy named Howard who's been cooling his heels all the time she's been away overseas.' Fleur wondered whether she merely imagined the heavy waiting silence that ensued. Apparently not, however, she realised the next moment as the photographer glanced uncertainly around the table. He said diffidently, 'Don't take too much notice of me, though, I'm just a new-chum around here, might have got my lines crossed.'

As the talk resumed around her with its discussion of farming matters, stock and weather, Fleur remained silent. There it was again, she thought, the dark cloud of suspicion that hovered over everything, blotting out all the laughter and fun-talk, whenever Bart's name was mentioned. The impression of important matters left unsaid, cruel accusing words concerning him. My goodness, she told herself, it's time I came home and Bart has someone to stick up for him in his absence. All at once there was a pause in the flow of talk, and impulsively she rushed into speech. 'Of course there's no mistake about Bart and me!' Once again she was acutely aware of Logan's deep penetrating glance. 'Nothing's changed between us! How could it?' and she saw Bruce's face cloud over.

'Don't give up too soon,' his mate told him with a grin, 'you never know your luck. Fleur might change her mind yet!'

'Change my mind?' Swiftly she sprang to Bart's defence. 'Why ever would I do that?' Even to her own ears her tone was a little too defiant, her voice a shade too high, out of control. It was almost as if she had to convince everyone, even herself, that despite a year's separation, her feelings for Bart hadn't altered one little bit. 'Listen, everyone,' she called, 'I've got news for you! Bart and I are getting married just as soon as we can!' She raised eyes sparkling with anger and defiance to Logan's satirical glance. 'And there's just nothing anyone can do to prevent it!'

The next moment she caught a fleeting impression of her father's stricken face, then once again the conversation around her became general. Somehow, though, her appetite had vanished and she picked at the meal that Daphne had prepared with such care—the succulent roasted lamb served with golden baked kumera and beans and peas picked from the garden, that a few moments earlier had seemed so appetising.

Later she helped Daphne to clear away the dinner dishes and glasses, and presently she was once again drying the dishes that Daphne was washing in the sink. 'It's funny,' Fleur was giving voice to her thoughts, 'but sometimes I feel as though I'd never been away.' She added slowly, 'Except for Logan, that is. What do you think of him, Daph?'

'He's all right.' Clearly the housekeeper wasn't giving anything away. 'He seems honest enough,' she vouchsafed in her blunt, no-nonsense way.

Honest? What an odd word to use about him, Fleur mused. Aloud she mused, 'What I can't make out is why he bought that tumbledown old property down the road. There's someone living in it now, I noticed smoke coming out of the chimney when I was up in the hills today.'

Daphne nodded. 'That will be his friend.'

Fleur stood very still. 'You don't mean a—woman friend?'

'Oh yes,' Daphne rinsed a crystal brandy glass in cold water, 'he told me all about it. Seems this woman friend of his has been through a bad patch lately, and according to Logan she needed some peace and quiet, somewhere where she could be away from everyone she knew to put the pieces together again and get herself sorted out.'

So there was a woman in his life, Fleur was thinking. Someone who mattered a great deal to this autocratic, overbearing man. One thing was for sure, her thoughts ran on, he wouldn't be confiding anything of his love life to her. Not that she was the slightest bit interested, of course, it was just that it seemed ... strange ... the arrangement between Logan and his 'friend'.

She could well imagine the type of girl for whom Logan would form an attachment. Someone who was insecure, clinging, dependent on him. Maybe this girl was recovering from a nervous breakdown. For surely only a negative type of woman could put up with his high-handed ways and aggressive male dominance.

That night she took a late swim in the pool, but later, as she tossed restlessly through the night hours, it seemed that nothing could make her sleep, her excitement about the meeting with Bart tomorrow saw to that, and as time dragged on she felt more and more wakeful. Maybe, she decided at last, if she read for a while it might help to quieten her nerves.

As she went quietly down the carpeted hall towards the bookcase in the lounge room she noticed to her surprise a strip of light shining beneath the door of the small room that had always been known as the office. Suddenly fear shot through her. Suppose her father was in there? What if he had been taken ill? He could be helpless and alone in the silent room. Thoroughly alarmed now, she turned the door handle and opened the door to find herself staring directly into Logan's surprised face. He had swung around on the office stool to face her. 'What the devil——'

She stood still in amazement, a small girl in cotton shortie pyjamas, a cloud of burnished copper hair tumbling over her shoulders. She summoned a smile and said briskly, 'Sorry—I thought Dad might be in here working. It seemed so late for him to be up and I got an awful feeling that he might be ill—or something.'

'It's okay.' To her relief he spoke absently, his mind evidently still centred on the calculator and the figures on the pad lying on his desk in front of him.

Fleur tried to lighten the awkward moment. 'Must be important, whatever it is you're working on, to keep you going at it so late.'

'It is.' His tone was strangely off-putting. 'Let you in on it in the morning—or your dad will!'

She eyed him in bewilderment. 'I don't know what you're getting at——'

'You will, tomorrow,' said Logan grimly, and swung himself back to face the desk. He couldn't have made it more clear, she thought angrily, that she wasn't welcome here.

'Good night, then.'

''Night.' He didn't even turn as she closed the door behind her.

The next morning when Fleur strolled out into the yards, the pens were crowded with milling sheep. Overhead the helicopter that had been used yesterday to spy out hidden pockets of sheep in rocky outcrops now hovered over the homestead area. The idea is to take more pictures, I suppose, she told herself, waving a hand to the pilot as he chug-chugged above her, on the orders of the new owner—*part*-owner, she corrected herself.

At the thought of Logan, she could feel herself getting angry all over again. It was childish and absurd, she chided herself, to allow herself to get so emotional over him. After all, he was useful to her at the moment. There was no harm in accepting his offer of a plane trip to town, and afterwards she need never see him again.

As she moved towards the stockyards she was scarcely aware of the hovering helicopter above or the crowded pens. The sounds of sheep calling mingled with the lowing of steers being driven into the yards, but Fleur's thoughts were with Barton and the decision she had made. But everything would work out, of course it would. Already she had placed in her Maori flax kit a minimal of essential belongings—purse, toilet bag containing make-up, sun-lotion and hairbrush. A change of underwear, a couple of T-shirts, jeans. A somewhat meagre wardrobe with which to start a wedding journey, but there was no sense in making her father and Logan suspicious of her movements. She hated herself for the lie she had told her father—a visit she intended making to a sick friend, a girl who had worked with her earlier in the year with World Vision. If necessary she might have to stay with her friend for a day or two. Apparently both Logan and her father accepted her story as the truth, although as far as Logan was concerned, she reminded herself, you never could tell. He was a man who kept his own counsel. As to her father, he had always found difficulty in refusing his beloved daughter anything she wanted. His 'Fox' was the apple of his eye, she couldn't help but know it. All at once she was pierced by a pang of guilt. What was she giving him in return for all the loving? Lies and evasions, and most hurtful of all would be her marriage to Bart, whom her father had no longer liked or trusted, or so it would seem. But in the end it would work out, and when she and Bart came back here together all the stupid misunderstandings would be cleared away. She rationalised away a niggling feeling of apprehension. What other courses had she but to do things this way—Bart's way?

All at once she was possessed by a spirit of restlessness, and to use up her energy she decided to take Sally for a canter over the hills. A short distance away she could see Logan, his tall figure rising through the dust of the stockyards as he moved among the milling steers. Now she need have no fear of meeting up with him on the lonely slopes. Presently she was carrying saddle, bridle and sheepskin up the winding path leading to the horse paddock.

Away on the green slopes time flew by on wings as

she let her mount have her head. At times the mare picked her way down stony slopes or climbed steep slippery rock faces, sailing over fallen logs and galloping along the straight. Fleur's coppery-coloured hair, loosened from its knot, streamed behind her ears as the exhilaration of wind rushing past her face dispelled the worrying thoughts that had bedevilled her since her return home.

When at last she rubbed down her mare and returned to the house, Daphne was preparing the evening meal and the men were in the small washroom off the verandah, freshening up after their day in the yards.

The next day Fleur was ready early and waiting impatiently on the creeper-hung verandah, a slim figure in well-cut jeans and a pale blue T-shirt, a capacious Maori flaxkit in her hand and only the deep glow of her eyes betraying an inner excitement that held her in its grip.

The approaching Land Rover told her that Logan was on time for their appointment, and as he dropped down from the vehicle and came striding towards her she couldn't help the thought that today he looked very much a man of power and authority. His impeccably cut jacket accentuated the powerful shoulders, his thick dark hair struck glints in the sunlight and his smile was a flash of strong white teeth against the sun-bronzed skin. All the same, it was a smile she didn't quite trust, not really friendly but more in the nature of a mocking, twisted grin.

He took the steps two at a time and her father, who had come out to bid her goodbye, greeted his partner with a friendly nod. 'She's all yours,' he quipped, and Fleur found herself irrationally irritated by the joking remark. It was an effort to force a smile and not to show her feelings too plainly, for after all, she reminded herself, she was dependent on Logan for today's journey and she simply couldn't afford to fall out with him . . . unfortunately.

'All this rushing off all of a sudden,' did she discern a serious note, Fleur wondered, in her father's tones? '— There are matters I wanted to go over with you, Fox, things that must be said.' She intercepted a swift significant look that passed between the two men, over her head. 'But it will have to wait. No sense in holding you up when your sick friend's needing you to help out.'

She said on a breath of alarm, 'What's wrong, Dad?'

His thin lined face broke into a reassuring smile. 'Nothing that can't wait for a day or two until you get back. Anyway, come to that, Logan can let you into all that—if he cares to take on the job?'

Her eyes widened in alarm, and the colour left her cheeks. 'It's nothing about your own health, Dad? Tell me, I'd rather know!'

'Lord no! The doc tells me I'll be fine so long as I don't throw any more hefty rams over fences. With Logan taking over the business side of things, I've nothing to worry about in that direction. No, no, Fox, nothing like that! You take off and get on with your nursing job. 'Bye now. See you tomorrow, Logan.'

Fleur's eyes misted over and she threw her arms around her father's neck, her fresh young face pressed close to his lined cheek. 'Take care, Dad.' Silently she added, 'And forgive me.'

The next moment she realised the housekeeper had joined the group on the verandah. 'Goodbye, Daph!'

Daphne didn't even smile a farewell. 'Goodbye.' Her grim expression didn't relax one little bit—but then, Fleur consoled herself, ever since she could remember Daphne had looked with disapproval on practically everything Fluer did, and it really didn't mean a thing. Beneath her austere manner, her grumbling and devastatingly truthful opinions, freely expressed, she was fiercely loyal to Fleur and her father. Daphne couldn't possibly be aware of Fleur's real reason for the hurried trip today. She breathed a sigh of relief. Thank heaven for that!

'Let's go!' Together she and Logan went down the steps and he flung open the door of the waiting Land Rover and saw her inside. Lifting a hand, he sketched a farewell to the two on the verandah, then he spun around in the driveway and they shot up the dusty track winding up the hill. Soon they were dropping down into a bush-filled gully, to emerge into full sunlight and run along the mown grass of the airstrip.

Presently she was climbing into the small Cessna and Logan folded his long length into the cockpit beside her.

He shot her a sideways glance. 'Belted up, Fox?'

She didn't trust the glint of amusement in his eyes. 'Of course.'

'Right, here we go!'

She felt the plane taxi along the runway to rise in the air, only to drop down with a sickening lurch on the grass. Almost immediately the procedure was repeated and she was flung from side to side. At last, as the plane finally lifted and took off to rise high in the air, she gasped breathlessly, 'What was all that in aid of?'

'What was what in aid of?'

'You know what I mean!' she threw back at him. 'All those acrobatics!' They were gaining height now, passing over the high hills of the station. 'If you're counting on showing off your piloting skills to me, you're wasting your time. I'm not a bit impressed!'

He tossed her a triumphant sideways glance. 'And you a station owner's daughter!'

Fleur said huffily, 'What's that got to do with it?' She was still feeling annoyed with herself for those involuntary moments of panic.

'Hell, don't tell me you didn't see those lambs down on the runway?'

She eyed him suspiciously. 'No, I didn't.'

'Well, I did, and I took scare tactics! You won't find sheep crowding the runway, they've got too much sense, but lambs, they're the ones you have to watch out for. You've got to scare the daylights out of them and keep right on doing it until they get the message!'

She eyed him suspiciously, uncertain whether or not to believe what he said. 'I'll take your word for it,' she murmured doubtfully.

She caught his challenging grin. 'Now you're talking!'

They were passing over the homestead now, the drafting yards crowded with milling sheep looking like plastic animals, she thought, in a child's farm set. A tractor appeared a miniature toy, a shepherd taking a winding hill track was a tiny doll-like figure against the vast backdrop of dried slopes. Could that really be the road, she marvelled, the narrow ribbon twisting and turning as it snaked its way over the hills?

Fleur, busy with her thoughts, was content to sit in silence, watching the vista spread out below. The green mounds that were sheep-dotted hills and always the sun-sparkled waters of the blue Pacific, endlessly washing up on sandy beaches edged with rocky cliffs. Aloud she murmured, 'How long will it take us to get to the city?'

'We should hit the drome in Auckland in a couple of hours,' Logan told her. 'That suit you?'

'Oh yes, that's fine with me.'

He made no comment, and as they went on, Fleur's thoughts were all for herself. Would Bart notice any difference in her appearance, after a whole year? Would he look the same? More mature, maybe, his thin alive face filled out a little. One thing was for sure, he seemed to have no shortage of money, so they might even travel to England. It didn't really matter where they went, all she wanted was for them to be together.

Lost as she was in her musing, the unaccustomed sound, or rather, a lack of it in the engine of the plane failed to register. Then with a quiver of alarm she realised that quite clearly, even to her untutored ears, there was a definite miss and the engine noise was uneven. Gradually it was cutting out at more frequent intervals, and that meant—that meant—'Logan!' Fear dilated her eyes as she flung him a desperate glance and saw that his attention was concentrated on the bush-clad slopes ahead. 'Don't worry,' his face was set and stern, 'the engine's playing up a bit, that's all.'

'That's all?' she echoed on a swift indrawn breath. Now that her senses were alerted to the danger, she was aware all over again of the engine silence that filled her with terror. After what seemed to her an age the spluttering sound was back. All at once there was no sound at all. It was as if the silence was shouting a

warning of imminent danger and she knew with a sick
sense of certainty that very soon the failing engine
would cut out for good. This is it! she thought, and felt
as though she was another girl seated here in the
cockpit with Logan, waiting . . . just waiting.

'Don't be scared, Fox!' His terse voice cut across her
frozen senses.

'Is there a chance?' Her voice came in an anguished
croak.

'We'll make it! Keep your fingers crossed that I can
get her over the hill and find somewhere on the other
side to land her.' All at once his tone was filled with
urgency. 'Listen to me, Fox! The big danger is fire. So
the moment we hit the ground you've got to cut loose
and run like hell!'

A terrifying possibility shot through her mind. 'But if
you're hurt——'

'Forget it! Don't wait for anything. I'll be right with
you, but you've got to get free of the wreck as fast as
you can. Got it?'

'Yes, yes!' The next moment she held her breath as
they cleared the summit of the high hill ahead with only
feet to spare. Below she glimpsed flat land covered in
tall trees, bush and scrub.

'Hold tight!' shouted Logan. 'I'm going to aim for
the gap between those two big trees!' He couldn't
possibly get through the opening, she thought. They
were losing altitude rapidly and Fleur sat tense and
stiff, braced for the coming impact. *'Please God,'* she
prayed, *'let him bring us down safely. Please. Please!'*

CHAPTER 5

'Now!' Logan's voice rang in her ears, then the next
moment sky and tree-tops tilted around them in a crazy
kaleidoscope. Swiftly the plane was dropping out of the
sky, shearing off a wing as it shot through the narrow
gap between towering trees, to plunge through the

forest canopy and come to a shuddering stop among the broken bushes.

Dazed and shaken, Fleur picked herself up from the shattered timber and debris of the wrecked cockpit, hearing Logan's urgent tones as from a distance. 'Are you all right, Fox?'

Bewilderedly she put a hand to her head to finger a swelling bruise on her forehead. 'Yes, yes—I can't believe it!'

'Thank the Lord for that!' His voice was full of relief. Then he was struggling with the jammed door, using all his strength to force it open. At last it broke from the hinges and he swung around to face her. 'Out you go, Fox, and run for your life!'

For a moment she hesitated. 'But how about you? You're not hurt——?'

'*Out!*' His tone was so fierce that she scrambled through the opening to drop down on the ground, oblivious of the branches that tore at her face and arms. Soon she was out in the open, running, running across the grassy clearing. A backward glance flung over her shoulder told her that Logan was close behind her. The next minute she tripped over a hidden tree root and went sprawling to the ground. Swiftly he pulled her to her feet, clasped her hand in his and half dragged her with him as they hurtled on. All at once there came the sound of an explosion, and as they turned, Fleur, still trying to recover her breath, watched with him as leaping tongues of fire licked the woodwork of the wrecked plane. Even as they took in the scene, flames soared high in the air, turning the wreckage of the Cessna into a raging inferno.

All at once she was seized by a trembling she couldn't control and once again Logan's gravelly voice seemed to come from far away. 'Fox! Fox! Are you all right?'

With an effort she raised heavy eyelids and gave a shaky laugh.

'Of course I am.'

'Sure? There's a hell of a bruise on your forehead— and how about that?' His deep tones were laced with concern and dazedly she followed his gaze to the trickle of blood that was running down her leg and staining her sneaker.

'It's nothing,' she told him, 'I didn't even know I had that cut or scratch, I didn't feel a thing!'

'Let me take a look.' He was kneeling at her side, rolling up the denim material of her jeans. 'Sorry, Fox,' his low tones were oddly husky. 'I wouldn't have you hurt for the world!' The next moment he had whipped a snowy handkerchief from his jacket pocket and was binding the makeshift bandage around the deep gash. 'It's not too painful? I've got to make it tight.'

She shook her head. 'How about you?'

'Not a scratch. We've been lucky, you and I.'

'I can't believe it,' she murmured, trying to fight her way free of the swirling grey mists that were closing in around her. 'Another minute and we would have been trapped in the plane, burned alive.' She shuddered.

'Don't think about it,' Logan said gently.

But she couldn't stop the thinking any more than she could control the stupid tremors that were shaking her from head to foot, and scarcely aware of her actions, she swayed dizzily towards him. It's the crash, she told herself faintly, that's making me feel this way, and buried her face in his warm sinewy chest. Shock and a vast sense of relief swept over her and she clung to him, while the tears ran unchecked down her pale cheeks. 'We're all right!' she sobbed. 'We're all right!'

'Take it easy, little one.' Dreamily she was aware of the strength of his arms holding her close and the tenderness of his touch. Who would have believed, she thought hazily, that Logan could be this way? It just went to show, the idea moved sluggishly through her mind, what a good fright could do to anyone! The tears she couldn't seem to control spilled over and she just wanted to stay here for ever, safe and infinitely content, in Logan's strong protective arms. It was a feeling that was out of this world, a sensation too good to last, she mused as gently he loosened his hold and gazed down at her.

The next moment she realised he was handing her another handkerchief. 'Goodness,' she smiled tremulously, 'you seem to have a goodly supply of these!'

'Not any more.' He grinned down at her. 'You've just used up our entire survival kit, such as it was!'

Fleur blew her nose, blinked away the tears in her eyes and slowly, slowly, the world swung back into focus. Logan appeared to have forgotten that his arm was still around her waist. Aloud she asked, 'Will there be any chance, do you think, of someone noticing the burning plane?'

He shook his head. 'Not a hope in hell! We're at the foot of a mountain, and if there was some smoke drifting around it would be taken for a scrub fire.'

'We won't be missed, then,' she was giving voice to her thoughts, 'until after dark?'

'That's the story. It's up to us to get ourselves back to civilisation.'

Her despairing gaze swept the high slopes around them, shadowed in the late afternoon sunlight. There was nothing to be seen anywhere but the steep hills covered in densely-growing native bush. 'It seems like the middle of nowhere,' she murmured on a sigh.

'Not to worry, it's not all that bad.'

It was funny, she thought, how just the sound of his deep voice made her feel confident that they would find their way out of this green wilderness, gave her the feeling she would be safe so long as Logan was with her. She wrenched her mind back to his reassuring tones.

'I've flown over this territory a couple of times on the way to town, and according to my calculations there's a river not too far away with a farmhouse over on the other side. All we need do is keep walking thataway,' he gestured in a direction ahead of them, 'and we'll hit the river late today or early tomorrow.'

Fleur, however, had taken in only part of his words. 'What you're trying to tell me,' she said slowly, 'is that sooner or later we'll come across water to drink? That we won't die of thirst.'

'We won't die, Fox.' His eyes were deep dark pools. 'The worst can happen to us is that we'll have to spend a night together in the open.'

Her startled gaze flew upwards to meet his, but there

was no reading the enigmatic expression in his eyes. To change the subject she said hastily, 'Hadn't we better get started, then?'

'Soon.' He was eyeing the wrecked aircraft. With unbelievable rapidity the timbers were being consumed by leaping flames and the fuselage of the Cessna was charred and blackened. 'A spot of rest won't hurt you. Take a seat.'

She dropped down to a fallen tea-tree log and he stood gazing down at her. 'I have to hand it to you, Fox,' she surprised a reluctant approval in his tone, 'you don't panic easily.'

She felt a wave of pleasure out of all proportion to his remark. Blame the note of approval in his deep tones. For approval, she reminded herself, was something she had come not to expect from him during their brief acquaintance. She heard her own voice saying, 'What was the use? I just felt—I don't know, sort of resigned, frozen.' Something deep down inside her prompted her to acknowledge her debt to him. 'You were the one who did all the quick thinking, getting us through that gap between the trees.'

'We were just lucky there was a landing spot handy.' Logan was tugging at his tie and tossing it into the bushes, unbuttoning the top buttons of his shirt. 'We've got some hiking ahead of us to get out of the bush, may as well travel light.'

Fleur watched him throw his tailored jacket over his shoulder. 'Why take your coat with you, then?' she asked.

He threw her a cryptic glance. 'The answer to that one, young Fox, is that chances are you and I will have to bed down for the night, and it can get mighty chilly out in the open, even in summer.'

'Oh, camping out doesn't worry me!' Did her voice sound as light and carefree as she intended? she wondered. Breathlessly she hurried away from a loaded subject. 'I've been on lots of tenting holidays way out in the country,' she remarked airily.

To her relief he seemed less than interested in their sleeping arrangements. But of course, the thought shot through her mind, he had good reason for his apparent indifference in the matter. How could she have forgotten, even for a moment, that he made no secret of his dislike for the boss's daughter? A night spent together in the wilderness, and the enforced intimacy of their remote surroundings wouldn't stand a chance against his unconcealed disapproval.

Why, even before setting eyes on her, he had written her off as a girl who was spoilt and selfish, hard and self-seeking. He mistakenly believed that she had let her father down at a moment when he most needed her, and he despised her because she was Bart's fiancée and determined to remain loyal to him despite all she heard against him. Anyway, what did she care what this autocratic stranger thought of her? And yet . . . could it be because of their having survived a plane crash together that somehow she did care? Fortunately she told herself the antagonism they felt for each other was a two-way thing. All at once she caught her breath as she recalled her crazy antics of a few moments earlier— flinging her arms around his neck and weeping all over his shirt! But he would put such emotional behaviour down to shock and reaction, of course he would. Considering their recent fiery encounters he would know, who better, how she *really* felt about him!

'We've been lucky, you and I——' Logan's deep tones cut across the crackling of burning timbers.

'I know, I know.' Her gaze was on the leaping flames, shimmering in the hot sunshine, and in her nostrils was the acrid smell of smoke.

'I'll tell you something, though,' she became aware of his probing glance, 'you won't be keeping that appointment of yours in town today.'

'No.' All at once the shattering significance of that missed meeting with Bart struck her like a blow. When she failed to arrive at the appointed place he would jump to the conclusion that, influenced by malicious gossip, she had lost all faith in him. The awful part of it was, she caught her lower lip in her teeth, that he had told her that whether she accompanied him or not, he was leaving the country almost at once, and she had no address, nor had she any method of contacting him to let him know the truth. Fate had handed her just one chance of happiness and she had blown it! The anguish of the realisation of all she had lost through that missed appointment surged over her and she felt herself pinned by Logan's hazel-eyed gaze. 'Don't look like that, it can't have been all that important!'

Only the most momentous meeting of my whole life! But she said the words silently. Becoming aware of the ironic curve of his lips, she roused herself to say challengingly, 'Anyway, how about you? You had an appointment in town today too that you won't be keeping. Important business, wasn't it?'

'Oh, that,' he shrugged broad shoulders beneath the cotton shirt. 'Another day won't make much difference. It's not the end of the world for me,' the deep gravelly tones were heavy with meaning, 'not like you!'

Fleur pretended not to understand. Damn him, how much did he know of her affairs? The next minute she told herself that he was only guessing. He couldn't possibly be aware of her telephone conversation with Bart. Swiftly she switched the conversation back in his direction. 'All the same, you must have been put out by not being in town today?'

'I was planning on seeing someone, but not to worry,' she caught an amused glint in his eyes, 'it'll keep.'

Some devil of retaliation sparked her to say, 'You mean, she'll wait?'

To her surprise Logan burst into a shout of laughter. He seemed not a bit put out by her remark but merely remarked cheerfully, maddeningly, 'She'll have to, won't she?'

Selfish brute! she thought angrily. Just because he looks so—so impressive he seems to imagine he can treat women any old how. What does he care that some unfortunate girl will have to wait for him today for hours, with no explanation of why he doesn't turn up to meet her?

She seethed inwardly. He couldn't care less about the luckless female he was to see today, not him! Probably, she mused hotly, he treats all his women friends with the cool contempt he's always handing out to me. All at once she remembered his unexpected tenderness towards her after the plane crash. Well, nearly always!

'Looks like the flames are dying down,' his level tones broke across her resentful musing. 'Just as well, we don't want a ranging bush fire on our hands. Let's get cracking, shall we? How are you on hiking, anyway?'

'I've done lots of it a few years ago——'

'You're in for a lot more!'

Fleur got to her feet and together they moved over the long, sunwarmed grass, threading their way between the sparsely growing tea-tree with its fresh tangy aroma and showers of starry white blossoms. Then presently they were entering the green gloom of the native bush clothing slopes and valleys that stretched endlessly ahead.

'Wait,' said Logan, and stepped ahead of her. 'I'll lead the way and you follow.'

Typical autocratic Logan-talk! Fleur thought scornfully, and realised the next minute that he was preceding her in order to clear a way through the densely growing undergrowth. He was pushing his way through clumps of flax and bushes of five-finger, thrusting aside vines of bush-lawyer with its sharp thorns and reaching overhead to pull aside great hanging ropes of supplejack that trailed from trees high above.

In the filtered light, magnificent native giants reached for the sky. The towering trees were so far above them, Fleur thought, that she and Logan might have been in some primeval forest. All around them, the hum of insects was loud in the humid air and underfoot was the damp earthy smell of moss and rotting leaves. As she pushed her way through the undergrowth in Logan's wake, tiny fantails darted on outspread wings around her and somewhere in the branches of a tree high above, a tui's musical chime echoed on the still air.

On and on ... Fleur lost count of time. Her watch had stopped ticking since the plane crash, but the shadows were deepening around her. No wind cooled the moist heat of the forest and Fleur's jersey top clung

damply to her body. Tendrils of reddish-gold hair clung
wetly to her hot prespiring forehead, long scratches
made by encroaching vines reddened her face and arms
and she would give a year of her life, she vowed, for just
one drink of cold water. As time went on and the bush
around them grew darker, her footsteps flagged. The
wound on her leg was bleeding again, she could feel the
blood seeping down her ankle and for all her
determination not to surrender to the weariness that
was creeping over her, she was finding it difficult not to
fall too far behind Logan. If only he'd slow down!
Didn't he realise, for heaven's sake, how much more
ground he covered in his long strides than she could
achieve with her hurrying steps.

She pushed her way forward automatically, for
fatigue and shock were taking their toll and a deadly
inertia was taking possession of her. Bart ... Don't
think of Bart. It was no use, the despairing thoughts
persisted. By now he would have given her up, finally
and completely. Patience had never been one of his
virtues. Thinking of her as he would now, he wouldn't
contact her from his new address. He would never have
an opportunity of hearing her side of the story. Eyes
misted with tears, she stumbled blindly on. When at last
Logan paused to tug aside a rope of trailing supplejack
barring the way she rallied herself to fresh effort, and
hurried towards him. Something of her state of
exhaustion must have got through to him, however, for
as she neared him, his gaze rested on her wan, dust-
stained face.

'You're limping, Fox. How's that wound of yours?
Not too painful?'

'It doesn't hurt much,' she lied. Was he apprehensive,
she wondered, that the injury might delay them on the
enforced journey through the bush to find their way out
of the wilderness or, more important still, to discover
drinking water?

'Time to take a break anyway.' Thankfully Fleur
dropped down to a fallen, creeper-covered log.

Too weary to argue, she rolled up the bloodstained
material of the leg of her jeans and as he whipped aside

the crimson handkerchief binding the deep cut, blood spurted from the wound.

'Stay right there, Fox,' he had turned aside, 'first aid treatment coming up!' He strode towards a cluster of trees, to return a few minutes later with gossamer-like threads trailing from his hands.

'Spiderwebs?' She brushed away the sweat from her face, leaving a long trail of dust across her cheek. She felt a wild urge towards hysterical laughter. 'I don't believe it!'

'You will.' With infinite gentleness he was placing the webs over the wound. Who would believe, she asked herself in wonder once again, that a hateful, arrogant man such as Logan could have such a gentle touch? 'Now for the bandage,' he was saying. 'It's shot, but we've got nothing else.'

'Is this part of your bushcraft lore?' Her voice was incredulous.

'Not exactly. I got this idea from a Maori friend. It's one of the old traditional remedies his tribe used to call on long before the coming of the *pakeha*. And believe me, it works!'

She shook her head in bewilderment. 'I'm sure finding out things on this trip!' I'm learning things I never dreamed of about Logan too—she brushed the fugitive thought aside, for somehow she had no desire to pursue the subject. 'He despises you,' she told herself sternly, 'and you'd better not forget it, my girl!'

They had resumed their journey through the sombre shadows of the bush when suddenly Logan retraced his steps and come to join her. For once she thought his eyes didn't register the contemptuous look he seemed to keep just for her. 'Getting tired?'

She lifted her small square chin, wrinkled her nose at him and willed her voice to a light, uncaring note. 'Not a bit. Just thirsty, I guess.'

'We can fix that problem.' Surely she must be imagining the note of compassion in his tone? 'Do you hear what I hear?'

She pushed the hair back from her damp forehead and stood motionless, listening intently. 'You mean, like creek water running over stones down there in the gully?' A surge of renewed vigour swept her and she grinned up at him. 'Lead me to it!'

'Give me your hand, then.' She found a sense of companionship in his clasp as they hurried through a clearing and scrambled down a mossy bank. Almost immediately the immediate sense of comfort changed to something different, a riot of emotions that was wildly exciting and strangely disturbing.

Soon they had dropped down on the lush grass bordering a low bank, leaning over the creek to cup their hands and scoop up the crystal-clear water. Water that was cool, fresh, life-giving, Fleur thought as she gulped it down.

'It's heavenly here.' She was splashing water over hands and face, washing away dirt and sweat and dried blood from cuts and bruises. A cool breeze stirred the lacy fronds of the pungas that clustered the gully like hundreds of green parasols. The sun was setting behind the hills and a purple gaze veiled the bush-clad slopes rising around them. 'Couldn't we stay——' She stopped short as her mind shied away from thoughts of the approaching hours of darkness. 'Just for a while,' she added, and hoped he hadn't caught her betraying moment of hesitation.

Unexpectedly he grinned, the heart-knocking smile that was doing things to her composure. 'Good thinking, Fox! But I've got a better idea.' She followed her gaze to wisps of steam that were rising among sparsely growing tea-tree. 'Hot mineral pools! How does that grab you? We've got it laid on, Fox, steaming hot pools that are just what you need to hurry up the healing, get rid of the aches.' She caught his cryptic glance. 'Guaranteed to give you a good night's sleep!'

'On the hard ground?' Nervously she ran on, scarcely aware of what she was saying. 'Don't they say that people can die of exposure sleeping out in bush country?'

'Ah, but they didn't know their bushcraft!'

The confidence in his tone sparked her to say with spirit, 'And I suppose you do?'

Logan grinned in his maddening way. 'Why do you think I lumbered myself with this jacket?'

Of course, she told herself, he's thinking of his own well-being. She brought her mind back to his deep voice. 'And if that doesn't work there's always the happy thought that when it comes to sleeping out in the outback, two together are a lot better than one.'

'For warmth, you mean?' She couldn't tell whether he was serious or merely having her on.

'What else?' His heavily marked brows rose in simulated surprise. 'But you wouldn't go along with that theory, would you, Fox?' All at once his voice changed, deepened. 'Bart mightn't like it.'

Fleur's soft lips were set firmly. Even though she didn't dare risk looking at him she just knew his mouth would be twisted in that hateful mocking twist. '*I* might not like it!' she flung at him.

'A fate worse than death?' The gravelly tones were threaded with amusement. Now he was mocking her, she thought angrily, and flung him a furious look. 'Don't be absurd!'

His cool direct gaze flickered over her stormy face. 'You don't like being teased, do you, Fox? I suppose it comes of having no brothers around. You've never learned to take the knock-backs.'

'I'm glad I hadn't,' she threw at him, 'if they were all like you!' Hating herself for descending to such infantile retaliation she couldn't resist saying, 'I bet you didn't have any sisters!'

'Three of them,' he said cheerfully. He added smoothly. 'They did their best, but I managed to get the better of them—most of the time!'

'Bully for you!'

'You'll feel a whole lot better in the morning.' His deceptively soothing tones were infuriating to her taut nerves. 'If you're worried about tonight——'

'Of course I'm not worrying about tonight,' she cut in. The unconcern she was endeavouring to infuse into her voice was somewhat spoiled by hands nervously plucking at the grass. 'It doesn't matter to me where we camp.' Deliberately she pretended not to understand the meaning underlying the light words. 'All I care about is getting out of here before we both die of starvation.'

'Oh, I wouldn't let that happen to you, Fox!' No doubt he had sensed her unease about the night hours, she thought. She never could keep anything from him, but thank heaven he was following her lead. His amused tones broke across her tumultuous thoughts. 'How do you think the Maoris got along for food in the forest before the Europeans came along?'

'Don't ask me,' she said exasperatedly. 'I suppose they ate fern roots and whatever they could find in the bush.'

'Oh, they did much better than that, so my Maori friend told me.'

She was feeling unutterably weary, hungry too, and now she had to cope with Logan in this maddening cheerful, teasing mood.

'I'll take your word for it,' she said deflatingly.

It was no use, he took not the slightest notice. 'Seems that cabbage-tree shoots pack a power of nutrition, there's swags of vitamins in the puha plants growing all around here, and as a special delicacy, I might even find you some hu-hu grubs.'

'Yerk!' she shuddered at the thought of the fat white grubs she had often come across in holes in puriri trees. On another level, however, her mind was still with Logan and the hours of darkness that lay ahead. If only she could leave well alone, she told herself the next minute, for some devil deep inside her had prompted her to say tauntingly, 'Aren't I lucky that you simply can't stand the sight of me!'

'You're wrong, you know. I like you a whole lot better——' Swiftly he reached forward to pluck a twig from her hair. The next moment, with a deft movement of his hands, he had unpinned her topknot, sending the bright hair cascading around her shoulders, '—like this!'

She swung around to face him, eyes wide with indignation. 'Why did you do that?'

He met her accusing glance with his outrageous grin. 'Just showing you the way I like you!'

'Now you've lost my hair-comb.' With hands that trembled in spite of herself she fumbled amidst the long grass beside her. Logan made no attempt to help her in her search, and after a moment she gathered the long strands together over her shoulder and began to twist them into a thick plait. Some instinct warned her that the way to safety tonight lay in their mutual antagonism for each other. As for herself, she *had* to hate him, or else—— She gathered her defences together, and the anger and frustration she felt for him came rushing back.

Logan was eyeing her with his penetrating gaze. 'You don't believe me?'

'Why should I?' she slung at him. 'You didn't believe *me*,' she said very low, 'when I told you I didn't get that letter from Daphne about Dad not being well! Of course I would have cancelled everything and taken the first plane back had I known what was happening at home. What sort of girl do you take me for—No,' she rushed on in a flurry of words, 'don't answer that one!' Two spots of colour burned on her pale cheeks. 'Spoiled rotten by that doting father of hers, selfish as they come. Didn't even trouble to cut short her overseas commitments and hurry home when she knew her father needed her! Well, it's not true!' she cried defensively. 'I hadn't a clue as to what had happened at home until I got back, and I don't care,' she cried wildly, 'whether you believe me or not!' and waited for his cutting retort.

'Oddly enough, I do.' The glint of amusement was back in his eyes. 'Maybe I did jump to conclusions, something about the way you look, that turned-up little nose of yours and the way you seemed to think nothing could possibly have changed while you'd been away. Guess it got under my skin.'

To her horror Fleur felt her mouth wobble. Damn him, he never reacted in the way she expected.

'Oh well,' he leaned back on the cushiony grass, arms crossed behind his head, 'now that we've got all that sorted out——'

She threw him a challenging look. 'We haven't, you

know!' Once again her fingers plucked nervously at the grasses at her side. 'Not while you've got something aginst Bart that you won't let me in on! Are you afraid that I could blow your story sky-high? Because I could, you know!' Suddenly it all built up inside her, the shock and fatigue, the missed meeting with Bart that spelled the end of all her hopes. She would never see Bart again, and it was all Logan's fault! She had to know the truth behind all the insinuations about Bart, get things out into the open. She took a deep breath, said very low, 'I can't take your word about—other things.'

He was eyeing her attentively. 'Like what, Fox?'

Anger mushroomed up inside her in a black cloud. 'I happen to know Bart a whole lot better than you do, and I know that he'd never do anything the slightest bit underhand——'

'You're a fool, Fox!' His curt voice cut across her words. 'A blind trusting little fool if ever there was one! Hanging on to Bart like grim death, believing every word he tells you!'

'Why shouldn't I believe him?' she protested fiercely. 'We're going to be married! I *have* to take his word for things!' she cried defensively, and pushed aside the thought that came unbidden to her mind. Who are you trying to convince, Logan or yourself? 'Oh, I know,' she ran on angrily, 'that you managed to talk your way around my dad. He's sort of trusting with people. For some reason I can't understand he seems to have the mistaken idea that you're someone special and that he can rely implicitly on you, a stranger, goodness only knows why!' She raised eyes sparkling with fury, 'But me—you won't fool me so easily! You may as well know right now that you won't be able to pull the wool over my eyes, so it's no use your trying to get around me!'

'Get around you?' His ironic tones were infuriating. 'Why,' he drawled, 'would I want to do that?'

Her eyes slid away from his satirical glance. 'Oh, you know what I mean! All those lies and insinuations about Bart. What's he ever done, for heaven's sake?'

'What's he done?' All at once Logan sprang to his feet and stood looking down at her, a powerfully built man

who looked oddly menacing in the fading light. The thought shot through her mind that even his voice was different, all the lightness gone and the gravelly tones low and intimidating. 'Shall I let you in on a few things, Fox? Think you can take it? Your dad wasn't looking forward to putting you in the picture about your boyfriend, so you may as well have it from me!'

Uneasily she shifted her position on the grass. 'I don't know what you're getting at. Anyway, whatever it is, it won't worry me—I know Bart. So go right ahead if you like. I suppose,' she added with assumed carelessness, 'that was what Dad was trying to tell me when I left home this morning? The two of you,' she added bitterly, 'must have had some matey little chats running down Bart's character, adding up all those wild rumours about him, whatever they are.'

'Not rumours, Fox,' he shot the words at her like bullets, 'plain truth! If you want me to give it to you straight, your Bart has been getting rich the quick and easy way while you've been overseas. Cheques have been drawn with forged signatures, and there's a little matter of over a thousand sheep taken away in lorryloads at night and later sold up-country. It was no trouble for him to get away with it all in his position as manager, and your dad trusted him implicitly. Spiriting away the sheep was a matter of working in with another guy who wasn't fussy as to how he made a quick buck or two. Gerry Nelson's his name——'

'I've never heard of him!'

'You will! He's due to appear in court next month on charges relating to mobs of sheep taken from another station further up the coast. Bart,' his mouth tightened, 'happens to be in luck in that he's got himself tangled up with you. There won't be any charges laid against him, your dad is much too wrapped up in his only daughter to let that happen!'

Fleur had turned very pale. She pushed away the small shadow of doubt his words had evoked and sprang to Bart's defence. 'There's been some awful mistake! Bart couldn't—he wouldn't—You've made it all up!' she flung at him wildly.

'Why would I do that?' His voice hardened and she got the impression that he might just as well have said, 'Unlike Bart, I have no need to pretend a romantic interest in the boss's daughter!' 'Tell me,' she brought her mind back to the steely masculine tones, 'seeing you're so active in Bart's defence you might let me in on just why you think I would go to all the trouble of discrediting him.'

'So that you could get rid of him and take his job for yourself!' she cried triumphantly.

He sent her his ironic grin. 'Nice try, Fox. Actually, your dad told me that he'd had suspicions about that missing stock for quite a while, but he couldn't prove a thing, not until I came along.'

'You!' she said bitterly.

'That's right. When I took over a half share in Te Haruru the first thing I did was to go through the books, and that was when——'

'I don't believe you!' Fleur cut in hotly. 'It's all your say-so and you're telling me this just to try to blacken Bart's character. You said yourself,' she cried triumphantly, 'that there was no proof of what you're saying about him.'

'There is now.' His tone was grim. 'Even you can't get away from the evidence of your own eyes!'

'So you say,' she scoffed. 'What evidence?'

'The count that was done after the muster, that's what! Those pictures the photographer snapped from the air yesterday! Your dad and I were in the office until three this morning, counting the stock in those photos. We checked and rechecked and we always came up with the same answer, and that meant there was a hell of a lot of sheep unaccounted for.'

'So that was why the 'copter was over the yards,' she said slowly,' and I thought the photographer was taking pictures of the homestead.' All at once the full significance of what he had told her reached her. 'There's some mistake! There's got to be!' Eyes blazing with anger, she cried accusingly, 'You made it all up to suit yourself!'

At last, she realised the next moment, she had got

through to him, for a muscle jerked in his cheek and for a tense moment she imagined he was about to shake her by the shoulders in an attempt to ram home to her the truth of his assertions. Even in the shadows she caught the hard line of his mouth. To her relief, however, when he spoke his voice was impassive. 'Check the figures yourself when we get back if you like.' All at once he seemed weary of the subject. 'What's the odds when you won't believe me?'

Turning aside, he picked up his jacket and threw it over his shoulder. He regarded her with his formidable glance. 'Now that we've got that little matter sorted out, shall we try out our own private mineral pool?'

'Why not?' Fleur was feeling utterly deflated and weary. One thing, though, she encouraged herself as she got to her feet, she had scored a victory over him in that he no longer believed her guilty of ignoring a summons to return home three months ago.

In silence they made their way over the shadowed grass where tiny blue moths fluttered around their ankles and high above, an opalescent sunset sky merged into dusk. All the time a small voice deep in her mind niggled. 'You don't believe all that Logan told you, then?' 'Of course I don't!' 'Honestly now, can you really see Logan as a liar? And how about your dad?' Because there was no satisfactory answer to that line of reasoning Fleur pushed the small voice aside and tried to concentrate on the clouds of steam she could see rising among the twisted trunks of closely-growing tea-tree.

The mineral water springs, however, appeared to her to be further away than she had expected. Or did she merely imagine that to be so? she asked herself as she trudged doggedly on through the deepening shadows, because she was tired and hungry and stuck with Logan of all men in the world. Logan, with his overbearing, autocratic ways and utterly mistaken opinions to which he clung so doggedly.

The next minute his deep voice cut across her musing. 'That cut of yours not troubling you too much, is it?'

'It's all right,' she assured him, and hoped she hadn't

been limping too noticeably. 'One thing,' she added, 'your Maori remedy has magicked away the bleeding!' Deep down she was thinking, if he chooses to ignore that stormy scene beside the creek, that's fine with me!

She brought her mind back to his steady tones. 'You'll find it will be worth the extra mileage,' he encouraged, 'once we get there. Mineral waters are great for curing aches and pains and all those scratches and grazes of yours!' His gaze went to a long jagged cut across her forehead.

They had gone on for only a short distance when all at once the air was pungent with the smell of sulphur and in a grassy clearing ahead Fleur caught glimpses of the dark sheen of water in a setting of native green bush. The soft haze of evening hung over the shadowed pools, open to the sky, flax and tree-ferns clustered around the low banks, vines trailed green branches in the water and clouds of steam drifted among nearby manuka trees with their showers of starry white blossoms. The only sound was the soft plop-plop of bubbles rising to the surface from turbulent fires deep underground.

All her weariness forgotten, Fleur hurried ahead, pushing her way through the bushes past the first pool and moving through the stiffly growing flax spears edging a second pool a short distance away. 'This one doesn't look to be so hot,' she called back over her shoulder. Kicking off her jandal, she ventured a toe in the steaming mineral pool. 'Lovely!' All at once her spirits rose, and she turned to Logan who had come to join her. 'Beat you in!' Already she had turned away. 'You're on!'

He moved on with his long stride and swiftly she dropped to the grass, pulling her dust-smeared shirt over her head. Soon she was stepping free of bloodied jeans and discarding panties and bra. She tossed her rubber jandal beside its mate, because she couldn't afford to lose sight of it in the near darkness.

She lost no time in divesting herself of her garments, and now she hurried along the flax-bordered bank, her body pale among the shadows, as she sought an easy approach to the water. For without the protection of clothing the thickly growing knife-edged flax bushes that edged the steaming pool presented a real hazard.

At last, just when she had been about to give up all hope of avoiding the razor-sharp spears, she stumbled on a muddy area between the giant bushes. Drifting steam veiled the dark surface of the pool below, but no matter. Leaving the shelter of the bushes, she dropped down to the water below. The next minute she found herself caught in a firm grip. Heavens! Her heart seemed to stop, then plunge wildly—she had leaped right into Logan's arms! In the warm sensuous water she felt his body pressed close, close to hers. Her senses rocketed and for a crazy moment a star tangled in the branches of a tall manuka tree seemed to be performing acrobatics overhead.

'Ever been kissed in a mineral pool, Fox?' His deep exultant laugh sent her emotions spinning in wild confusion. 'Or didn't Bart ever take you to one?' The next moment his seeking lips found hers in warm and lingering pressure.

A fiery sweetness was spreading through her veins and wildly she struggled against the throbbing excitement that was taking over. At last he released her and she was moving away from him through the dark water.

They stayed in the mineral pool for a long time while the warmth of the water brought the blood to their faces and beaded their hair with drops of moisture. Soon Fleur felt a delicious languor stealing over her senses, born of the special qualities of the mineral water that was miraculously easing away weariness and exhaustion. It was a joy, she mused, to float on the dark surface of the water or to drop down to feel the soft earth between her toes.

The rising moon, a glowing yellow pumpkin in the dark bowl of the sky, shed its soft radiance over tall flax and manuka and shadowed Logan's strong features with odd planes and angles. Logan ... All at once she caught her breath. They were alone here amid primitive surroundings, a man and a woman—'A man and a woman who loathe each other,' she reminded herself.

'And just as well too,' the thought came from nowhere, 'when his kiss affected you the way it did.' She brushed the thought aside. What was a kiss? An impulse? A nothing thing?

Glowing with warmth and filled with a delightful sense of relaxation, at last they left the pool, and Fleur climbed the muddy bank to put on her stained and dusty garments.

In no time at all, it seemed to her, Logan was coming towards her through the shadows. He was pushing his wet hair back from his forehead and she thought that in the moonglow he looked younger, more carefree. She was finding pleasure in looking at him, just looking. It's just, she tried to rationalise away the direction in which her thoughts were drifting, that if I had to be stranded in the wilderness with a man, Logan would be the one I'd choose. Only because he knows New Zealand bush lore and survival tactics. Personally I can't stand the man!

Once again she realised the danger of emphysema, the silent killer that crept through the darkness to attack travellers who were sleeping out in the open in the New Zealand bush, without sufficient covering or a fire to keep themselves warm. Thrusting the terrifying thoughts aside, she brought her mind back to Logan's deep voice. He seemed to tune in on her thoughts. 'What I'd give right now for a box of matches!'

'I know, I know.'

'We may as well camp right here,' he was saying. 'It's not too far from the creek and with a bit of luck we'll get to the river in the morning. What do you say?'

She avoided his gaze. 'That's—fine with me.'

'You don't sound too enthusiastic about it——' He broke off. 'What's on your mind, Fox? Don't you want to spend the night with me? I get it!' A hateful grin split the dark face and she caught the flash of white teeth. 'It's not the morning that's on your mind, right?'

'It's nothing to do with you!' she flung at him.

'Just,' there was an odd unreadable note in his voice, almost as if it mattered to him, 'that you're not used to spending the night out with a man? True or false, Fox?'

She was so confused by the unexpected query that she spoke unthinkingly. 'True, true, true!'

'You've nothing to worry about, except the cold.' He had turned aside and was gathering small leafy branches and dried fern, then bundling them into a heap on the ground.

'Here's your pillow.' He handed her the ferny bundle. 'Try that for size.' After a startled look Fleur dropped down on the grass, stuffing the makeshift pillow behind her head. 'It's pretty scratchy.'

'Stop complaining!' He was gathering together ferns and bracken and covering her from shoulders down to her feet with greenery. Fleur giggled at the thought of what she must look like.

'Don't laugh,' he told her, 'you'll be glad of any sort of covering later on in the night.'

'I don't need *that!*' He was tossing his jacket over the mound of leaves and bracken.

'All the same,' his voice was flint-hard, 'you're going to have it.' He straightened and looked down at her. 'You'll be all right, Fox?'

'I guess so.' For a heart-stopping moment she wondered wildly if he was about to kiss her, but he turned away. 'Don't forget I'll be within call if you need me. Yell out if the cold and damp get too tough for you.'

'I'll be fine!' Inwardly she vowed that a midnight appeal for help would be the last thing she would consider. It opened up too many dismaying possibilities. She would rather die of the cold.

Covertly she watched Logan as he moved a short distance away from her. Soon he was gathering bracken and greenery, dropping to the dew-wet ground and pulling the ferny covering over him. Fleur lay looking up at the stars, brilliant in the soft dense darkness of the night sky. The Milky Way was a silver pathway dusted with stars and the Southern Cross above her head was a scintillating kite traced in gold. A night for love, she mused on a sigh, and she was here with Logan with his high-handed ways—well, most of the time—while Bart, with his beguiling smile and caressing voice, was far away. Bart? The thoughts chased one another through her troubled mind. Of course Bart was innocent of the theft of stock from the station he had managed. Oh, Bart, if only you were at Te Haruru still, if only none of this had happened! The slow tears coursed down her cheeks. He wouldn't risk the loss of well-paid employment by taking such risks—Swiftly she caught herself up. Anyway, he was honest as they come. It wouldn't enter his head to be a party to such dealing.

'No?' jeered the dark imp in her mind who never seemed to sleep. 'Bart's got expensive tastes that even his manager's job might not be able to gratify.' His words over the telephone a day or so ago returned to haunt her. 'We can go where we like, live where we want to, anywhere in the world except Te Haruru.' Why not Te Haruru? Could it be because he had been falsely accused there, had lost his job or——? Fleur shied away from the appalling alternative. But he hasn't lost *me,* she told herself, and pushed away the tiny niggle of doubt at the back of her mind.

The ground was becoming harder with each passing minute and the fern pillow did nothing for comfort. Worse, it was becoming cooler. Who would have believed that following the heat of the day had come a heavy dew and chilling temperatures?

In spite of everything, however, exhaustion must have had its way with her, for at some time during the night she awoke, feeling cold and stiff, to find the scene around her flooded with bright moonlight. In the intense stillness of the country she caught the harsh call of a kiwi somewhere deep in the bush, the mournful 'More-pork' of the native owl and the rustle of some small creature in the undergrowth. Suddenly she froze at the sound of breaking branches and heavy thuds, as if at the approach of a large animal. For a terror-ridden moment fear held her in its grip and she thought with horror of the wild pigs hunted by her father and the young shepherds out in the bush. The movements were becoming closer now and she jerked herself upwards in alarm. How could she have forgotten the savage animals that roamed the depths of the forest? Suppose a wild pig were to attack her and she had no defence, nothing—except Logan. Driven by panic, she sprang to her feet, hurried across the dew-wet grass and crept down at his side. At least, she thought, the peril of the night was eased, and so long as he remained asleep . . .

Yet still she couldn't sleep. She shivered with cold and her light clothing was damp with dew. Chilled, sick with worry over the events of the day, the plane crash that had resulted in that missed meeting with Bart tugged endlessly at her mind. Tears flooded her eyes and she tried in vain to stifle the sobs.

'*Now* what's the matter?'

The brute, she thought angrily, he was awake all the time! Aloud she muttered, 'I'm so c-cold,' and raised a hand to dash away the tears from her wet cheeks.

'You shouldn't have tossed off the fern.'

'I hadn't time to worry about that,' she said stiffly, 'with all the crashing and banging that was going on in the bushes. I got scared,' she admitted. 'I'm sure it was a wild pig.'

'Probably.' Logan's tone was careless as he rose to his feet and moved away to collect the bracken and his jacket from the spot where she had discarded them in her flight. He tossed the greenery over her, followed by the warm jacket.

'It doesn't make much d-difference,' muttered Fleur through chattering teeth.

'It's the best I can offer.' He dropped down at her side, arms crossed behind his neck.

Belatedly she said, 'You should have kept the coat yourself.'

He ignored that. 'If you really want to warm up there's only one way, and that's for us to get close, you and me.'

How close? she wondered over a suddenly pounding heart. Uncertain of what he was getting at but taking no chances, she said crisply, 'It's all right.'

The gravelly voice cut across her rioting thoughts. 'Bart wouldn't approve?'

Relieved at the change of subject, she said irritatedly, 'I don't know why you keep on about him.'

'No? I'll tell you something, Fox. You've had a lucky

escape today. You should thank your lucky stars for that plane crash.'

She caught her breath. 'What—do you mean? You knew?' Too late she realised she had given herself away. 'How did you find out—about me?'

'It's fairly obvious.' She could imagine the ironic twist to his well-shaped lips. 'You were so dead keen to keep that date in town. Anyone ever tell you, Fox, that you've got a tell-tale face? You should watch it if you want to keep things to yourself, things like sneaking away and going off with Howard——'

'It wasn't sneaking!' Fleur protested hotly, then stopped short, aware that once again she had betrayed herself. 'Anyway,' she ran on, flustered, 'how could we get married any other way, the way things are at home . . . and everything?'

All at once he seemed weary of the subject. 'Try and get some sleep, Fox. The sun will be up before you know it.'

But she was too cold to sleep, and much later, in the hours before dawn, icy chills seemed to creep through her bones and her body was racked with tremors. She thought desperately that if only she could be certain that Logan was asleep she would creep close to him for body warmth. The trouble was, with Logan one could never be sure of anything. The man never seemed to sleep. Before long, however, damp and chill became so crippling that nothing else mattered but warmth, any warmth, and she edged nearer to him. The next moment a strong arm shot out to draw her close and on a shuddering breath she crept blissfully close to Logan's strong sinewy body. Oddly comforted, she felt her shaking limbs relax. Her last thought before sleep claimed her was that who could imagine the word 'comfort' in connection with Logan's forceful nature!

CHAPTER SIX

FEELING stiff, cold and aching in every muscle after a
night spent lying on the hard ground, Fleur opened her
eyes in the morning to find Logan standing over her.
'Better get moving, Fox.' Putting out a hand, he helped
her to her feet.

A vividly tinted fan in hues of flame and orange was
outspread over the eastern horizon, but Fleur was in no
mood to appreciate the spectacular sunrise. Shivering
with damp and cold, she tried to infuse a cheerful note
into her voice. 'Water's the first priority, I guess?'

'Right!' The thought shot through her mind that he
was regarding her in the oddest way, a quite un-Logan
look that she couldn't fathom. Compassion? Concern?
She was unaware of tangled hair, the look of strain in
her face and dark shadows under her eyes. His tone of
voice, however, was as matter-of-fact as ever. 'Keep
your fingers crossed that we hit the farmhouse on the
other side of the river in time for breakfast!'

'Breakfast!' she groaned. 'Don't talk about it!' At the
thought of food her stomach felt emptier than ever.

Logan turned away and with an effort she managed
to keep up with his long strides. Even if it killed her, she
vowed silently, she wouldn't allow herself to lag behind
and force him to wait for her! Before long they had
reached the bank of the stream, to kneel on the dew-wet
grass, cupping their hands and gulping down the cold,
crystal-clear water.

Logan was the first to rise to his feet. 'On your way,
Fox! We'll make good time while we can. Later on the
sun gets as hot as Hades!'

Over her shoulder she flung him a bright smile—at
least she hoped it was a bright smile. 'Don't I know it—
after yesterday! Ready when you are!'

Afterwards she could never recall with any degree of
clarity the details of the walk through the bush, only the

95

unutterable relief of emerging into the sunshine in view of a swiftly flowing river. 'Hallelujah!' She turned a shining-eyed face to Logan. 'What do you know, there really is a farmhouse over the river!'

He grinned down at her. 'You don't think I'd put you wrong, do you?'

It was precisely what she did think of him, but at the moment she felt too hungry and exhausted to argue the matter. After all, she reminded herself, he had guided them out of the bush and to a point directly opposite a dwelling. The farmhouse was so near that she could see a man striding up a path towards the open door of the rambling, red-foofed farmhouse. 'Lucky for us,' she brought her mind back to Logan's deep gravelly voice, 'that the guy over there tossed a tree over the water, saves me time looking for a fallen tree, a ready-made bridge.'

'Bridge!' she echoed. His words seemed to come from a distance and a strange hazy feeling was making her feel woozy. 'Where?' She steadied her quivering nerves. 'Oh, that——' nervously she eyed a smooth narrow tree-trunk thrown from bank to bank over the swiftly running water.

'Don't worry, it will do. Come on, Fox,' his tone was oddly tender, 'I'll be right behind you!'

But then, she thought bemusedly, he was like that, being nice to her when for one reason or another he was feeling sorry for her. And she didn't want pity, not from him. A strange disembodied sensation was creeping over her and she tried to push away the wave of giddiness that threatened to overwhelm her. Since childhood she'd had a thing about heights, she couldn't help it, and even though the makeshift bridge didn't altogether come into that category she knew that to keep her footing on the damp and slippery tree-trunk would be like walking a tightrope. Not that she would admit her trepidation to Logan. So she straightened her shoulders and lifted her small square chin and hurried along at his side. It was no use, she admitted to herself as they reached the tree-shadowed river. A feeling of nausea lodged itself in her midriff and the moving water merged into a haze. All at once she became aware of Logan's perceptive gaze, his eyes clear and aware. The next moment she found herself scooped up in his arms, and carrying her light weight effortlessly, he moved swiftly and confidently over the narrow tree-trunk.

The wild barking of dogs heralded their arrival as they neared the weathered old house set against a backdrop of towering native trees, and as they opened the small gate a young woman, a man and two young boys clad in pyjamas hurried down the path to meet them.

The farmer was the first to greet them. 'You're not the survivors of that plane that crashed over the hill yesterday?'

Logan grinned, 'We are, you know——' and Fleur broke in, misty-eyed, 'You've just no idea of how glad we are to be here!' In spite of herself there was a catch in her voice.

'Come right inside!' The lively, dark-eyed young woman and her slow-speaking husband led them into a sunny dining room while the two children eyed the strangers with wide, curious eyes. 'What would you like first? I'm Ann McLain, by the way, and this is Ted— What's it to be?' she asked in her quick bright way, 'breakfast or a shower? Just say the word!'

'The telephone for me!' came Logan's decisive tones. 'I'm hoping we haven't been missed, that they'd take it for granted over at Te Haruru that I'd stayed in town overnight. Fleur wasn't due back for some days anyway.'

'Not a chance, mate,' Ted told him. 'A gang of forestry workers heard the plane engine cutting out, then they watched it vanish over the big hill. They tried to find out what had happened, but when it got dark they didn't have a show. Since then the phones have been red-hot all around the district and search parties are all geared to go into the bush at first light. They're probably starting off now—phone's over there on the bench.'

'I'll soon put things right!' Logan was striding towards the instrument and dialling a number. In the silence Fleur caught his deep reassuring tones. 'Is that you, Stan? Logan here. Sure, we're okay, hungry but okay. Yes, yes, Fleur's fine. You can ask her yourself if you don't believe me. She's right here beside me and we're at the McLains' place, just over the river.' He held out the handpiece. 'Over to you!'

Already she was listening to her father's voice. 'That you, Fox?' His broken tones told her of the agony of suspense he had endured through the long hours of darkness. 'Thank God you're alive!'

'I'm all right, of course I'm all right!' The silly emotional tears filled her eyes. 'Thanks to Logan!' The words seemed to come without her volition and she knew that despite all her antagonism and resentment towards him, there was no getting away from the truth that she owed him a great deal.

She brought her mind back to the masculine tones. 'Bruce is right here beside me. He's looking as pleased as punch at your good news. He was just about to take off in the helicopter to make a search in the bush—hang on,' he broke off for a moment, 'he wants me to give you a message, says to let you know that the rescue squad is on the way. The McLains' place? Logan said. Bruce knows the farmhouse well, he says.'

'That's terrific! See you soon, then. 'Bye!' Fleur dashed the tears from her eyes with the back of her hand and swung around to meet Logan's level gaze. 'It's all arranged, Bruce is coming over in the chopper to pick us up.'

Soon she was taking a quick shower, avoiding, after one horrified glance, her own reflection in the mirror. Who wanted to take a second glance at that pathetic-looking waif with leaf and twig-encrusted hair, face and arms crisscrossed with scratches and dried blood, a dark bruise on her forehead? Presently, clad in Ann McLain's borrowed T-shirt and slacks several sizes too large for her and held together at the waist by a safety-pin, she made her way into the kitchen, fragrant with the aroma of percolating coffee and sizzling bacon. The hot drink was reviving and the plate of bacon and farm eggs that Ann magically produced the moment Fleur came into the room was like no other meal she had ever tasted.

Presently she was relating to the kindly couple seated at the table her experiences of the past two days while the two small boys listened with rapt attention. All the time, however, on another level of her mind, she knew that the sick disappointment and shattering knowledge of her failed meeting with Bart was there ready to pounce. During the past few hours, all but drugged with fatigue and cold and hunger, the aching sense of loss had lain quiescent, but she knew that soon the pain would start. Pain because of the crashing of all her plans for a new life with Bart? Or could it be because of the insistent niggle of doubt that she couldn't seem to banish from her mind because of all that Logan had told her about Bart. Not that she believed Logan, of course, not for a single moment, and yet . . .

She watched him as he entered the room, his thick dark hair waving damply after his shower. As always, she thought, he looked lazily relaxed yet at the same time he exuded a sense of leashed power. At that moment their glances clashed, and catching the glint in his hazel eyes, her glance slid away and a tinge of colour crept up her pale cheeks. Was he remembering the enforced intimacy of a night spent together under the stars? The trouble was, she admitted ruefully, that she hadn't behaved as though the intimacy were enforced—on the contrary. Swiftly she took her runaway thoughts in hand. Put it down to reaction, she told herself, the effects of shock and stress. What else could it be, that crazy attraction between a man and a girl who despised each other?

She and Logan were finishing their second mugs of coffee when the chug-chug of a helicopter in the sky alerted them to Bruce's impending arrival. Hurrying to the window, Fleur watched as the 'copter passed over the high bush-clad hill behind the farmhouse to hover low over a cleared paddock not far away. It wasn't long before the young pilot was coming in at the door, his eyes dark with concern, seeking Fleur's face. 'You're not hurt?' He let out a long breath of relief. 'You really are all right?' He seemed totally unaware of anyone else in the room.

'Oh, I am! I am! Thanks to Logan!' She was determined to accord him the appreciation due to him for his skilful piloting of the damaged plane.

'What happened?' Bruce asked her. The next moment everyone was talking at once, and it was left to Logan in the end to explain in a few terse words their narrow escape from death. Within a few minutes the group moved out to the waiting helicopter and farewells were made to the couple at the farmhouse. Their new friends stood waving goodbye as the 'copter rose in the clear morning air, skimming over bush-clad slopes and moving on in the direction of Te Haruru. The noise of the machine made conversation difficult, and Fleur, pressed close to Logan in the close confines of the cabin, was dreamily content to relax in the plastic bubble. At one point of the journey Logan pointed down to bush-clad slopes below, and straining her eyes, she caught sight of a wisp of smoke rising among tall forest trees.

When they reached the homestead, cars and trucks were lined up on the driveway. As Logan braked to a stop Fleur was out of the vehicle and running up the verandah steps to greet her father. His warm hug as he clasped her in his arms left her in no doubt of his heartfelt delight at seeing her safe and well. 'Great to have you back, Fox!' His voice was husky with emotion.

'I know I'm lucky!' She gave a low laugh at his tender protective glance. In truth she was shocked by his appearance. He appeared to her to have aged overnight, for surely those were new lines in his thin face. Aloud she said reassuringly, 'I'm not hurt a scrap, honestly!'

'Didn't know what had become of the plane,' she could scarcely catch the low uneven tones, 'couldn't bear to face up to what might have happened to you——'

'There's nothing to worry about now, Dad—My goodness!' she took in the vehicles that were manoeuvring for a space on the crowded driveway below, 'don't tell me all these folk are here because of the crash?'

'Sure are!' As the group from the 'copter entered the lounge Fleur realised that the big room was crowded with people. Some faces were unfamiliar to her, acquaintances of Logan's, no doubt, she thought fleetingly. Friends of the family were among the groups, many of whom must have travelled a long way to come here today, and there were young folk well known to her in the isolated district. At that moment the telephone shrilled from the hallway and Daphne hurried from the room, to return with a message that the Inspector of Air Accidents wanted a word with Logan.

Immediately Fleur found herself surrounded by an excited chattering crowd, eager to ply her with questions or to congratulate her on a narrow escape from disaster. Presently Daphne was at her side, a tray held in her strong capable hands. 'Good to have you back, young Fleur! Coffee? I'll bet you need it!'

'Do I ever? It's only my third lot this morning!' Dropping down to the carpeted floor, she cradled the steaming pottery mug in her hands. 'You know something, Daph? There were moments back there in the hills when the plane engine had cut out and I didn't think we were going to make it. We wouldn't have done either if Logan hadn't brought the Cessna down in a clearing. He was just fantastic!'

'Any pilot would have done the same!' She hadn't realised that Logan was standing close by until the deep gravelly voice cut across her fervent accents. 'Self-preservation,' he drawled, 'isn't that what they call it?'

Fleur felt her face grow hot. He was intimating that her presence in the plane had been a matter of no importance to him. She was seething with anger. He needn't have put her down like this, she told herself resentfully. How could she have imagined him to have changed in any way from his usual arrogant self? During their ordeal in the bush it was only pity for her that had made him soften in his feelings towards her. Oh, she might have known that it wouldn't last, not with him!

As the minutes went by the chink of glasses merged with the buzz of conversation in the crowded room. Then all at once a throaty feminine voice cut across the murmur of voices. 'Logan!' All eyes were drawn to the tall woman who stood in the open doorway, her anxious gaze searching the room. The most beautiful woman, the thought pierced Fleur with an odd stab of the heart, that she had ever seen. Sparrow-thin, even by today's standards of feminine attractiveness, with a hauntingly lovely face and, clearly, all the careless confidence of an acknowledged beauty. At that moment Logan entered the room from a door at the other end of the lounge and in the electric silence a single word rang out. 'Darling!' Oblivious of watchers, the stranger was pushing her way through the crowd as she hurried towards the tall masculine figure. The next minute she reached Logan, flinging her arms around his neck and clinging wildly to him. 'I've just heard the news, but I had to make sure! I thought I'd lost you for ever ... for ever!' Her thin shoulders were shaking and sobs racked her body. At last she raised her head from his chest, the tears running unchecked down her cheeks. 'You're really back!' All at once she was laughing and crying at the same time. 'And looking just as though nothing awful has happened to you! I'm so *glad*! You wouldn't believe,' the words tumbled huskily from her lips, 'but I prayed for you to come back safely. Can you imagine it—*me*, praying! And now, look, my prayers have been answered!' The throbbing voice ran wildly on. 'Such a long night, I thought it would never end, thinking of you, seeing you go down with the plane. I couldn't bear it! And now you're really back here with me!'

As if becoming aware of others in the room for the first time, she swung around to face the onlookers, tears sparkling on the long black lashes making her eyes like blue stars. 'Forgive me, folks,' the throaty voice was tremulous, 'but I couldn't help getting carried away. It's just,' she confided to the room in general, 'that I've been worried sick about Logan. You see, I've known him all my life——' a secret glance passed between them, 'well, near enough! The thing is, I simply can't imagine how I could get along without him!'

Fleur's gaze was fixed on Logan's face. How would he react to this emotional outburst? she wondered. For his inscrutable expression gave nothing away. Logan who delighted in putting her down, or trying to do so, with his sardonic glance or knife-edged remark. But not this time, not with this woman—*his* woman, she told herself the next minute. For an indulgent smile lifted the corners of his well-cut lips and clearly he was actually revelling in the unconcealed hero-worship and slavish devotion being lavished upon him. Fleur strained her ears to catch his response. 'Cuts both ways!'

The lovely face and throaty appealing voice had captured the attention of everyone in the room and all eyes were on the stranger as she ran on. 'It's not the first time this has happened,' the rapid tones were tinged with hysteria and she still clung to Logan. 'Once before, ages ago, he crash-landed in the bush, but I was with him at that time and it didn't seem so bad when we were together. Anyway,' all at once she appeared to pull her thoughts together and become aware of her emotional outburst, 'I guess you're all wondering who I am——'

'Christina!' Logan cut in in his deep voice, and you could *hear* the ring of pride in his voice, Fleur thought dully. 'She's our new neighbour—moved into the old Stanford property, just over the hill on the coast road.'

'That's right!' Tears misted Christina's dark blue eyes, but her smile was dazzling. 'I've leased the place for a year. Once I get things sorted out I'm planning to set up a riding instruction place where kids can come and stay for a week or a weekend—older ones too if they wish—Oh, I know everyone around here is bound to be well clued up about riding, but they might want to brush up on the advanced stuff, show-jumping and all that. My horses are being brought up from the South Island next week and Logan's got a man coming to set up the jumps and put in new fencing. I don't know if I could kick off the project with him, and now he's back——' Her warm glance clung to his face as though she could never look away.

'A load of rubbish!' Logan disclaimed, grinning. 'Christina is perfectly capable of organising the whole set-up single-handed!'

'Not without your helping hand!' She was almost as tall as Logan and her smile swept towards him, then she glanced around at the crowd. 'I wanted to go somewhere out of the rat race and Logan came up with this riding school idea. Oh, I know the place is run down right now, but the grounds are ideal for my purposes and Logan's arranging to have the house made livable in and have new stables and outbuildings put up. With transport it won't be too far from civilisation.' Her tender glance beamed towards Logan said quite plainly, Fleur thought, 'or from you!'

The next moment talk and laughter and eager questions echoed around Christina. After a few minutes, however, she and Logan left the group gathered around them and made their way towards Fleur. Christina held a sherry glass in her hand and her scornful glance as she approached made Fleur unhappily aware of her own dishevelled appearance and ill-fitting garments. Christina said carelessly, 'You're the land girl here, I take it?'

Fleur drew a deep breath of indignation, but before she could summon up a sufficiently crushing retort, Logan cut in smoothly, 'Among other things!' At the glint of amusement in his eyes Fleur found herself hating him all over again. 'Fleur's father and I,' he added blandly, 'happen to be partners in Te Haruru station. Right now Fleur's a survivor. She got out of the plane crash with me and did a marathon to the nearest farmhouse.' It was the only time, Fleur thought in astonishment, he had ever accorded her praise or appreciation for anything. His words came as such a shock to her that she was lost for an answer.

'Oh—*that* girl!' Christina's husky tones sharpened and her brilliant blue eyes took on a glitter that Fleur didn't care for one little bit. 'You were out all night in the bush?'

'That's right,' Logan agreed cheerfully, and for the merest second Fleur surprised a softness in his glance. The next minute, aware of his offhanded tones, she decided she must have imagined it. 'Not an experience to be envied, eh, Fox?'

Now, however, she had her runaway emotions firmly in hand. 'Anything but!' she said crisply. 'I've never been so cold in all my life, and I was scared out of my skull by the wild pigs rooting around.' Why was she defending herself like this? she wondered. There was nothing to defend or explain away. It must surely be the effect of those blue eyes, dark with suspicion and—yes, jealousy—she was sure of it, that had sparked her to such indignation.

She wrenched her mind back to Logan's tones. 'Being my passenger in the Cessna,' for a fleeting moment his glance met hers, 'was bad news for Fleur in more ways than one!'

Christina, however, appeared uninterested in Fleur's affairs and seemed scarcely conscious of her idle question. 'How do you mean?'

'Oh, just that the crash interferred with her plans quite a lot,' Logan's deep tones ran on, 'put finish to an important date she had with someone in the city.' Fleur's eyes were sparkling with anger, but he eyed her imperturbably. 'Isn't that right, Fox?'

'It didn't matter,' she muttered, and hoped no one else in the room had caught the furious glance she flung in his direction. And to think, she stormed silently, that she had actually come to believe, during the perilous hours they had shared, that he might have changed in his attitude towards her!

'Bad luck for Fleur's girl friend,' she realised her father had come to join the group, 'seeing she's ill and on her own in town and needed Fleur's help——' He broke off to eye Fleur. 'You'll be wanting to ring your friend and explain what happened?' he suggested.

'Yes, of course. I will—soon,' she agreed, hating herself for the lie.

She realised the next moment that friends were clustering around her. 'You haven't told us a thing about the crash yet. It must have been a horrific experience! Did you have anything to drink all that time you were in the bush?'

'Creek water was fine!' She went on to describe the desperate journey through dense bush, the delight in drinking the crystal-clear creek water. All the time she was aware of Logan's interested look. Did he imagine, for heaven's sake, that she was about to babble on about the dip in the hot mineral pools, the river crossing when he had picked her up in his arms because she was just too scared to make her own way over the makeshift bridge?

Presently Logan and Christina went to join a group at the other end of the room, and Fleur stared after them, the thoughts tumbling through her mind.

So this was Logan's 'friend', and clearly the other girl was anything but the helpless clinging type of female Fleur had imagined her to be. Experienced in the ways of the world, Christina radiated confidence in herself. Wouldn't any woman, given that fashion-model appearance, for Christina was reed-thin, even by today's standards of feminine beauty, and with that provocative tone of voice ... She's terribly attractive, Fleur acknowledged reluctantly, and deeply involved with Logan. He must have been joking, she mused, when he had told Daphne about his 'friend' who had had a bad deal in life and who now was anxious to pick up the pieces and make a fresh start. For clearly Christina was a woman who had everything, including Logan's love and trust. The odd thing was that Fleur had a niggling impression of familiarity concerning the stranger, as if somewhere at some time she had met Christina before. But of course, she told herself, that was impossible. One didn't, she had to admit, forget a woman of Christina's charm and beauty.

'Down this, Fleur! You look as though you could do with it!' Bruce's friendly tones broke across her musing and she glanced up to find him at her side. Probably he had been there all the time, she realised now, saying nothing and regarding her with his concerned dark eyes.

'Oh—thanks.' She took the glass of wine he was

holding out to her. With an effort she wrenched her glance away from Logan and Christina who were chatting companionably together. Just as though there was no one else in the room, she thought crossly. Suddenly she became aware of Bruce's low compassionate tones. 'You've had a rough time——'

'But we got back!' She stared down at the ruby-coloured wine in her glass. 'It's a funny feeling, being a survivor. Everything happened so quickly at the time of the crash. The worst moment of all was when the plane was falling out of the sky and the hill below was coming nearer every second. Luckily Logan guided the plane down between two big trees and we went through—Whoosh!' she sketched a gesture in the air with her hand, 'losing a wing on the way! Then just a few minutes after we climbed out of the wreck,' she shuddered at the thought of the leaping flames and crackling timbers, 'came the fire.'

'Don't think about it,' he said softly.

She smiled tremulously, 'All right, then, I'll think about you instead! How come you're here when you had a job jacked up on another property miles and miles away?'

'That's an easy one to answer. I was due to take off on some aerial spraying early this morning, but when word got through last night about the missing Cessna, I planned to fly over the bush country at first light. Getting word from the farm by the river that you'd turned up there was the best news I've ever had in my life! If anything had happened to you,' his low voice was husky with emotion, 'if I'd had to find you out there, too late——' He took her fingers in his warm clasp, 'I couldn't have faced that, not *you*——' his voice thickened.

To lighten the moment Fleur said with a smile, 'It was a big thrill for me to see you in your chopper coming through the clouds this morning! I never expected to get home so quickly!' All at once she realised that he must have been standing nearby ever since her arrival in the room. After all those hours exposed to Logan's arrogant company, there was something definitely comforting, she mused, in being treated as a girl who was someone special, and not merely because she happened to be the heroine of a recent dramatic plane crash!

Scarcely aware of Bruce's words, her attention was riveted on Christina, who was clearly the centre of the admiring group gathered around her. 'I've got to go, folks,' she flashed a brilliant smile. 'I'm expecting a call from the nice builder man who's promised to make my disreputable old place into a real equestrian centre. See you!' A melting glance from those startling blue eyes thrown towards Logan, then she was threading her way through the crowd, her model's walk taking her past Fleur without a glance in the other girl's direction.

All at once Fleur became aware of Bruce, who was eyeing her intently. 'Look, when can I see you again? I'll be around this part of the world at the end of the week,' he grinned. 'I've made it my business to work things that way. Any ideas?'

'I don't know,' she answered vaguely. 'What would you like to do?'

'What would I like?' His dark eyes softened. 'Just to get you to myself for a while, without all this!' He waved a hand towards the groups still lingering at the doorway. 'We'll work something out when I get back.' Then, taking in her wan appearance, 'Take care!' He turned aside and Fleur, aware of a reporter with a camera slung over his shoulder, who was moving in her direction, slipped from the room. Let Logan take care of the newspaper man, she thought resentfully, and went into the kitchen.

Daphne, busy over the electric range, sent a shrewd glance over Fleur's pale face. 'What you need,' she said reprovingly, 'is to rest up for a bit.' Then, catching Fleur's indignant look, 'And don't tell me to mind my own business! That's right, isn't it?' she appealed to Fleur's father, who had come into the room.

'Absolutely!' he agreed.

As he and Fleur strolled up the long hall together, she hooked her arm in his. 'Tell me, Dad, how did you know the Cessna was in trouble? Logan was hoping you'd take it that he'd changed his mind and spent the night in town instead of coming back here.'

Her father shook his head. 'I'd never buy that! He's not a man to alter arrangements without letting me know.'

Fleur's soft lips tightened. Logan ... Logan ... He seemed to have bewitched her father into imagining his partner to be an entirely different man from what he actually was. She should know! Pushing aside the angry thoughts, she said quietly, 'What did alert you that something was wrong?'

'When he didn't show up when it got dark I knew he'd run into difficulties in the plane. I phoned through to the president of the Cattle Breeding Association in the city and he reported that Logan hadn't shown up at the meeting. All through the night the phone was ringing non-stop with people wanting to know if I'd had any news of the Cessna. When a forestry worker reported seeing a plane disappearing over a hill, then hearing an explosion, that was when I really went through hell. There was just one ray of hope, and I clung to it all the time——'

She eyed him curiously. 'I can't imagine what that could be?'

'That's because you don't know Logan as I do. He's piloted a plane for years, and I knew that if there was one chance in a thousand of getting you both out of the smash safely, he'd make it.' He threw her a swift glance. 'Know what I'm getting at?'

Logan again! she thought huffily. Aloud she answered, 'Not really.'

Her father, however, appeared not to notice her lack of enthusiasm in response to his query. 'After the crash, you two had to put in a lot of time on your own. You got to know Logan a bit better after all that, hmm?'

She swung around indignantly. 'I don't know what you're getting at——'

'Take it easy, Fox-girl! You've got your lines crossed. What I'm getting at is something that's been on my mind quite a lot. A little matter I was hoping Logan might have straightened out for you. You did talk things over between you?'

Instantly she was on the defensive. 'Oh yes, we talked all right, and if you want to know, he told me a lot of lies about Bart and missing sheep and forged cheques and all the rest of it.' The words tumbled wildly from her lips. 'He made quite a point of it. Not,' she ran on bitterly, 'that it did him any good. I told him I simply didn't believe him and I won't ever believe it, not until Bart tells me himself—and I know that when he does,' she finished, tossing her head defiantly, 'he'll be able to explain everything satisfactorily. It's all just a stupid misunderstanding!'

He was staring at her in disbelief. 'Are you telling me you've still got faith in Bart?'

'That's right.' She lifted her small chin. Somehow she was getting into the habit of lifting her chin whenever Bart's name came into the conversation, 'Anyway, I'm getting sick of hearing about all that and I'd rather not discuss it any more. Right, Dad?'

He hesitated for a long moment, then he said on a sigh, 'If that's what you want.' All at once a smile illuminated his thin face. 'I'm willing to put up with anything now that I've got you back with me safe and sound.' He added after a moment, 'Got to thank Logan for that!'

'Oh, blast Logan!' The words came without her volition. At her father's expression of open-mouthed astonishment, she said hastily, 'Oh, he's a good enough pilot of a plane, I grant you, but personally I can't stand the man!'

'So I gather,' came the dry tones. He sent her a shrewd glance. 'Better watch it, young Fox. Ever thought that all that hate you're always on about for Logan might just be a cover-up for something quite different, something you won't admit, even to yourself?'

Fleur knew very well what he meant. 'Never!' she said firmly, and because she felt she had to convince herself as well as her father she added, very positively, 'Not with me!'

The next day she awoke early after a restless night, conscious of a dull sense of loss. Who wouldn't feel that way, she rallied herself, after having lost for ever the man she loved? For she knew that Bart with his aggressive male pride and easily pierced armour would allow her no second chance. Even to herself she refused to admit that her heaviness of heart could in any way be connected with Logan and the startlingly lovely woman who had followed him to the isolated district. Correction, she told herself, the woman for whom Logan had made arrangements to live not far from him. At the thought of Logan she seethed with anger. The brief interlude in the wilderness night, when some madness had drawn her to him despite her hatred of him, had been just part of the nightmare events of the past two days. Now that she was back in the real world she loathed the man more than ever, if that were possible.

The hours went by slowly as she stayed indoors, making a pretence of reading a magazine, then sorting through her photographs of the refugee camp overseas. All the time, however, her ears were alerted to the shrill summons of the telephone bell. Not that she expected to receive a call from Bart in Australia, she told herself. She knew he wouldn't get in touch with her, not now, but still she couldn't seem to tear herself away from the house. All through the morning the telephone rang almost continuously, always for Fleur and with the same questions to which she gave the same answers. Yes, thanks, she was feeling fine! No, she had no after-effects from the night spent in the wilderness. Are you sure? whispered the dark goblin deep in her mind, but she thrust it aside. Once or twice over the wire she had to parry veiled insinuations regarding the night spent in the darkness with Logan, but she had her answers ready for that too. So lucky for her, she said brightly, that Logan happened to be well experienced in bushcraft and survival in the wilderness ... all she could remember of the period was the intense cold and the rooting of wild pigs in the bush around her.

It was one of the rare days when Logan happened to be working close to the homestead, and at lunch time he came to join the others at the table. He was seated opposite to Fleur and she was all too aware that her nervous jump at the pealing of the telephone did not go unnoticed by him. 'Expecting a call, Fox?' His hard gaze challenged her.

'All the time!' she flashed back. About to spring from her seat, she forced herself to sit motionless and allow someone else to answer the call. She put on her brightest smile. 'I keep telling them I'm quite all right. I was just lucky to have you around!' The next moment, catching the glint in his eyes, she regretted her choice of words and was grateful for Daphne, who came hurrying towards her at that moment. 'It's for you, Fleur. A man—long-distance.'

This time she was too excited to hide her eagerness and she all but ran out of the room. Maybe this was the call she had been waiting for. She snatched up the receiver. 'Hello! Hello! Is that you, Bart?'

'Hi—Bruce here! I've been thinking about you, wondering if you're still feeling okay after the big drama yesterday?'

'Yes, yes, of course I'm all right.' She could scarcely contain her disappointment, and it was with an effort that she concentrated on the warm masculine voice. What was he saying?

'I've been caught up here with an urgent job that's going to last all week. The devil's own luck! And the weather's no help, fine and clear without a breath of wind, perfect for aerial spraying. But I'll get back to see you before long or die in the attempt!'

'That will be great——'

'You don't sound too enthusiastic!' Had the instrument that so clearly registered nuances in speech, she wondered, betrayed her complete lack of interest? His next words confirmed her suspicion. All at once his voice was low and persuasive. 'No strings, love. Just a chance to see you again, a night out together—what's wrong with that?'

'Nothing, I guess.' Why not? she asked herself as she replaced the handpiece in its cradle. There was no sense in wasting her life in useless regrets. Slowly she made her way back to the dining table, her eyes thoughtful. But that doesn't mean I'm going to believe any of those lies Logan has told me about Bart, she thought. A promise is a promise and that's that! Engrossed in her thoughts, she raised blank eyes to meet Logan's piercing gaze. Almost she could read the question in his probing look. Was that call on the phone from Bart or not? Well, at least she could set Logan's mind at rest on that score. 'Just another wellwisher.' She poured herself a fresh cup of coffee. Aware of Logan's enigmatic gaze, she said lightly, 'We sure hit the headlines with that plane crash! It's a funny thing, but everyone expects I must have some after-effects from the crash or the fire or——' meeting Logan's deep compelling glance, she found herself regretting having begun this line of talk, 'the night spent out in the cold,' she finished in a rush of words.

'But you haven't?' he enquired in his bland, detached tone.

She couldn't bring herself to meet his deceptively innocent gaze. 'None at all,' she said lightly, and flashed him a 'couldn't-care-less' smile. 'Of course you can't count a few scratches and bruises, but nothing that really *matters*!'

He shrugged broad shoulders. 'You should know!'

The double-edged remark set her seething. If he had the nerve to be referring to that closeness in the long reaches of the wilderness night when she'd crept near to him because of the cold ... The next moment, as she watched him rise from the table, his expression unreadable, she wondered if she had been mistaken in her suspicions.

'Excuse me, folks,' at his matter-of-fact tone she decided she must have imagined the note of significance in his voice, 'I've got to take a look over at the pine plantation. I told Mick I'd meet him there this afternoon.'

'Do you want to take a passenger with you in the Land Rover?' The older man nodded towards Fleur. 'She just might——'

'No, thanks,' she cut in hurriedly, and searched her mind for a plausible excuse. 'I have to wait in for a telephone call,' she added, and was horrified to realise that her words were spoken in unison with Logan's deep tones. His derisive look sparked her into saying the last statement she had meant to give voice to. 'But it's not all that important.'

'Come along, then!' He sounded anything but pleased at having her company thrust upon him, and she found herself wishing her father would refrain from interfering in her arrangements. Now she was trapped into accompanying Logan on a long ride to another part of the station, far from the homestead. Logan, the last man in the world she wanted to be with at this moment! And suppose Bart happened to ring through in her absence? For a moment she considered letting Daphne into her confidence, asking her to take a message should a call come through from Australia, but the next moment she realised the absurdity of such thinking. Daphne would no more bandy words with Bart than he would think of ringing his ex-fiancée. She must forget about the telephone, about Bart, put him out of her mind for ever.

CHAPTER SEVEN

Soon Fleur was seated in the Land Rover beside Logan as they swept up dusty tracks winding over sun-dried hills and plunged down into tree-fern-filled gullies. Despite the rough terrain, he drove at speed and Fleur found herself bumped and thrown from side to side of the vehicle as they sped on. But seeing she had practically invited herself to accompany him on the ride, she told herself grimly, she was darned if she would give him the satisfaction of complaining about the discomfort of the journey.

His sideways glance took her by surprise. 'Interested in pine plantations?'

'Oh yes!' For a moment she forgot the identity of the man seated at her side. 'I love the fresh spicy smell of them and the way they grow so straight up into the sky.

Although,' she added thoughtfully, 'I'd just hate to see Te Haruru covered in pine trees. Sometimes they look so dark, cutting out all the light, especially on a dull day. Not like our own native bush that lets the sunshine through.'

'You've got a point there.'

Long before they came in sight of the plantations, the acrid smell of burning timbers was in the air. She turned an apprehensive face towards him. 'Someone's been burning off around here?'

He nodded briefly. 'The other side of the hill. It's due for planting in seedling pines when the ground's ready——'

'Oh *no*!' There was a note of alarm in her voice.

'Why not?'

'*Why not?*' she echoed with feeling. 'There's a stand of native bush over that way. It runs down to the sandhills and it's the finest stand of bush on the whole station. I couldn't bear it to be destroyed! You know how it is with virgin bush? Once it's gone it's gone for ever! Besides, the seabirds that nest along that strip of the coast are practically an endangered species. You know? When I was a kid,' she ran on, 'I used to find wild orchids growing there and I used to pick the red rata blossoms. If Dad's put a match to that bush while I've been away,' she vowed, 'I'll never forgive him! I've been on at him for years and years to see that it was protected, but he never seemed to take much notice. He doesn't feel the way I do about conserving the native bush we've got left in this country. I guess he's not a nature-lover, like me. If he's dared——'

'It's all right,' the deep voice cut across her heated outburst, 'it's still there. Everything's taken care of and that particular stand of native bush won't ever be destroyed. The official wording goes something like——' His voice took on a ponderous intonation: '"To be set aside as a special area of virgin forest to be left totally developed so the native trees and plants can be studied in their natural surroundings."' He tossed her a grin. 'How does that grab you?'

'That's super!' Fleur clapped her hands delightedly.

'And to think I've always had the notion that Dad didn't have an idea what conservation was all about——' She stopped short. 'There it is now!'

They had swept over the brow of the hill and as Logan braked the vehicle to a stop Fleur's gaze took in the area of densely growing bush that covered the hillside and swept down to the dark sandhills below. Sunshine burnished tall clumps of flax and threw into relief the softly waving fronds of giant tree-ferns against their dark green backdrop. Kauri trees, growing straight and tall, towered above totara and the feathery rimu and the wind from the sea sent cabbage-tree spears tossing against the translucent blue above.

'It's so beautiful,' she breathed. 'Funny how you have to go away from your own country before you can appreciate all this!' She turned towards him animatedly. 'Do you know, this is one of the few stands of native bush anywhere in the north island where the kiwis still live in their burrows in the ground? You can hear them calling sometimes in the darkness, that queer harsh cry. I heard the kiwis calling last night too when we were——' She broke off, aghast at the direction in which her words were leading.

'Were what, Fox?' Logan's voice was very low. 'Together?'

'In a way,' she said breathlessly, not daring to meet his gaze for fear of the emotion he might read in her eyes. How could he, she thought angrily, how *could* he amuse himself by saying such things to her in that intimate tone when all the time he was in love with another woman? She had been so sure that now that she was aware of his involvement with Christina, she could handle the situation. All she need do was to steel herself against the masculine attraction he held for her, and now . . . Her thoughts were in a turmoil and wildly she rushed into speech, saying the first words that came to her lips. 'What I can't make out is what happened to Dad to cause him to change his mind about protecting this stand of bush. He's always had a thing about logging!' She flashed him a sideways glance and caught the enigmatic glint in his hazel eyes. 'Oh, now I get it,' she said slowly, 'you managed somehow to talk him into the idea. Tell me, however did you do that?'

He tossed her a sideways grin. 'No problem. This stand of bush happens to be a part of the land I've taken over from him.'

'Oh ... I see. Of course,' she muttered the next minute, 'I should have realised that these hills come into your territory.'

To her taut nerves the smug satisfaction in his tone was infuriating. 'That's right.'

'I might have known,' she sighed. Nervously she twisted a strand of coppery-coloured hair round and round her finger. If only he didn't so obviously delight in putting one over her! If only she didn't so often hand him a chance to score over her! The thoughts shot through her mind. What had induced her, she wondered, angry with herself, to make such a blunder? Why must she keep forgetting that Te Haruru no longer belonged entirely to her own family? Some Freudian twist of the mind, because she wanted to forget?

She wrenched her mind back to Logan's tones. 'Seems we think alike,' he observed dryly, 'about some things!' And maddening though it was, she had to admit the truth of his words.

'Just for once!' she responded edgily.

It was a long way further to the pine plantations. The sun, a silver dollar in a clear blue sky, blazed down on them as they took the twisting tracks formed by a myriad sheep, that threaded the sun-dried hills. Logan appeared to be disinclined for conversation. And just as well, mused Fleur resentfully, seeing they seemed unable to avoid striking sparks in each other no matter what they spoke about. He was so darned autocratic, anyone would imagine that he owned the station, she thought crossly. Well, of course he did, half of it, she admitted reluctantly to herself, and went on hating him. What made the position even more intolerable for her was the inexplicable way in which her father, who had known Logan for so short a period, appeared to regard the younger man as though he were one of the family—well, almost!

Long before they reached the plantations Fleur
caught the aromatic tang of the pines, then at last they
came in sight of hillsides planted in symmetrical rows of
seedlings and mature trees. Presently they turned into a
firebreak cutting between dark curtains of sombre green
that clothed the hillside. The fresh tang of the pines was
strong in her nostrils and a lace pattern of sunlight
flickered over the firebreak.

'Wait for me, will you, Fox—won't be long!' Logan
had pulled the Land Rover to a stop and soon he was
striding up the track that was covered in pine needles.

Idly Fleur's gaze strayed towards a truck into which
two men were loading logs. No doubt, she mused, this
was a working party organised by her father. Or by
Logan, she reminded herself bitterly, for of course the
area was all a part of his property. She watched him as
he conferred with the other men. How tall and erect he
stood, and there was something about his strong face
that held her despite the feelings of antagonism and
resentment he invariably aroused in her. He's so
authoritative and arrogant, she told herself irritatedly,
and tried not to think of the moments of peril during
the plane crash when he had probably saved her life.
Don't forget that he was looking after his own skin as
well, she reminded herself. The thought was comforting
to her bruised ego. So she didn't really owe him
anything, not much anyway!

When he returned to seat himself once more in the
vehicle she turned towards him. 'So these pine
plantations belong to you now?'

'That's right,' he said easily. 'Your dad didn't seem to
mind parting with the pines, so I took them over.'

'No,' she agreed, 'he's a cattle and sheep man and
always has been.' She spoke absently, for looking up
she found his gaze fixed on her face, and at something
in his deep glance her stupid heart was behaving crazily
and a wild feeling of sweetness was running through
her, quickening her pulses, making her lose her grip on
reality. It was something to do, she thought faintly,
with the intoxication of his dark masculine face so close
to her own. It's a trap, she told herself as she tried to

gather together her tremulous senses, that masculine aura of power and attraction that he projects so strongly and that I find so difficult to resist! Even as she swayed towards him, with another level of her mind she was fighting her instincts every inch of the way.

He said very low, 'What's the matter, Fox?'

'Nothing!' she said breathlessly, and with an effort she jerked herself back to some sort of sanity. 'Where—are we going now?'

'Not far,' his words seemed to come from a distance over the wild confusion of her senses, 'we'll take the coast road for a change. I've got to make a call at Red Gums on the way——'

'Red Gums!' That did it! She jerked herself away from him as all the important things, like his not being able for long to keep away from the woman he loved, came flooding back to mind. And just in time too, she told herself grimly.

All at once his voice was steel. 'Any objections?'

'No, no, of course not!' Suppose, she thought on a sick feeling of dismay, that he had mistaken her sudden coolness towards him for jealousy of Christina? The thought impelled her to put all her effort into the most nonchalant voice she could summon. 'Why should I care? I just wondered.'

Out on the road that followed the coastline, the track was deep in black sand tossed from the beach below by winds blowing endlessly over the ocean. The winding road seemed to go on for ever, skirting sheer cliffs, and always there was the sound of the turbulent surf as it thundered against rocks and foamed into dark caves. Far below an endless expanse of sand flashed in the sunlight like a myriad black diamonds, and some distance from the rugged shoreline, a ship with Japanese markings tossed on the waves.

For something to say Fleur commented, 'So iron-sand is still being piped from here and shipped over to Japan?'

His gaze was on the surf-clouded shoreline merging away into a haze of distance. 'Doesn't look as though the supply of iron-sand will ever run out—I won't be long at Red Gums.' His closed expression she thought gave nothing away. 'Just a check-up to see if Christina's got any problems.' All at once the deep voice was charged with pride. 'She's game enough starting up a new venture from scratch, but one thing's for sure, she'll make a go of it!' He added on a voice so low she scarcely caught the words, 'She's got to!'

Fleur thought waspishly, How could Christina help but be a success, with your help and encouragement every inch of the way? Once again her habit of speaking without stopping to think caught her unawares. 'Isn't Red Gums a bit out of the way? Do you really think prospective pupils will come away out to the coast for training?'

'They'll come.' The supreme confidence of his tone sparked Fleur to snap, 'She must be quite a girl!' and she could have kicked herself for the sharp note in her voice. Fortunately, she told herself the next moment, Logan didn't appear to have heard her. His gaze was fixed on the road ahead, his face hard and set. The heavy thoughts chased one another through her mind. She must be someone for whom he cared a great deal, this Christina. But why if she meant so much to him did he look so stern and unhappy when he talked of her? And what had Logan's problems to do with her anyway? Yet somehow the shining lustre of the sunshiny day had dimmed.

Engrossed in her thoughts, all at once she realised they were turning into a tree-shaded driveway where a gate hung open on rusty hinges and along the winding overgrown pathway towering gum trees flung their blossoms in a blaze of crimson high against the blue. Soon Logan was pulling up outside the rambling farmhouse with its sagging verandah timbers and peeling paintwork. The next moment a German Shepherd, barking excitedly, leaped towards the Land Rover.

'Don't mind Prince,' Logan told her, 'he won't hurt you!'

'I'm not scared,' Fleur said with dignity, getting out of the vehicle. It was clear to her that the dog

welcomed Logan as a friend. And why shouldn't he?
The thought pierced her with an odd pang, 'Logan
comes here often enough!' She need not have bothered
telling him, she realised the next moment, for he hadn't
heard her, his attention was all for Christina, who came
running down the steps and hurrying towards the Land
Rover.

'If I'm not glad to see you! I thought you were never
coming! There's so much I want to see you about——'

Logan had jumped down from the vehicle and the
two stood talking together. Fleur thought, I might just
as well be invisible for all the notice either of them are
taking of me! Logan has completely forgotten about
me. He simply can't see anyone else in the world when
Christina's around. And Christina? I get the feeling that
she's deliberately ignoring me. I know she resents me, I
can see it in her eyes every time she looks at me.
Goodness knows why. She's no need to be jealous of
me on Logan's account, not when he's looking at her
the way he is right at this moment, as if what she's
telling him matters more to him than anything else in
the whole wide world! Who else but Christina, she
acknowledged reluctantly, with her Twiggy-thin figure
and hollow cheeks, could look so appealing, even with
smudges of dust on her lovely face, and wearing shabby
jeans and a shapeless knitwear top? But with those
brilliant blue eyes ... Once again, out of nowhere came
the odd impression of having seen Christina somewhere
before. The next moment she thrust away the thought
as absurd. For who, meeting the other girl, could ever
forget the haunting loveliness of Christina's face?

She jerked her mind back to the man and woman
who seemed entirely oblivious of her presence.
Christina's husky voice was running on ... and on. 'I
never dreamed that starting up a venture like this could
pose so many problems. Honestly, if it weren't for
having you around to turn to when things get too much
for me——' Her voice broke, then she added in a low
tone, 'I'd give it away right now!'

'No, you wouldn't. Not you, Chris! You'll make it, I
know you will!'

It seemed to Fleur that his encouraging tones had restored some confidence to Christina, for she was smiling mistily up into his face. 'Anyway,' she invited in the throaty tones that matched the hollow-cheeked appeal of her thin face, 'come along and have a look around.'

As if becoming aware of the girl seated silently in the Land Rover, Logan tossed a careless glance over his shoulder. 'Coming, Fox?'

'Oh, I shouldn't think,' Christina cut in, 'that Fleur would be interested in horses and stables.' She flung Fleur a cool glance. 'Didn't someone tell me that you're in the nursing line? You wouldn't have much time for riding.'

'You'd be surprised!' Fleur returned with spirit, and jumped down from the vehicle. A moment earlier she had had no intention of accompanying the other two on their inspection of the grounds, but at Christina's obvious attempt to get rid of her she changed her mind.

Christina, who had taken a few steps forward, turned back. The look she directed towards Fleur was icy. She hates me—once again the conviction shot through Fleur's mind. Because of the night spent out in the open with Logan? If the other girl only knew, she had no cause to feel jealous of her on that account. Deliberately she slowed her pace as she moved to join the other two.

Seen in the harsh white light of full sunlight, Christina now appeared older than Fleur had at first imagined. Tiny lines fanned out from around the blue eyes and the bone-structure of Christina's face was sharply defined. Not a girl by any means. But evidently Logan preferred the allure and experience of an older woman. There was no doubt either that Christina was supremely confident of Logan's care and attention. Why not face facts? she told herself. *His love.*

'Why on earth,' the husky feminine tones broke into her musing, 'does Logan call you Fox?'

Fleur's quick temper rose and she drew a deep breath. Before she could speak, however, Logan had broken in smoothly, 'It's fairly obvious. You don't mean to tell me you haven't noticed her hair?'

'Oh, that?' Christina tossed Fleur a careless glance. 'Now I get it!' Did she imagine, Fleur thought, incensed, that she had earned the nickname because of a reputation for low cunning?

'Of course,' tossed off Christina, 'I remember now. You're the little girl who was Logan's passenger on the plane trip.' Now Fleur knew she had made no mistake concerning the suspicion and resentment in the blue eyes. She had, however, had more than enough of this treatment.

'That's right,' she said cheerfully, 'I'm the *girl*——'

But already it seemed that Christina had decided not to betray any further interest in Fleur's involvement in the crashed plane. 'I was so worried about Logan I didn't give a thought to his passenger in the plane.'

'Oh, Fox was there right enough. She gave a great account of herself!' Logan's championship was unexpected. 'We shared quite a time together, eh, Fox?'

Fleur saw the older woman's lips tighten and the glance she threw her was dark with suspicion and dislike.

Let her think what she likes, she thought angrily.

The group moved past a car and a stock transporter standing on the long unkempt grass, then Christina led the way towards a spirited bay hunter. 'You remember Charisma?' Her laughing glance went to Logan. 'And Cadiz?' She had moved to stroke the velvety nose of the half-Arab gelding.

'He always was your favourite.' He too was caressing the grey horse. As he and Christina went on to discuss the competitive and challenging world of dressage and show-jumping in which apparently they had both been involved, Fleur was conscious of feeling more than ever left out. Watching the other two as they stood together in the sunlight, she couldn't help the thought that, both so tall and dark and attention-getting, they made a striking twosome. They were so completely in accord with each other, her thoughts ran on, for they chatted with the easy comradeship of old friends. Or old-time lovers, she amended, and wondered why the thought should hurt so much. They seemed to have a lot to say to each other, she mused bitterly, and for all the notice they were taking of her, she might just as well have been miles away. Turning aside, she began to stroll away, and it took her a full two minutes to realise to her chagrin that the other two hadn't even missed her!

She wandered down a weed-choked path leading towards tumbledown sheds, then paused to glance around her. If Christina planned to run a riding school here, she reflected, the other girl would need to have a lot of work done on the property. For all around was the evidence of age and neglect—empty implement sheds, a stable where doors swung open to reveal a single saddle, stained with mould and draped in cobwebs, hanging from rusted supports.

Presently she made her way back towards the house. The dwelling seemed to her a depressing sight, for salt winds blowing endlessly from the ocean had long since bleached paint from the timbers, and around the rotting floorboards at the base of the building the grass grew rank and long.

She was passing a high hedge where straggling green tendrils reached towards the sky, when Christina's throbbing voice, coming clearly through the green barrier, arrested her. Something in the timbre of the low distraught tones shocked Fleur. 'Sometimes I get to wondering,' the husky tones broke, 'what I'm doing here.' Fleur caught the sound of a terrible sobbing. She was rooted to the spot, fearful that to move away would betray her presence. Could that really be Logan's forceful voice? she wondered the next moment, for his deep voice was threaded with a strange compassionate quality she had never heard before.

'You'll be all right, you'll see! If it's the expense that's on your mind—forget it! I'll take care of all that—I want to.'

'I know, I know.' The heart-wrenching sobs had died away and the feminine tones were empty and drained of all feeling. 'I just—can't help worrying . . .'

'You won't feel that way once we get things straightened out.' His gravelly voice was husky with emotion. 'What was the problem?'

'Just—oh, it seems so stupid when I talk about it—but everything seemed to pile up on me. The transporter company rang through to say the hacks and ponies will be arriving next week. And the fences—you know what they're like! And it's so dry here, there's no good grazing.'

'That all?' Logan's tone was infinitely comforting. 'Don't give it another thought. I'll get a couple of fencers on the job right away and I've got swags of hard feed I can give you to keep the horses going. Once the rains come, you won't need it.'

'You're so good. I'm not often like this,' came the tremulous tones, 'not now.'

'You'll feel differently once we get the show off the ground. Another month,' came Logan's encouraging tones, 'and you won't know the place! Then you can slap an ad for pupils in the local papers and—zoom, you're in business!'

'We!' corrected Christina shakily.

'That's my girl!' The warmth and confidence in Logan's voice was enough to cause any girl to lose sight of her problems, Fleur thought. 'I knew you wouldn't let me down!'

As the voices faded from earshot Fleur hurried back the way she had come, slowing her footsteps to allow Christina time. Time for what? she asked herself wryly. A loving embrace with Logan, who had taken over all the other girl's problems in his high-handed way? The odd thing about it all was, she mused, puzzled, that Christina, with her self-confident manner, she would have imagined would be the last woman in the world to allow herself to be indebted to anyone. Yet clearly she was positively grateful to Logan, happily dependent on him for help in every possible direction. But of course, Fleur reminded herself, they were a twosome, a partnership, and it was only she herself who was the outsider—unnoticed, unwanted.

Unhappy? queried the dark goblin in her mind, but she refused to admit that. The aching sense of loss deep in her heart was because of Bart. Logan's love affairs meant absolutely nothing to her, why should they?

By the time she had joined the others, they appeared so perfectly composed that if she hadn't overheard their conversation she would never believe it had happened. Nothing could be more matter-of-fact than Logan's level tone. 'How about the house?' he was saying to Christina. 'The bedrooms are crying out for redecorating, but they'll be okay then for putting up a crowd. No leaks from the roof, no rusted window catches that can't be opened.'

'No, no, they're fine.' Christina tossed Fleur a glance. 'Oh, hi, Fleur.' Fleur had to look closely to discern the traces of tears on Christina's exquisite face. Any other girl would appear ravaged and unattractive after a storm of weeping, the thoughts ran through Fleur's mind, but Christina's emotion-wrung face held a wistful haunting quality that touched the heart. Even, for some reason she couldn't understand, Fleur thought in some surprise, her own.

That evening after dinner was over and Fleur had helped Daphne to clear away the table and wash the dishes, she came into the lounge room to find her father busy setting up the film projector. He turned towards her with a grin. 'Now's the time for you to show us those slides of the refugee camps that you brought back with you. You've put a lot into your letters, but pictures are a lot better than words!'

'Right!' She went to her room, to return with boxes of colour transparencies in her hand. 'They're not exactly cheerful viewing——'

'Never mind,' Daphne settled herself comfortably in a chair, 'we'll get an idea of what you've been doing over there in the camps.'

Fleur's father turned away. 'Wait a minute. I'll go and fetch Logan——'

Swiftly Fleur caught his arm. 'Don't bother—he wouldn't be interested in this sort of thing!'

The older man looked surprised. 'You're off beam there, Fox. He——'

'Let's keep it to the family, shall we,' she cut in, and smiled cajolingly into his lined, puzzled face, 'just for tonight?'

'If you say so.'

Presently she dimmed the lighting in the room and standing by the projector, she fed slides into the machine. All the time she was giving a commentary as best she could of people and places in a life style far removed from anything Daphne or her father had known.

'This is me,' she told them, 'arriving at the camp. I couldn't get over all the beds, rows and rows of them. And the refugees!' She flicked on another picture. 'You can see what pitiful physical condition they're in—sores and sickness and malnutrition, the lot! But it was amazing how they picked up after a while with some care and attention. The trouble was,' on the screen there flashed a photograph of a fresh lot of emaciated people, 'there were always new arrivals and the camp got more and more crowded. Sometimes we ran out of medicines and bandages, and that was worst of all. Here's a shot of the local witch doctor—don't laugh, he wielded such influence over the refugees you wouldn't believe! We had to go along with him to a certain extent or we'd never have been able to treat them at all!

'Here's one of the doctors and some of the other nurses.' She ran through the pictures, then paused. 'This one is special, that's why I've kept it till last.'

The next moment there flashed on the screen the picture of a child—a small girl, tragically thin, with enormous dark eyes in a waif like face and a wistful smile. For a moment the tragedy and heartbreak of abandoned children she had known in the camp flooded her mind. Children who were without homes or parents, lacking even the bare necessities of life.

'Who's that?' Her father's words jerked her back to the present.

'That's the little girl I sponsored.' Fleur's voice had softened. 'She really went to your heart, so undernourished and yet quiet and loving and—Oh, I don't know, there's something about that little girl that tears you apart! That's why I made myself responsible for her education. I'll look after her as well as I can from this distance, see that she has good living conditions with a caring family, pay the fees for her education. One of these days I'll go back to the village where she lives and see how she's getting along. But meanwhile she'll be able to write to me and I'll write to her. We'll keep in touch. It's not much to do for such a pathetic mite,' her voice saddened, 'but at least it's something!'

'She looks a sweetie.' Daphne's eyes were fixed on the tragic little face.

'Oh, she is, such a little thing, only seven years old and so loving and good. For her, being sponsored is a sort of lifeline. You'd be surprised how much an organisation like World Vision is doing for refugees in that part of the world. Honestly, you've got to see it before you realise . . .' Her voice trailed into silence as she caught sight of Logan, lounging by the door in the shadows. How long had he been there, she wondered, looking, just looking at the slides thrown on to the screen? Watching her, listening to her, no doubt with that satirical twist of his lips. The thought made her flustered. 'That's all for tonight, folks!' She switched on the light, flooding the room with brilliance. Her glance sought his face—and wouldn't you know, his gaze was cold and forbidding, a glint of mockery in his eyes.

'Oh!' She blinked in the sudden glare. 'I didn't know you were there.'

'I wasn't at first, but I didn't want to interrupt the show.'

Forgetting the others in the room, she looked him straight in the eye. 'What did you think of it?'

'Pretty harrowing——'

'That's nothing to some of the scenes we saw there,' she said spiritedly, 'especially the state of some of the patients. They were just skeletons—lack of food, frightful living conditions.'

His cold dissecting gaze swept her. 'And yet *you* stuck it out. Why?'

Fleur swallowed, aware of a crashing sense of disappointment. What had she expected from him? That the visual evidence of the caring work she had done with the refugees might give him a new perspective on her? Change his ready-made disparaging opinion of her? Clearly, however, instead of the reaction she had expected, he was merely puzzled that selfish, self-centred Fox should have chosen to spend time in unpleasant surroundings and conditions, for the purpose of caring for those less fortunate than herself. Incredible!

She decided to ignore the personal angle to his comment. Schooling her voice to a light conversational note, she enquired, 'The pictures gave you an idea, then, of what the camps were like?'

'They sure made an impact,' he agreed equably. 'What I can't make out,' the satirical gleam in his eyes spelled out the damning implication of his words, 'is what you were doing over there, working in the camps, a girl like you?'

She threw him a suspicious glance. Others might take the words as a teasing remark, even maybe a compliment to her youth and attractive, copper-haired appearance. But she wasn't so easily fooled, not with that cold implacable gleam in his eyes. Well, if he wanted to play it that way ... She said on a careless note, 'Why not me? After all,' for some reason she could no longer sustain the flames that seemed to glow in his eyes, and busied herself sorting out the slides, 'someone has to do something about the volunteers that World Vision is always calling for.'

'Don't take any notice of Logan,' her father's eyes crinkled with amusement as he glanced from the younger man's impassive face to the mounting colour in Fleur's cheeks. 'He's just trying to get a rise out of you!'

'Oh, he doesn't worry me,' Fleur responded quickly. 'You can't really make an opinion on all this, can you, Logan?' She was carefully avoiding his eyes. 'I mean, you haven't been over to Thailand. You can't really *know*.'

'True,' his lazy tones reached her, 'but I know *you*!'

'Now you two have got that sorted out——' Her father, Fleur thought, incensed, appeared to take Logan's remarks as good-natured teasing. If he only knew ... She brought her mind back to her father's voice. 'There are a few things I'd like to chew over with you in the office.'

'Sure, I'll come with you.' The two men rose to leave the room. In the doorway Logan paused to throw back over his shoulder. 'Thanks for the slide show, Fox.'

'I didn't ask you to come,' she muttered under her breath, but already he had disappeared through the opening. Daphne too got up to go to her own room, so there was no one to hear. It was odd, to Fleur the thought came unbidden, how empty the big room seemed once Logan had left it. Probably, she told herself, because of the verbal fireworks they invariably engaged in—and she began to dismantle the projector.

CHAPTER EIGHT

THE next morning as the phone continued to ring regarding the after-effects of a plane crash Fleur told Daphne, 'I'm off. You can cope with the telephone calls, they won't be for me anyway. Everyone I know has rung through already, so I'm not expecting any calls,' unconsciously she sighed, 'not now.'

Daphne sent her a shrewd glance, but she said nothing beyond, 'Are you going to the rodeo over at the Morgans' place on Saturday?'

Fleur was stuffing a carrot into the pocket of her jeans. She picked up an apple from a dish on the sideboard. 'I wouldn't miss it for worlds! I'm way out of practice, but all the same I'm going to have a go at the barrel race!'

'You won the event last time the rodeo was held up this way,' Daphne reminded her.

'Mmm, but that was a while ago. Sally and I both need to go over the course, I'd better do something about it. 'Bye, Daph!' she ran down the steps and out into the sunshine. Not far from the house in a sheltered enclosure with long benches, she glimpsed the two young shepherds, Jim and Colin, preparing a hangi. Soon she was approaching the tea-tree screened, grassy area.

Colin glanced up at her, a grin on his open face. 'Hi, Fleur! Guess you wouldn't have had this kind of a meal over in Thailand?'

She laughed, 'There's nothing quite like hangi food. Tell me, is this a private party tonight or can anyone come?'

To her surprise Colin's boyish face was oddly evasive. 'You're coming?' he said at last. 'You will, won't you?'

His mate Jim, lanky and red-haired, said persuasively, 'Sure?'

'I'll be there. Tell me,' she asked curiously, 'who else is coming?'

It seemed to Fleur that both shepherds were looking embarrassed, she couldn't imagine why. 'Don't know for sure,' muttered Colin, and Jim said vaguely, 'Guess we'll see who shows up.'

'I don't know why you're both so cagey about it!' Fleur said smilingly. She watched as the two men completed a procedure with which she was long familiar as they placed river stones over burning tea-tree logs in preparation for the food that would be cooked for long hours in the steam oven. 'Oh well,' she said at last, 'I'll just have to wait and see, won't I? Must go and practise for the barrel race at the rodeo—goodbye!'

Up in the hill paddock she forgot about the hangi in the pleasure of being with her beloved mare once again. The thought came unbidden that had it not been for Logan's training of Sally in Fleur's long absence from the station, she wouldn't have had a chance of getting her mount in trim for the single women's event at the forthcoming rodeo. Why was it, she asked herself irritatedly the next moment, that her thoughts so often reverted to Logan? She glanced towards a fenced paddock not far away, looking for his high-spirited stallion, but Joker was nowhere to be seen, so evidently Logan was riding him.

Catching Sally, she slipped the bit into the mare's mouth and springing lightly on to the broad back, guided her mount down to the stables. Presently she was rolling out the oil drums stacked in a shed, placing them at intervals on the flat grassy ground, and for the remainder of the morning she guided her mount at a canter around the corkscrew route of the makeshift course.

Engrossed in her routine as she strove to re-train Sally in the twisting route of navigating the course, Fleur was unaware that she had an audience until riding back to the starting point she found Logan. He had pulled in his restive mount and was regarding her with a quizzical grin. 'Sally's a bit slow,' he observed. 'You'll have to put on a better performance than that if you're going to get anywhere in the race!'

'I know!' she snapped, and sent him a goading glance. As if she had asked for his opinion! She faced him with bright angry eyes. 'Could *you* get Sally to give a better performance?' she challenged him.

'Sorry!' She caught the flash of strong white teeth in the sun-bronzed face. 'They won't let me enter for the women's events at the rodeo!'

'How about your friend Christina, then?' The words were out before she could stop them. 'From what you've told me she should give a good account of herself. She is going to the rodeo, I suppose?'

'Christina?' His expression darkened, all the banter and teasing replaced by a cold set look. 'I'm taking her along with me,' his voice was steel, 'and if I can talk her into entering for the barrel race——'

'Oh, I'm sure you'll have no problem there!' What was the matter with her today? Fleur asked herself the next moment. But he had asked for it!

All at once the glint of laughter was back in his eyes, his well-cut lips curved and relaxed. 'You reckon I'm just about irresistible to women, then? If only,' the deep tones ran on, 'you'd let on to me about that when we were together the other night——'

'To *some* women, I mean,' Fleur cut in repressively. Turning away, she set her mare to a canter and horse and rider swerved at an angle as they rounded the first barrel of the course set out on the dried grass. All the time on another level of her mind the thoughts were with Logan. If he persisted in reminding her of the night they had shared out in the wilderness, innocent though it was, she told herself, she had best see as little of him as she could. Not, she thought wryly, that avoiding him would present much difficulty, for clearly all his spare time would be spent with Christina, helping the other girl establish herself with her project. Then afterwards . . . She switched her thoughts aside, her mind shying away from following the thought to its logical conclusion.

That afternoon she took a long ride along the beach, splashing through foaming breakers at the water's edge and urging her mount to a steady canter along the endless stretch of sand. Out in the fresh salt-laden air where the wind whipped colour in her cheeks and beaded her hair with sea-spray, problems and frustrations fell away and there was nothing in the world but the sheer sandstone cliffs and bays curving away into a haze of distance.

The long twilight lingered as in the stables, she rubbed down her mare. Then, back in the house, she showered and changed into a cool frock of crisp white cotton, tying the cords of string sandals around her bare ankles. Just for fun she fastened around her tanned throat the long chain with its embossed gold pendant that had once belonged to a great-aunt.

When she went into the living room, there seemed no one about, but no doubt, she mused, everyone would be at the hangi. *Except Logan,* a voice deep inside her whispered, and guess where he would be spending the evening? Moving out into the soft dusk, she took a short cut leading from the house to the cleared area with its windbreak of tall tea-trees that had been used for hangis and barbecues on so many summer evenings in the past. Strains of stereo music echoed around her, but it wasn't until Fleur entered the enclosed grassy area that she found herself suddenly surrounded by laughing, chattering groups. 'Welcome back, Fleur! Surprise! Surprise!' They clustered around her, young people with whom she had grown up and who were now, like herself, spending the summer holidays with their parents in far-flung homesteads.

Fleur regarded them laughingly. 'You've sneaked up on me! Where did you hide the cars?'

'Where do you think?' came a chorus of voices. 'Away around the back of the house among the bushes!'

Around them the hills were bathed in a purple haze and a single star glittered in the darkening sky. Fairy lights were strung among the tea-tree and wisps of steam rose from earth ovens.

On long benches that served as tables in the outdoor area, there were carafes of wine and cans of beer. Daphne had provided long crusty rolls of garlic-filled bread and great pottery bowls overflowed with fruit gathered from the orchard—grapes, melons, peaches, passion fruit.

Presently, as day faded to smoky blue night, Colin and Jim took from the earth ovens woven flax baskets holding succulent pork, chicken and mutton as well as golden kumera and pumpkin. As the hangi meal progressed bursts of laughter rose above the muted murmur of conversation, and later Fleur was asked over and over again to recount to a receptive audience details of her recent experiences in the refugee camp on the other side of the world. At one point in her narrative, a serious-eyed youth eyed her in disbelief. 'Surely conditions over there wouldn't have been all that hairy?'

'They were, you know!' Fleur's voice was abstracted. 'There was one woman——' At that moment waves of stereo music drowned out her words. But what did it matter? she asked herself. For how could the groups gathered around her tonight possibly envisage the hunger and poverty and downright despair of the lucky ones who had managed to reach the refugee camps? Any more than she herself could have understood such things, one year ago!

'Dance, Fleur?' She realised that Colin had come to stand at her side.

'I don't know that I will,' she pouted, looking up into the boyish face. 'You might have let me in on what you were up to this morning when I saw you making the hangi!'

His eyes widened in mock dismay. 'And ruined the

surprise? The others would have skinned me alive! Daphne passed on the word that you were out of the house all day or we'd never have got away with buzzing everyone for miles around to come along to Fleur's Welcome Home wing-ding.'

'Glad you did.' She rose to her feet. 'It's fun!' Together they moved to the foot-tapping rhythm of the latest pop tune that pulsed from the stereo plugged on to its long lead. Soon everyone was dancing, the coloured bulbs strung among the tea-tree overhead flickering over the light dresses of the girls and the sun-tanned faces of the men.

It was during a pause in the music that a girl with a round freckled face approached Fleur. 'You don't know me yet,' she had an endearing smile, Fleur thought, 'Tom and I have only been here for a few months. He took the job here just after we got married. I'm Jane Foster.'

Fleur smiled back. 'Isn't Tom the shepherd all the men here talk about as being so talented? The guy who sings and plays the guitar so well?'

Jane's face glowed with pride. 'Everyone knows about Tom and likes him! He's one of those sort of people you just can't help liking!' Her voice rang with enthusiasm. 'Wait until you hear him sing—he's terrific! He's brought his guitar along with him tonight. Here he comes now—listen!'

A fresh-faced young man with a mop of curly hair dropped down to one of the long forms set under the trees, his fingers plucking idly at the strings of his guitar. 'What would you like, folks?' As a deafening chorus broke out, he held up a hand in protest. 'One at a time, if you please! Did I hear someone say——'

'Play one of your own compositions!' His wife's clear young tones rose in the moment of silence.

He sent her a teasing glance. 'You mean the one I made up just for you?' A secret message flashed between them.

The next moment the throbbing notes fell on the night air and as Tom's voice took up the melody a silence fell over the group, for the singer's tones

possessed that special magical quality that touched the
heart.

> 'Your eyes tell me that you love me,
> And yet your lips say "no" . . .'

The pulsing notes fell into a silence, then almost at
once there was a quickening of the tempo and soon
everyone was joining in the rousing beat of the country
ballad.

> 'I'm a country lad from way back
> Where the wind is fresh and free;
> You can have your city pavements,
> It's the open road for me.'

Jane's round face was alight with pride and love.
'Everyone knows that song,' she told Fleur. 'That's
because Tom sang it at a charity concert on television
last year. He composed the song too.'

Fleur said smilingly, 'You must feel very proud of
him!'

'Wouldn't you be,' said Jane happily, 'if you were
me?'

The hours fled by to the accompaniment of stereo
music and dancing, and in response to pressing requests
for items, the songs of the young guitarist. It was late
when groups began drifting away in search of cars and
trucks and Land Rovers.

When the last car had nosed its way down the
curving driveway Colin, stifling a yawn, approached
Fleur. ''Night, Fleur, see you in the morning.' The two
single shepherds moved away in the direction of their
own quarters.

Left alone, Fleur began to gather up wine bottles and
empty beer cans. The moon in the velvety darkness of a
star-ridden sky made the scene almost as bright as day,
silvering the flax leaves and burnishing bushes. She had
stooped to pick up a glass lying on the grass when a
sound nearby alerted her and she straightened to find
Logan approaching her. For a strange silent moment
she stared up at him, his face all angles and shadows in
the moonglow. 'Hello!' she said breathlessly, for there

was something about his unexpected arrival that sent her thoughts rioting in confusion. 'You're too late,' she told him, for something to say.

'Too late for what, Fox?' His voice was very low.

'Why—why, the party, of course.' She heard herself nattering on, despising herself for the betraying wobble in her voice. 'If you'd been here at the house tonight you would have known what was happening . . . all the cars and trucks . . . they've just taken off. It was a big surprise to me!' She was chattering on to fill the silence where she couldn't trust her emotions. All the time she was speaking the traitorous thoughts were running through her mind. *I wish he were free and that he were a different type of man. I wish he knew the real me instead of the self-centred nit of a girl he's dreamed up for himself.* Steady, she chided herself the next moment. Make your voice offhand, remind yourself *and him* that he had a more enticing engagement tonight than a hangi here at the house.

'Aren't you going to offer me a drink?' The deep voice cut across her tumultuous thoughts.

'You should have come along hours ago with the others,' she said, trying for lightness. 'I'm not sure that I can find you anything now.'

'Don't be niggly, Fox,' came the drawling voice, 'you've got a brand new bottle of champagne right there by your hand.'

Stupidly she stared down at the unopened bottle on the table. 'So I have!' Blast him! Why did he always manage somehow to put her in the wrong? 'Well, now that you're here,' she muttered tightly, and found a clean goblet.

Moving along the littered table, he picked up another goblet. 'Aren't you going to join me?'

'Oh, all right, then,' she sighed ungraciously, and watched his deft fingers drawing the cork from the bottle. He poured the bubbling liquid into the goblets, then lifting his glass, he pinned her with his hazel-eyed gaze. 'Here's to us, Fox. To you and me.'

Wrenching her glance aside, she stared down at the tiny stars rising in her glass. 'How do you mean?'

'Oh, come on, don't pretend you don't know! Better public relations all round?' She caught an enigmatic note in his voice, 'Even if it's only on the surface.'

'So long as it's only on the surface,' she said brightly, 'I'll drink to that!'

'Why, Fox,' the crystal goblets rang together and it seemed to her that his deep tones were threaded with an odd intensity, 'what else could it be between us?'

All at once her heart was behaving strangely, giving a sudden leap, then subsiding. She said huskily, 'I—don't know.' She wrenched her mind back to his voice.

'Sorry I missed your hangi tonight.' At his low regretful tone she could almost believe he was speaking the truth. Whatever happened, she told herself, she must keep her sudden rush of emotion from showing. With an effort she pulled her thoughts together, schooling her voice to a tone that was almost normal. 'You missed out on something great. Tom Foster's singing was terrific, he sounded like a professional.'

'He is, just about. Actually I had something else on tonight——'

At his words sanity returned with a rush. I'll bet you had, she thought fiercely. 'Don't bother to explain!' she flung at him. 'I quite understand about you and Christina. You and she——' She broke off in confusion. The champagne must be going to her head, she thought dazedly, and jerked her mind back to his even tones.

'The thing is, she needed me. There are problems I can straighten out for her and at the moment she's pretty much on her own. Oh, she's lived the country life for long enough to know the way the wheels go around, but starting off where she knows no one but me is something else again. Takes some get up and go!'

Now at last Fleur was back in charge of her runaway emotions. 'I would have thought,' she was choosing her words carefully, 'that Christina could handle just about anything she chose to. Especially,' the words seemed to come without her volition, 'when she's so lovely to look at.'

'Isn't she just!' The sudden warmth in his voice was

like a douche of water over her spirit. She had to
wrench her mind back to his enthusiastic tones. 'There's
no one to touch Christina when it comes to looks.
That's why——' abruptly he broke off. 'But that's
another story. Let's just say that she gave city living
away.' A wry smile curved his well-shaped lips. 'I
warned her she wouldn't be able to stick it for long,
that she'd have to come back.'

Back to him? To his love, his care? All that the older
woman could not live without? Was that what he
meant? There could scarcely be any doubt on that
score, Fleur's heavy thoughts ran on, now that
Christina had followed him, or he had brought her, to
his new life. Not that it mattered to her, of course,
Fleur told herself resolutely and tried to concentrate on
the masculine tones.

'I've had a word with Daphne to find out if she can
put us on to someone in the housekeeping line.' Us?
Fleur felt once again that odd pang of the heart. What
was he saying now? 'A local girl who's free to come and
stay at Christina's place. Someone who can do a spot of
housework, cope with odd meals and so on. You don't
happen to know of anyone suitable, do you?'

'No, I don't!' she said shortly. All at once she was
tired of listening to talk of Christina and her problems.
Why should she be burdened with the task of finding
domestic help for the woman he loved?

'And you wouldn't let on to me if you did,' came the
cryptic comment. 'Jealous, Fox?' The rumbling tones
reached her with heart-knocking significance.

'*Jealous*? *Me*?' she cried indignantly. 'What on earth
gave you that idea?'

'Just an impression I got.' All at once he moved close
to her. 'Good night, Fox!' Something in the timbre of
the deep voice sent a tingle of excitement pulsing
through her veins. The next moment she caught his
deep exultant chuckle as he drew her into his arms.
Wildly she struggled against the forbidden happiness
that was closing in around her like a golden cloud, then
everything else was forgotten in the passionate
excitement of his unexpected kiss.

When at last he released her she was trembling. If only he wasn't aware of the emotion his touch aroused in her, she prayed, the wild sweetness that so swiftly sent flying to the four winds all those resolutions she had made about resisting Logan and the powerful attraction he had for her! She flung herself away from him, muttering a brief ''Night!' then she fled along the moon-silvered pathway. Why am I running? she asked herself, and slowed her headlong rush away from Logan. A quick glance over her shoulder took in a tall masculine figure standing where she had left him. Follow her? Why should he do that? His caress was no more than a passing impulse, a nothing thing. Slowly she made her way towards the house, her thoughts in a tumult, striving to talk sense into her runaway emotions. 'A good night kiss, what's wrong with that?'

'Plenty!' The answer came unbidden. 'When he affects you so. When his kiss carries you away into a magic place, thrilling, exciting, way beyond the boundaries of ordinary living and into a magic realm she hadn't known existed. It was a physical thing, of course, she rationalised with herself, but powerful nevertheless. Too powerful for her own peace of mind. It came to her with a conviction that caught close to Logan's muscular body, his arms around her, even Bart meant nothing to her.

Tossing and turning through the long reaches of the night, she faced the truth that she was deeply attracted to him, that his merest touch had the power to send her emotions soaring into forbidden rapture. Really she hated him! She always had, and she had good reason to loathe the man. She just couldn't afford to let herself surrender to the attraction he held for her. 'Especially,' the dark goblin in her mind spoke up, 'as he's in love with another woman!' And that, she knew, was the part of it all that really cut deep, the important thing that she must never allow herself to lose sight of. However much Logan's kiss electrified her, to him the light caress was merely an impulse born of the time they had spent together in the wilderness, hours sharpened by her dependence on him and their narrow brush with danger and death.

Right at this moment, she told herself, his good night kiss would already have passed from his mind. He would be sleeping like the dead, while she—angrily she punched her pillow and flung it over to the other side. If one kiss could do this to her emotions, keep her wakeful all through the night . . . After this, she vowed, I'll care never to be alone with Logan, and if it does happen I'll let him know that I feel about him the same way as I did right at the start, that my feelings about him haven't changed one little bit. 'Liar! You know you can't resist him!' She thrust the dark imp out of her mind.

Gradually, as the days went by, her heart ceased to race madly each time she answered a long-distance telephone call. Bart was lost to her, she faced the truth at last, and there was nothing she could do about it. Except, she told herself stubbornly, refuse to listen to untruths concerning him and, especially, lies told her by Logan. Don't forget, she reminded herself, that Logan had a lot to gain by Bart's giving up the job of manager here. The niggling sense of heartache and unhappiness that possessed her lately she put down to the shattering blow of Bart's break with her. But she would banish all that by keeping herself busy, she vowed, and especially by schooling Sally in the routine of the barrel race, the single event in which women riders could enter at the rodeo soon to be held in the district. Deep down she had a sneaky wish to prove to Logan that she could beat his glamorous 'friend' at her own game, Arab mount and all!

So she spent long hours guiding her mare in the cloverleaf pattern around the spaced-out drums. Fleur was taking care all the time not to cross her own tracks and both horse and rider leaned far out at an angle as they endeavoured to come as close as possible to the drums without knocking them down.

Before long Fleur told herself with satisfaction that the long hours of daily practice were proving worthwhile, for Sally, great-hearted mare that she was, soon adaped herself to the routine and did her part in helping to cut down the seconds as again and again she cantered around the makeshift course.

In the afternoons Fleur rode far over the paddocks, her gaze alerted to the sight of a sagging fence wire or a dead sheep. All the time she took care to avoid any chance meeting with Logan. Even to herself she refused to admit that she found him dangerously attractive and disturbing to her peace of mind. Indeed, had it not been for Bart, and Christina, and all she knew of Logan, and the way he despised her ... The list was endless, but it all boiled down to the fact that for her own sake she had best avoid any further encounters with him, and so far she was doing very nicely, thank you! The odd thing was that she felt no triumph at the thought, only a curious sense of emptiness, of longing. It's time I started thinking about working for a living again, she told herself briskly. Tonight I'll write away applying for work in one of the city hospitals. Somehow, however, the idea was shelved and the days passed without her making any move in that direction. Deep down where it counted she acknowledged to herself that she had no wish to leave Te Haruru, that something held her here. It's just that Bart might find out the truth of what happened between us, one of these days, she told herself. He just might ring me, and I couldn't trust anyone in the house to pass his message on to me.

One morning she was leaning sideways in the saddle, guiding Sally around the oil drums, when she became aware that Jane Foster had come to watch the procedure.

'Hi, Fleur!' The other girl had the friendliest face, Fleur found herself thinking as she smiled a greeting. She finished the round and slipping down from the saddle, strolled towards Jane. 'I haven't seen you since the night of the hangi.'

'I know. I've meant to pop over and have a chat ever so many times but somehow I haven't got there. Never mind, this will do.' Both girls dropped down on the grass. 'Tom has been explaining to me all about the barrel race,' said Jane. 'Let's see, you get ten seconds knocked off for every time you knock over a barrel, you mustn't cross your own tracks, you get as close as you can get to the barrel without knocking it over and the fastest time wins! How's that?' She had a merry, engaging laugh, Fleur thought.

'Bang on! Why not have a go at it yourself? I could teach you——'

'No, thanks! I haven't got the nerve.'

Fleur laughed. 'Like that, is it?'

'Afraid so. I'm a townie and I'd never set foot on a farm in my life until I married Tom and came up here to live. Not that I'm complaining,' Jane's voice softened, 'not with *him*.'

Fleur felt a twist of the heart. 'No regrets, then? No problems? I'd say you two were very lucky meeting each other.'

'That's what we tell each other!' The low tones were warm with emotion. 'No, no regrets.' A shadow passed over the clear blue eyes and her voice sobered. 'Just one problem—well, not really a problem——' Nervously she plucked at a long blade of grass. 'It's just . . .' her voice trailed away into silence.

'You can tell me,' Fleur said quietly.

'It sounds so stupid really, out here in the daylight.' All at once Jane seemed to brace herself and Fleur was struck by an expression of naked fear in the other girl's eyes. 'It's just the rodeo——'

'The rodeo?' Fleur echoed incredulously. The next moment realisation dawned on her. 'Oh, I get it! Tom wants to take part in the events and you don't go along with the idea. Right?'

'Too right,' Jane said wryly, adding in a low distressed tone, 'It's the first, the only real row we've ever had. I always thought that Tom would do anything for me, but he refuses to give in on this. He's so good to me about everything else, never opposes me in any way if he can help it, but this time . . .'

Fleur said mildly, comfortingly, 'Sounds to me like he's ridden in rodeos before he came here and collected some trophies.'

'Has he ever! He's taken part in rodeos all over the country for years!' Jane added on a sigh, 'Only I didn't know him then, so I didn't need to worry about him!'

'Don't let it get you down,' Fleur advised cheerfully.

'If Tom's used to riding at the rodeo and he's survived so far, he'll be pretty good at taking care of himself. And if it means so much to him . . . I know how it is. The men working here talk of nothing else when the rodeo is on, they wouldn't miss a chance of competing for anything!' She tried to lighten the shadow of apprehension on Jane's young face. 'I remember years ago a man arrived at the door on crutches, wanting a job. He'd taken a toss in a buckjumping event, but by the next year he was as healthy and active as ever and getting ready for the local rodeo!'

'There you are, then!' cried Jane triumphantly, 'you admit that it is dangerous!' Before Fleur could argue the matter the distraught tones ran on, 'You don't understand how I feel about Tom. He's different from the other men working here. He's so gifted, you've heard him sing——'

'I know, I know. His voice is like honey. It touches you somehow.'

'That's what I mean. And the way he can play the guitar, just as if his hands were made to pluck the strings! His *hands*,' Jane whispered brokenly, 'if anything should happen——' She raised a tragic face. 'It's only a month before he has to compete in the National Country and Western Music Festival. If he wins the Singer of the Year Award it will put him on the start of a musical career, especially when his own compositions are so popular! I know that once he gets a start he'll never look back. But if he gets thrown and hurt at the rodeo——' her voice trailed despairingly away.

Fleur threw an arm around the other girl's shaking shoulders. 'You only feel that way because it's on your mind and you're thinking about it all the time.'

Jane hadn't taken in the words of comfort. 'I'm scared stiff of Tom being thrown and hurt,' her mouth wobbled. 'Stupid of me, isn't it, but I can't help feeling this way.' Nervously she bit her thumbnail. 'Tom wants me to go along with the others from the station and watch him ride, and I can't! I just couldn't bear to see it. He can't understand when I tell him that. He thinks,' she gulped, 'that I'm just being bitchy about it because I can't put him off the idea!'

'Listen, why not come along with me to the rodeo? Even if I'm riding in the barrel race I'll be with you all the rest of the time and so will Dad and Daphne. That way Tom will see that you're interested——'

'Interested!' Jane's voice broke.

Hurriedly Fleur ran on, 'Then once his events are over, you'll be able to enjoy yourself. You'll be there to cheer me on in the barrel race too—how's that for excitement?'

Jane's anxious expression cleared a little. 'Maybe you're right. I'll be there, and if something happens to Tom, I'll be on the spot.'

'Nothing's going to happen to him,' Fleur said cheerfully, 'and you'll be so glad you made the effort to go along, you'll see!'

All during the week the stockmen and shepherds employed on the outback station talked of little but the rodeo events. From their reminiscences Fleur gathered that they had attended a rodeo held in a nearby district while she had been away overseas and all had evidently given a good account of themselves. Especially Tom, who was evidently a top bareback rider and could had he wished have made a living by joining the matey, daredevil band of riders who followed the rodeo circuit all over the country.

'Too bad about Tom, a good man wasted,' Colin mourned to Fleur.

Puzzled, she said, 'But he's going to the rodeo——'

'And he's married,' put in his friend Jim, 'and trust Jane to press the panic button when he so much as mentions the word "rodeo". Tom get away for good on the circuit? Brother, he wouldn't have a hope in hell, not with Jane around!'

Fleur considered the matter. 'Does he mind, do you think?'

'Does he mind!' You've gotta be joking!' The youthful masculine faces regarded her incredulously. 'He could have made a career for himself, competed overseas, gone to meetings over in the States——'

'But he's such a fabulous singer,' she protested. 'I'm sure he could make a career of show business, hit the big time before long in the entertainment world——'

'Oh, that . . .' Clearly in the eyes of the young station hands a career in music was not to be compared with the colourful life of a rodeo rider who was prepared to brave the dust or a runaway bull as part of the fun for trying a quick buck or twist.

One day, as she continued with her daily practice seesion around the oil drums, Fleur realised that Colin and Jim had come to lean on the stockrails as they watched her progress, their comments clearly audible in the fresh morning air—Colin's, 'She's making good time, wouldn't you say?' And Jim's reply, 'I'll say. She's sure of a win!'

Colin's voice was threaded with a note of doubt. 'How about that riding school woman over at Red Gums? They tell me she knows the ropes fairly well, could make Fleur work hard for her victory.'

'Maybe, but my money's on Fleur every time!'

'Mine too!'

Fleur found that she was gritting her teeth. She just had to win that barrel race, she vowed, or at least gain a faster time than Christina. Somehow it had become desperately important that she beat the older woman. Jealous, Fox? Logan's mocking voice echoed in her mind, to be immediately thrust aside as she consulted her stopwatch.

'What do you think of Fleur's chances in the barrel race, Logan?' enquired Jim.

Fleur's heart gave a crazy lurch. Logan had reined in, pulling his prancing stallion to a halt, and as she caught the enigmatic glint in his eyes the thought flashed through her mind that he had no need to spell it out. The scarcely perceptible lift of heavily marked black brows said it all, pinpointing the utter absurdity of young Fox, for all her long practice with the oil drums, having the slightest chance of winning the barrel race at tomorrow's rodeo. Not when Christina with her half-Arab steed was competing in the race!

At that moment the black stallion reared high in the air and Logan, with a few quiet words and a firm hand on the reins, brought the restive animal under control. 'Tell you tomorrow,' he grinned, then he turned and cantered away.

CHAPTER NINE

On the morning of the rodeo Fleur got out of bed and parting the curtains at the window, took in the scene of activity outside. Men wearing checked cowboy shirts, high boots and flapping chaps revved up engines of vehicles that were parked haphazardly on the dried grass. A stockman had brought Fleur's mare down from the hill paddock and pale rays of early morning sunshine threw a nimbus around the flowing mane and silky tail that Fleur had brushed and combed so painstakingly yesterday afternoon.

Swiftly she showered, then slipped into fresh underwear, pulling over her head a shirt of crisp ice-blue cotton and fastening around her slim waist a leather belt with its beaten brass buckle, threaded through tough denim jeans. As she tucked a wayward strand of coppery hair behind her ear, then reached for well-polished riding boots, she felt she was ready for the challenge of the day ahead.

In the dining room she found her father and Daphne finishing an early breakfast, and she helped herself to coffee. Soon, a slice of toast in her hand, she was running lightly down the verandah steps, the pale blue chiffon scarf tying back her bright hair floating behind her.

As she threaded her way through the vehicles on her way to the stables, chaffing and goodnatured comments echoed around her. 'Hey, Fleur,' called a young stockman, his frankly appreciative gaze resting on her fresh young face, 'you've just gotta win that barrel race! I can't afford for you to lose!'

She tossed a smile over her shoulder, 'As if I would!' and wrinkled her nose at him.

'Got that lucky feeling, have you?' called another masculine voice, 'like this is going to be my day!'

'Sort of.' I would really feel that way if I were going to the sports day with Logan. Now where had that ridiculous thought come from? she chided herself the next moment. All the time she continued to parry the teasing remarks thrown at her by shepherds and stockmen she found herself searching the crowd for Logan's tall figure. Don't be an idiot, she scolded herself. He'll be over at Christina's place helping her to load that high-spirited mount of hers into a horse float and then driving her to the sports ground. Fleur couldn't understand herself. Seeing she couldn't bear the sight of either Logan or his woman friend, why should the thought of the other two together on the long ride to the rodeo grounds give her this strange forlorn feeling that had suddenly overtaken her? It must be, she explained away the matter to herself, that she was missing the constant fiery spats between herself and Logan that somehow made other male companionship seem dull and ordinary.

She was giving Sally a final brush down when she became aware of Colin and Jim, colourful figures in their cowboy gear, as they hurried towards her. 'Morning, Fleur! Mind if we hitch a ride to the showgrounds with you? Colin's car battery is on the blink——'

'Why not?' She tried to infuse a careless note into her voice. 'How about Logan? Is he riding in any events today?' At the young shepherds' surprised expression she added hastily, 'He's new to the station and I just wondered.'

They still looked astonished. 'Didn't he tell you?'

'I haven't seen much of him lately,' she explained, still wielding the brush. And that, she thought with a little pang, was true enough.

'He said something about having a go at the bulldogging,' Colin said offhandedly.

'The bulldogging!' For a crazy second the clear

sunshine was a-shimmer as Fleur was wafted away on a daydream. Logan, thrown to the ground, saying in his peremptory way as he was being carried towards the ambulance tent, 'Get Fleur! She'll know what to do. She can tell if there's any damage.'

Christina hovering nearby, agitated but helpless to deal with the situation. Fleur's prompt diagnosis after a brief inspection. 'It's all right, Logan, there's no damage done, no bones broken.' Somehow she couldn't bear the thought of any real injury to him, but a light fall followed by a moment or so of concussion would serve to make him appreciate her. No longer would he regard her disparagingly as 'a girl like you', a girl who had offered her services to work with World Vision on the other side of the world merely because she wanted 'something to do'. Now everything was different, because she had proved to him her skill as a qualified nurse, someone to be called upon in an emergency—skilled, cool-headed, wanted! Never again would she be that girl for whom he had nothing but contempt. Granted that a physical attraction sparked between them, but of course it meant nothing to him, it was something over which neither she nor Logan had any control. It just—took over and carried them away with its potent power.

With a start she realised the two young shepherds were eyeing her with some impatience. 'You've sure brushed that mane long enough. We've got to put Sally in the float—boss's orders!'

'Yes, of course.'

The mare, well accustomed to the horse-float, took the ramp without hesitation. Fleur tossed a well-oiled saddle, bridle and fluffy skeepskin underblanket into the back of the Land Rover and the two shepherds climbed into the back seat, placing their wide sombreros carefully beside them.

Fleur took the wheel and when she reached the house she found Daphne waiting below the steps, a bulging island-type hamper at her feet crammed with the picnic lunch she had prepared the previous day—mouth-watering quiches, crusty home-made bread, filled hamburger rolls, shortcakes filled with pale green kiwi-fruit and fresh fruit from the orchard, peaches, plums, apples. In the chilli bins were fruit drinks and cans of beer for the men.

After the food was stowed in the vehicle, Fleur's father and Daphne seated themselves beside her and to the loud tooting of car horns, the Land Rover and float joined in the line of vehicles moving along the driveway. They were passing a blue ute when Tom Foster, fair hair hidden beneath a wide sombrero, flashed Fleur a grin and gave her a thumbs-up sign. As she smiled back at him the thought went through her mind that today he looked happy and confident. No doubt he realised that as a past champion in the hazardous sport in events held in other parts of the country, a lot was expected of him from the men employed at Te Haruru station, where the annual rodeo had become a tradition and a way of life. Fleur caught a passing glimpse of the girl seated at his side. Jane's round, almost childish-looking face was pale, her expression strained, and she appeared anything but happy at the ordeal that she had steeled herself to endure. Catching Fleur's encouraging wave of the hand, however, she forced an uncertain smile to her lips.

Out on the main road the twisting highway climbed to meet the horizon, and as they moved over the rise Fleur strained her gaze, peering ahead to a Land Rover trailing a horse-float. Logan and Christina? She wrenched her gaze and her thoughts aside and driving carefully because of the mare in the float, went on along the highway that curved between sheep-threaded hills with their clustered fans of cabbage trees and gullies green with densely growing native bush. In the still heat-hazy day the sea far below was a pale burnished sheet of blue. Vaguely she was aware of the murmur of voices around her. For the first time she became aware that Jim was new to rodeo riding, but if he had any apprehensions about the dangerous aspect of the sport, he hid them well. 'Me, I'm for the Youth Steer Ride,' he said proudly to his mate.

'Just watch,' Colin told him, 'that you don't get

kicked by one of the horses or get your foot caught in a stirrup and dragged along the ground! Watch the way Tom does it. He's dynamite when it comes to the rodeo, got glue on his pants! He won the championship last year and this year he's up against pretty fierce competition—a crack rider from the States and three buckjumpers from Queensland. Not that he's worried at all, you couldn't keep him out of the events today if you tried. Not even Jane stood a show of changing his mind. As if she need to have any worries about Tom! He knows the way to fall and can take care of himself.'

'I only hope you're right about that!' Fleur made the comment silently.

A silver milk tanker swung around a bend and flashed past, and as they moved along the country road bordered with fern and wild white daisies, Fleur swerved sharply to avoid a dead possum lying on the road, a casualty of the hours of darkness when the animals were caught in the glare of the car headlights. All at once a notice board nailed to a tree-trunk loomed ahead—*Rodeo*, with a black painted arrow. Soon they were passing through a small township, an old timbered hotel on the roadside and opposite, a petrol station and general store. Then they were joining in the cavalcade of trucks, cars and transporters moving along the road in the direction of the sports grounds. Already they could hear the lowing of steers and presently they were sweeping down towards the big tea-tree fenced enclosure below sun-dried hills that formed a natural amphitheatre.

Flags unfurled lazily against the blue and gates enclosed chutes near a corral where the horses that had been brought in from a nearby station earlier this morning now awaited their turn in the sawdust-covered ring. Trucks parked beside the railings formed excellent grandstands, brightly coloured sun-umbrellas blossomed on grassy slopes and a few sheep wandered among the picnickers. On a truck huge Maori men were having a tug-of-war, pulling on a thick rope to the loud applause of their friends. Maori women seated on a truck nearby cheered on their men to victory while young children silently watched the entertainment with velvety dark eyes.

As she guided the Land Rover and float between clusters of vehicles moving down the slope Fleur took in the scene around her. Ambulance men were pitching their tent near a tree-lined enclosure filled with calves and steers, Maori riders strolled past them, colourful figures in their wide felt hats, high boots and sheepskin leather chaps. Family parties relaxed on the grass beneath sun-umbrellas, the women's brightly coloured summer frocks vying with the vivid tonings of men's shirts in shades of scarlet, mauve and tangerine. A young Maori boy selling wedges of silvery-pink water melon moved among the crowd.

Fleur braked the vehicle to a stop near the arena and got out to loosen the bolt of the float and lead her mare down the ramp. A fleeting glance around her showed no sign of Christina or Logan. Anyway, she chided herself, why must she be always searching for Logan? The man seemed to invade her thoughts by night and day, she couldn't imagine why, and she refused to acknowledge the answer that the goblin, so adept at handing out home truths, whispered deep in her mind.

Soon the men were carrying stools and picnic baskets from the Land Rover, throwing rugs on the ground while the spicy pungent smell of pennyroyal rose from the trampled grass. The next moment Fleur realised that Logan was manoeuvring his Land Rover and double horse float in their direction. As he passed the party from the station with a brief nod, his glance slid over Fleur before moving on to the others. Christina, an eye-catching figure in impeccably tailored jacket and white figure-hugging jodphurs, lifted a hand in acknowledgement, then Logan moved on to park the Land Rover beside the railings a short distance away. Fleur watched him as he moved to the horse float, but it appeared that although his own sturdy stock horse caused him no concern, the half-Arab horse had its own ideas in the way of transport, and it was only after a lot of coaxing that Logan at last succeeded in leading the high-spirited mount down the ramp and on to the ground below.

It was amazing, Fleur marvelled, how much patience Logan had brought to the task, yet he treated her any old how. Just look at the way he insists on calling me 'Fox', she thought, when I've told and told him it's not my name, and he refuses to believe a word I say in defence of Bart and his being innocent of the wild rumours that are flying around about him. Is it any wonder that I loathe the man! Especially when he has such a low opinion of my capabilities and makes no secret of his feelings in the matter! If he and Christina prefer their own company to joining in with the rest of us, why should I care?

Almost at once other vehicles were drawing up around them and a buzz of conversation punctuated by loud bursts of laughter rose in the air as the party from the outback station prepared to enjoy the picnic atmosphere.

A short time later, as she gave a swift glance towards Logan and Christina, she told herself that if the other girl was enjoying herself at the sports ground, her face didn't show it, for Christina wore her customary withdrawn expression as if she wasn't really interested in the activities going on around her.

Incredibly, Logan was grinning towards his companion and evidently he was attempting to lighten her mood. Logan! Who had never shown the slightest concern for Fleur's feelings (not counting the shock and hazards of the plane crash, that was). But of course, she told herself, the truth was inescapable. Christina was the woman he loved and he would do anything to make her happy. Lucky Christina!

Fleur was tying Sally to the fence, then giving her a final brush-down in preparation for the barrel race, when a familiar gravelly voice reached her. 'How's it going, Fox?' Taken by surprise, she flung around to find herself looking directly into Logan's glinting eyes. Vibrations were running through her. Could it be something to do with the way he looked today? she thought wildly. Like the other men from the station he wore calf-hugging jeans, and the checked crimson-and-black Western-style shirt suited his mahogany-tanned skin. A wide felt hat was nicely angled over his eyes, low but not so low as to hide the hazel eyes that seemed to flicker with tiny lights, challenging and exciting— especially exciting! Fleur's heart was behaving strangely, thumping in her chest, and it took every ounce of determination she possessed to force her voice to a light uncaring note. 'Fine, just fine!' She searched her mind for ordinary things to say, words that might serve to hide the excitement he must have glimpsed in her eyes. At last she came up with, 'I heard over the grapevine that you're entering for the bulldogging——'

'That's right.' He seemed scarcely aware of what he was saying, his gaze fastened on her face. Because she could no longer sustain his so-alive glance she dropped her eyes and once again found herself groping for words. 'Have you done much rodeo riding down South?'

'Not for some years. I'm way out of practice right now.' The warmth in his grin made her forget everything else, and once again she was swept by the wild sweet excitement that sent the sunlit scene shimmering around her and her spirits soaring.

'Good luck, then!'

'Thanks, Fox. You too!'

At that moment she caught sight of Christina approaching them as she led her restive mount towards the fence. Fleur's spirits plummeted and she glanced away. Of course he didn't mean the good wishes for the race—how could he when it was Christina for whom he would be barracking in the one 'Girls Only' event of the day? She couldn't understand how she kept forgetting about the other girl.

'Hi, Fox.' Christina's chilly blue eyes moved over Fleur's face and the beautifully curved lips tightened. 'I hear you're going to give me a run for my money today, you and your mare.' Her cool disparaging glance rested on the sturdy grey who, blinking in the hot sunshine, appeared to be half asleep. She would have little to fear in the way of competition in the barrel race in that direction. Was that what Christina was thinking? Fleur reflected angrily.

'I'm going to give it a try.' She raised clear eyes to the older woman's lack lustre gaze, and said spiritedly, 'I'd rather you didn't call me "Fox". Actually my name's Fleur. Do you mind?'

Christina regarded her rather in the manner of a long-suffering parent who was slightly amused at the antics of an exasperating child. 'Really? Does it matter to you as much as all that?'

'Yes, it does!' Fleur snapped.

'Oh, I get it.' Christina's hollow-cheeked face wore an expression of boredom, yet to Fleur the words cut like a knife. 'I take it "Fox" is specially reserved for Logan?'

Fleur's glance flew to the man at her side, but to her relief he merely regarded her with a goodnatured grin. He drawled easily, 'And her dad.'

'Well . . .' Christina's delicately raised eyebrows left no doubt as to her annoyance, but turning aside, she began tying her horse to the fence. 'Give me a hand here, will you, Logan!'

She spoke just as if, Fleur thought with an unconscious sigh, Christina and Logan were two people who loved and understood each other so well they had no need for polite pleasantries. Oh, Logan might be skilful at concealing his real feelings where the other woman was concerned, but there wasn't the slightest doubt but that the other two were involved in a deep and lasting relationship with each other. Fleur tried to push aside the dark cloud of unease that threatened to envelop her. 'See you later.' She turned and moved away.

When she got back to the picnic spot everyone seemed to be talking at once, and excitement quickened as the men entering for the coming events went to check in at the nerve centre of the whole operation in the secretary's office and her father strolled away with them.

'All by yourself?' She realised that Jane Foster had come to drop down at her side. The other girl's smile wavered. The round face was pale, the eyelids puffy, Fleur noticed, as if Jane had wept throughout the night. The next moment she burst into a rush of words. 'I don't know whether I should have come here today or not! If Tom is badly thrown today I won't be able to bear it—' With a trembling hand she pushed the fine fair hair back from her forehead.

'Don't worry,' Fleur said cheerfully, 'he won't be!' She glanced towards the fair, curly-haired young man wearing Western-style garb who was talking and laughing with the others as they approached the secretary's office.

'How can I help worrying?' Jane's voice was low and troubled. 'Oh, I know *he* doesn't feel that way,' she ran on. 'He tells me that a fall at the rodeo is just all part of the act.'

'If he's been all right at rodeos up till now,' Fleur pointed out, 'nothing's likely to happen to him today, you'll see.'

Jane regarded her with her heavy-lidded gaze. 'Tell me that after the seventh race and I'll believe you.'

'The seventh race?' Fleur echoed bewilderedly. 'Isn't that the calf-roping?'

The other girl nodded. 'I know this sounds crazy, I haven't told anyone else, but I keep having this dream.' Her voice was a flat monotone. 'It's a day like this with bright sunshine and the crowd, everyone here, they're all so happy—except me. At first everything is fine, and then,' her voice thickened, 'it's the seventh event and Tom——' Her voice broke. After a moment she went on in a low distressed tone. 'I pleaded with him that if he wouldn't stay away from the rodeo today, to give up that one event just to please me, but he wouldn't even listen . . .' Her voice trailed despairingly away.

'Don't worry about it,' Fleur sought to comfort her, 'it's only a dream. It will be different today!'

'Oh, what's the use of talking to you!' Suddenly Jane's low tones were fraught with emotion. 'You don't seem to *care*! It's different for you. You haven't got anyone riding today who you love so much you just can't bear the thought of their getting hurt!'

Haven't I? To Fleur the thought came unbidden. I couldn't stand seeing Logan thrown and injured, really badly injured. I'm only calm and collected about watching him ride in the bareback and the bulldogging because he's so arrogant and so darned sure of himself that I just can't imagine him coming to grief in a rodeo event.

'What's the matter?' She became aware of Jane's puzzled tones. 'You look so sad somehow. I thought that your boy-friend was somewhere miles away. Bart someone, isn't it?'

'Nothing's the matter!' Fleur forced her voice to a brisk cheerful note. 'I don't know how you got that idea!' On another level of her mind, however, other thoughts had surfaced. Bart. It was strange how all at once he seemed to have receded into the past, no more than a man she had once been fond of. She still believed in his integrity, of course, but she was no longer in love with him. They had been apart for too long.

Jane's voice broke across her musing. 'I didn't think there could be anyone here today——'

'No, of course there isn't!' Fleur thrust away the shaft of fear that, just for a moment, had darkened her world. 'How could there be?' Her gaze flew to Christina. Unlike the rest of the party from the station who were enjoying the happy picnic atmosphere, the other girl had elected to remain apart. And why not? The thought came with an odd stab of the heart, when Logan would be returning to her side at any moment, pinpointing the fact that he preferred the company of the woman he loved and had no wish to share her with others. Without warning, pain twisted her heart. If Logan and she were man and wife, if she were the one he loved deeply, what then? She knew that she would never become accustomed to the dangerous sport.

'Listen!' Jane's voice was sharp with fear. There was a hush among the crowd as the first event of the day was announced and a call made for riders who had entered their names for the steer riding. The two young shepherds and Tom, who were sauntering back across the grass in their direction, turned back and began to hurry towards the chute where the steers were penned.

'Good luck!' Fleur's good wishes mingled with the various remarks shouted towards them from the rest of the station staff. Presently a chute was opened and to the crack of a stockwhip a steer rushed out, twisting and turning wildly.

Jane turned her face aside. 'I can't bear to watch. It's Jim, isn't it?'

'Yes.' The boyish figure kept a precarious hand on a thick rope for a brief time, then he was tossed into the dust of the arena. As the steer rushed wildly away Jim, apparently unhurt, snatched up his rodeo hat from the ground and hurried away.

'He's all right,' Fleur said to Jane, who opened her eyes and breathed a sigh of relief. 'Thank heaven for that!'

His mate Colin was next in line and managed to keep aloft for an even shorter time. He picked himself up unhurt and the pattern was repeated as more and more steers crowded the enclosure, until at last a man in a wide stetson and high boots entered the arena and sent them through a gate into a paddock.

Jane's face was pale as a chute was flung open and a steer pounded out with Tom keeping a precarious balance on the animal, one arm held aloft, another on the thick rope. Miraculously he kept his seat for an interminable few seconds when the hooter sounded and he dropped to the ground, bowing and smiling to the applause of the crowd.

'He's won the event!' Fleur spoke excitedly, but Jane's reaction was one of vast relief.

'That's the trouble with Tom,' she said unevenly, 'he always does!'

The picnic lunch was leisurely and enjoyable. There had been no serious accidents to mar the morning's programme and everyone was in a holiday mood. Everyone, that was, except Jane—and Christina, Fleur reflected. At lunchtime Logan had brought Christina to join the party from the station and the two sat together at the edge of the group, with them yet somehow apart from the others.

A loudspeaker blaring over the crowd as it called for the entrants to the bulldogging event roused Fleur from her thoughts. Out of the corner of her eye she saw that

Logan was getting up from his seat on the grass beside Christina, and as she watched him sauntering towards the arena, Fleur was pierced by a stab of apprehension. What was the matter with her today, for heaven's sake! It wasn't the first time she had attended a rodeo and up until now she had watched the performers with interest and enjoyment. Yet now she was aware of a chill feeling of fear. Pull yourself together, girl! she chided herself. Can you imagine Logan coming to harm in the event? And what is it to you what happens to him? She was jumping to her feet and hurrying towards the railings. A few minutes later a masculine voice shouted 'Wait for it!' and oblivious of the crowd pressing around her, Fleur drew in her breath sharply as a bull was released from the chute and came galloping down the arena.

A hush fell over the watchers as a rider galloped alongside the enraged beast, flung himself on the animal's back, grasping the horns and endeavouring to slip to the ground. Before he could do that, however, he went flying to the sawdust arena, then hurriedly picked himself up and hurried out of the ring. The procedure was repeated over and over again as various riders were eliminated. One bull that managed to break free of the enclosure was chased by two outriders.

Last of all came Logan, mounted on his sturdy stock horse. Fleur was scarcely aware of the party from the station crowding around her or the shouted comments that were flying through the air. 'Show 'em how it's done, boss!' She wasn't even aware that she was holding her breath as Logan jumped from his mount on to the animal's back, grasping the horns and slipping to the ground, digging in his heels as a brake. The next moment he had brought the enraged beast to the ground and as the hooter shrilled outriders ran forward, pulling him out of danger of the pounding hoofs, as the bull galloped away. A roar of applause went up from the crowd, and as Logan rose to his feet, his gaze sought Fleur's excited face and for an electric second, something unseen and potent pulsed between them. She raised her hand, waving excitedly, then he had turned and left the ring, but the heady sense of elation stayed with her. All at once she realised that Christina was standing beside her, and at the same time it came to her with a shock of surprise that the other girl's eyes were no longer apathetic but bright with resentment, and could it be—jealousy?

A few minutes later when Logan returned to join the party from Te Haruru he moved to Christina's side, goodnaturedly accepting the chorus of congratulations echoing around him. Only Fleur was silent. She must have imagined that moment in the ring, she told herself, when his glance had signalled that it was *her* approbation that mattered most to him when he won his event. She must have been crazy to think that!

The announcer's announcement of the barrel race jerked her mind back to the present. If only she could give such a good account of her riding ability. She realised that Christina had already left the group and was now guiding her mount towards the back of the chute and the restless horses penned in the corral. Logan's call of 'Best of luck, Chris!' shouted after the other girl reached Fleur as she went to untie her mare from the fence, and somehow it became overwhelmingly important that she win this event. She was scarcely aware of the goodnatured remarks thrown towards her as she rode away. 'Don't come back here if you don't make the best time!' and her father's quietly spoken, 'Give it all you've got, Fox! You'll make it!'

Presently the hooter blared and Christina emerged as the first competitor in an event that called for great horsemanship skill as well as speed. Horse and rider moved as one in those turns where every second counted and being too close could upset the barrel and cost a penalty of ten points. Fleur, watching from the back of the arena as Christina whirled her mount around the obstacles, realised that the other girl was a competitor whom it would be difficult to beat, finishing with an excellent time and the loss of only a few points.

Only by one the daredevil cowgirls took their turn in the demanding event, but no one in the race approached Christina's time and at last there was only Fleur left to compete in the event.

A ripple of excitement ran through the crowd as she rode into the arena. She was well known to many of the spectators as a winner of previous races, but the success of the unknown woman rider meant that the contest would be between the two outstanding riders.

Soon, leaning far out at an angle, horse and rider moved together, the mare's nostrils flaring and mane and tail flying in the breeze as Fleur whirled and swung her mount around the obstacles in a cloverleaf pattern. She could scarcely believe it when the signal from the hooter brought the event to an end and she was awarded the competitor with the fastest time. A cheer went up from the crowd gathered at the barrier, and among the shouting she recognised voices from workers at the station as stockmen and shepherds called to her as she rode out of the ring. All the time her gaze searched the sea of faces for Logan. For no matter what his private opinion of her, she thought triumphantly, today he would have to admit that she could ride!

'Congratulations, Fox!' His deep tones reached her without warning, and pulling on a rein, she swung around to face him.

'Thanks, Logan!' His bronzed face was aloof and forbidding, and as she met his flint-hard gaze all her excitement in the moment of victory died away. For what use his congratulations when he merely mouthed the conventional words? Swiftly she rallied herself and over the sudden ache in her heart, said brightly, 'I only just made it! If Christina hadn't lost those ten points at the beginning——'

'Don't give me that!' A reluctant grin twisted his lips. It was almost, she thought, as though the words were forced from him. 'It was a great performance! You derserved to win, Fox!'

Something deep inside her cried, 'Smile, then! As if you were *really* pleased that it was me and not Christina who gained the best time in the race!' The next moment the noisy crowd surged between them, making conversation impossible. Even as Fleur smilingly accepted the heartfelt congratulations of friends and family, all the fun of the victory was dimmed. Logan hadn't wanted her to win, not when his Christina was competing in the event!

When she rejoined the rest of the party from the station, Fleur realised that only Christina hadn't bothered to offer her the customary congratulations on her win. A swift glance showed her Christina and Logan standing a short distance away, and something about their complete absorption in each other made her scarcely aware of the enthusiastic comments echoing in her ears. 'We knew you'd pull it off!' 'Christina made a good effort, but not good enough!' 'Who needs an Arab horse when good old Sally can do all that's required?'

As the events continued one or two of the rodeo riders did their best to give spectators full value for their money, demonstrating the finer points of corkscrew technique as they stuck to the saddle. Other competitors risked life and limb in a fight with a bucking, unbroken horse. Fleur watched with the others, but the high excitement of the day had faded at the sound of Logan's cold forced tones. It came as a surprise when she heard the announcement of the last race, the calf-roping where the rider had only two chances with his lasso. He then had to jump from his horse and completely immobolise the calf by tying up its legs. Swiftly her gaze went to Jane, who was raising a chalk-white face to her husband. Clearly she was valiantly trying to fight threatening tears. Tom kissed her briefly, then strode away. Fleur hurried to the other girl's side. 'Don't look like that.'

Jane made no answer and in the wide eyes Fleur glimpsed an expression of naked terror. 'He promised me,' she said at last, 'that after today he'll give rodeo riding up for good. But Fleur,' her voice cracked, 'what if it's the last time he rides—ever?'

'Don't be silly!' Fleur endeavoured to laugh away the fears that did indeed have some foundation in reality in the dangerous sport.

At that moment a shout went up from the crowd, 'Here he comes!' as Tom, mounted on his stock horse, emerged from the chute. He leaned far forward in the saddle, his coiled lasso snaking through the air as he galloped in pursuit of a black calf ahead. Then suddenly as his horse wheeled and turned under the swirling rope, Tom lost his balance and was thrown heavily to the ground. The seconds ticked away as he lay motionless in the dust of the arena. The next minute ambulance officials were hurrying towards him, kneeling over the unconscious man and carrying him out of the ring and into a waiting ambulance.

As Fleur hurried with the others towards the officials, she realised that already Jane had run ahead. 'A spot of concussion,' a uniformed official informed her kindly, 'nothing to worry about so far as we know, but we'll take him to hospital for a check-up just to make sure there's no real damage done. It's always a bit of a toss-up in these cases.'

Jane's face puckered. 'But you really think,' she whispered unsteadily, 'that he'll be all right?'

'Sure as we can be without tests being taken. He's got a twisted ankle, by the look of things, but chances are he'll be fine in a few days, all set to ride in the rodeo another day!'

'No!' The vehemence in the soft tones surprised her listener. 'Never! He promised me——'

'Well then,' the middle-aged ambulance official regarded her kindly, 'you've nothing to worry about. Coming with us to the hospital?'

'Oh *yes!*' Jane got into the vehicle and seated herself beside the unconscious man inside.

'I'll come with you,' Fleur offered quickly, fearing that Jane was on the verge of collapse. 'May I?' she appealed to the driver.

'Sure, hop in.' Fleur climbed into the back of the van with its stretcher patient. 'You're all right, Jane?' she asked softly.

The other girl nodded. Her face was without a vestige of colour and she trembled uncontrollably. 'I will be, once I know that Tom will be all right.' Her anxious gaze never left the still figure.

When they reached the country hospital in the hills, Tom was taken away for tests and observation by a doctor and Fleur waited with the other girl in the empty waiting room as the time crawled by. At last, however, Jane was summoned into an inner sanctum and the white-coated doctor's words dispelled the fear that had haunted the young wife through so many sleepless nights.

'You're his wife, I take it?'

'Yes, yes, I am. Tell me the truth, doctor, he's not—badly hurt?'

The pleasant-faced doctor said with a smile, 'Right at this moment he looks a whole lot better than you do. I'll arrange for a nurse to give you a sedative to settle your nerves——'

'It doesn't matter about me, doctor,' the frantic voice cut in, 'he will get better?'

'Of course he will! He's deeply concussed at the moment. We'll keep him here for the night. He might not regain consciousness for anything up to forty-eight hours, so we've got to make sure there are no complications during that time. You can stay here with him if you like——'

'Oh, could I? That would be wonderful!' Jane was almost incoherent with relief. 'You see, doctor, we've only been married for six months.'

He smiled. 'So I gathered. Well, not to worry. A well-known rider like your husband has to expect a few falls along the way. Looks as though he was lucky this time not to be more seriously hurt.'

'I'm lucky too!' Her face fell. 'I will be if he's all right. You see, there won't be any more rodeo rides,' all at once she looked as though a weight had been lifted from her shoulders. 'He promised me!'

When Jane came back into the waiting room to join her, Fleur knew at once by the relieved expression of the other girl's face that the news was good.

'He's going to be fine, the doctor says, no serious damage.' Jane smiled mistily and blinked away the tears. 'I know it's awful for Tim to have concussion, but the doctor told me he's fairly certain that there's nothing to worry about. They're going to keep him in the hospital tonight just to make sure, and they want me to stay here with him. As if I needed an invitation!

The doctor thinks he'll regain consciousness some time in the next forty-eight hours. He's twisted his ankle too, but it all could have been so much worse! I've been nearly out of my mind with worry about today.' All at once she seemed to return to the present. 'Oh, Fleur, it's so good of you to stay with me all this time!'

'I wanted to. You're all right now, then? No problems?' Fleur got to her feet.

'None at all, thank heaven. And once Tom regains consciousness——' Jane broke off. 'But you,' she said anxiously, 'how will you get back to the station? The others will have gone back hours ago.' She glanced out into the darkness beyond the windows.

'Not to worry,' said Fleur with a smile, 'I'll ring from here and see if there's some sort of taxi service around somewhere——'

'Don't bother!' said a rumbling masculine voice behind her. 'You've got yourself one right now!'

Fleur spun around. 'You!' How long, she wondered, had Logan been standing in the opening of the doorway, waiting his chance to speak? She wrenched her mind back to the vibrant tones. 'Looks like the news is good, judging by your expression, Jane. Has he come to life yet?'

'No, not yet, but there's no serious injury.' Her shining eyes and the relief in her voice showed a release from a terrible fear that had haunted her for the past week.

'Great! Though Tom's too tough to get hurt too badly,' grinned Logan. 'I gather you'll be staying the night at the hospital?'

'Oh yes, *yes!*'

'Then I've only got Fox to worry about.' His eyes were dark and unreadable as his gaze went to her. 'No objection to getting a ride home in Tom's ute with me, have you?'

A thousand objections clamoured in her mind. You're the last man in the world I want to be alone with tonight! You're too damn good-looking and you affect me in a way no other man has ever done! Your touch electrifies me, and my only chance of sanity is to avoid being alone with you!

Instead, she heard her own voice saying with all the lightness she could muster, 'Why should I?'

Jane, as if tuning in on undercurrents running beneath the surface of the conventional words, glanced with puzzled eyes from Logan to Fleur.

'Let's get cracking, then, shall we?' Logan was saying. He turned towards Jane. 'I'll pass on the good news to everyone at home. We'll keep in touch. Fleur's father told me to let you know that there's no hurry for Tom to start work. If he has to spend a few more days here, it's okay.'

Jane raised the ghost of a smile. 'Even if he has to come back on crutches?'

Logan's grin broadened. 'We'd like him back any old way. Believe me, he'll get a great welcome! He's a nice guy.'

'I know,' a light sprang into Jane's eyes, 'I like him too!'

As she went with Logan down the hospital steps and out into the soft blue night, Fleur's emotions were in a tumult and she said the first words that came into her head. 'You haven't been waiting all this time for me——'

'And Jane!'

Why must she be so impulsive? she chided herself angrily. Of course there was nothing personal in his waiting to escort her back to the station. Since the night of the hangi she had managed to avoid seeing a great deal of Logan. Or could it be that he had at last picked up her signals that she wanted no more to do with him, especially his lovemaking? Even if she didn't have personal reasons for disliking him, this she couldn't tolerate. For him to be involved in a loving relationship with another woman, yet to imagine he could toss her a few light kisses, merely for his own amusement when the occasion offered ... Some devil of retaliation sparked her to say tauntingly, 'And now there's only me!'

'True, true.' Trust him, she thought crossly, to give nothing away. The deep voice broke across her rioting thoughts. 'Just the way I like it.'

As they took the winding path, pale in the gloom, Fleur's mind was playing tricks with her and a singing excitement was flying along her nerves. I didn't plan things this way, she tried to reason with herself, but now that it's out of my hands . . . Anyway, she was trying to subdue the heady excitement that just being with him could arouse in her, now that I know exactly where I stand with him, I'll know the best way to handle the situation.

'If you can!' jeered the goblin deep in her mind, but swiftly she brushed the tiny voice aside.

This time, she vowed silently, she wouldn't surrender to his masculine attraction that had so often caught her unawares. This time she'd be prepared, she wouldn't let him charm away all her resolutions to resist him. The trick was to think hard about Christina and to keep right on thinking about the other girl.

When they reached the car standing in the shadows of the tall oleander bushes, Logan saw her seated, then got in behind the wheel. He switched on lights and put the vehicle into gear, and as they took the pathway and turned into the highway, he flung her a sideways glance. 'Congratulations again on your win in the barrel race!'

'Thanks—again!' she said briefly, the thoughts rushing through her mind. Darn him, the man was a mind-reader! she thought hotly. He seemed to know that tonight she had steeled her heart and mind against any suggestion of intimacy between them, and he was playing along with her, no doubt because he realised he had to. She wrenched her attention back to his level tones. 'They tell me you ran off with the best score last time you competed in the race too. What's it to be next year? Women's Championship? Queen of the Rodeo?'

'Don't ask me!' she answered lightly, and couldn't resist adding, 'I got the idea you were pinning your hopes on Christina winning the event!' Belatedly she tried to infuse an impersonal note into her voice. 'I mean, she did have the best-bred horse, not just an old faithful like Sally.'

'I was, actually.' What had she expected him to say, for heaven's sake? she wondered wildly.

Aloud she agreed, 'Of course,' and felt her spirits sink with a plop.

In the heavy silence Logan's words struck her like blows. 'I had my reasons for wanting her to make it in the race. Tell you all about it some day!'

Tell me? What was there to tell? She longed to throw at him. Because you're in love with Christina, everyone knows that. Of course he would have preferred the other girl to win the race.

'Too bad I ruined things for you.' She couldn't resist the barb.

'Not to worry, Fox, you deserved to win! You put on a great effort!'

What was the use of saying nice things like that to her now? she thought bitterly. Oh, she might have known that he would find pleasure in putting her down, that as usual when it came to anything in which his precious Christina was involved, a victory over the other girl was the last thing he wanted!

With an effort she forced her voice to a nonchalant note. 'You didn't do badly yourself in the bulldogging. Once or twice I didn't think you could stick on for another second. I was holding my breath——'

'You were, Fox?' His tone was deep and soft. 'You never told me you felt that way about me?'

She ignored that, running on in a rush of words. 'Then wham! the hooter went and you had the bull down on the ground and there you were, smiling and taking the applause of the crowd!'

'I'm rather good at that, don't you think?'

At last, however, she had herself in hand. 'You weren't so good at getting away from the bull afterwards,' she pointed out coldly. 'If it hadn't been for the outriders rushing up and grabbing you around the waist and rescuing you——'

'All part of the act!' His tone was careless. That was one of the maddening things about Logan, she told herself as they sped up the rough metal road, you never could make an impression on him. You couldn't tell where you were with him. She wrenched her mind back to the deep tones. 'You have to hand it to the outriders,' he was saying as they swept up a dark slope, 'their act needs a hell of a lot of skill and stamina.'

'I guess it does.' Trying to keep the conversation on an impersonal level, she said, 'Isn't it great that Tom wasn't badly hurt in that fall he took today? Jane's been having nightmares about his riding in the rodeo today. Of course what was really on her mind was the awful thought that he might be badly injured or that he could damage his hands. He's such a fantastic singer and guitarist, and Jane's counting on him winning the big song contest in town next month. He's got the talent, and I guess,' she laughed, 'that a twisted ankle won't stop him having a go at his big chance in the entertainment business. Can't you just see Tom making a name for himself, travelling overseas, making recordings?'

'Good luck to him!'

They swept over a rise, then moved through a small township where lights streamed from a hotel and a roadside garage. Presently a shower of raindrops spattered the windscreen and Logan set the wipers working with their rhythmic beat. Soon they were out in the intense stillness of the country, where the darkness was more intense than within the radius of a city with its reflections of lights. Rain driven by the wind slashed against the windows and great drops coursed down the windshield beyond the half-moons of the wipers. Around them black silhouettes of trees and bush made a blurred outline against the dark hills, and the car was a small world of their own, dimly-lighted, enclosed, intimate.

At that moment the headlamps pinpointed the body of a dead possum, lying directly ahead of them, and Logan swerved sharply, throwing Fleur heavily against him. His arm around her drew her close, sending vibrations tingling through her. She stirred in a half effort to free herself from his encircling arm, but all at once it seemed in her relaxed state of mind absurd for her to make an issue of such a trivial matter. The next moment car lights illuminated the side of the road and a possum sprang forward, then paused, dazzled by the approaching headlights. Once again Logan swerved to the side, his hold tightening around her shoulders.

'Do you know,' she took a deep breath, striving to make her voice steady and impersonal, 'dead possums on the country roads who've been killed at night in the glare of the headlamps of cars is something I'd forgotten all about since being away in Thailand.' Even to her own ears her laughter had a forced, brittle quality. 'Like rodeos, and hangis and the fantastic loveliness of our own back country.' The thought flashed through her mind that she knew so little about him. 'Have you ever been overseas, Logan?'

'I've had the odd trip to the States and over to England, mostly on business. Farm study groups, taking in the cattle breeding scene in America, a spot of show-jumping in England.'

'Golly! I didn't know you'd been a show-jumper over there. How did you get on?'

He chuckled. 'Not good enough to carry off the championships, but I enjoyed the experience. It was tremendous! I met some good friends over there too. I was lucky.'

'Christina?' Why, she cried silently the next moment, must she always spoil things, introduce the one name she wanted to avoid when talking with him tonight? Stupid! Stupid!

'Not Christina,' the amusement in his tone puzzled her. 'I'd known her for a long time before that trip to Badminton.'

Having introduced the other woman into the conversation Fleur now had no wish to pursue the matter. If only she could forget about the woman he loved. Yet some devil of contrariness drove her on. 'I suppose by now she's about ready to take pupils at her riding school at Red Gums?'

'That's right!' His tone rang with enthusiasm. 'We're putting the ads in the local papers next week, then we'll see what comes along.'

We! The word cut like a knife, plunging deep. She couldn't understand the sense of hurt. It wasn't as if she even liked the man.

'How about love?' whispered the goblin deep in her mind.

Ridiculous! She lapsed into an unhappy silence, and Logan appeared to be concentrating on the vehicle he was guiding through the stormy night. Wind and rain slashed against the windows, a long stock transporter appeared around a bend, splashing the ute with mud as it ground past. The bush crowding the edges of the road hung wet and sombre, only the toe-toes tossed their shaggy rain-soaked plumes defiantly in the high wind.

'Had any word from your boy-friend lately?' The carelessly spoken words caught her by surprise. Instantly she stiffened, said defensively,

'Bart, you mean?'

'Who else?'

Just in time she caught at her common sense. 'Why do you ask?'

'Just wondering. You were pretty het up about him that night,' his deep soft tone played along her heartstrings, 'that we spent together in the bush.'

'It's nothing to do with you!' She attempted to wrench herself free, but his detaining arm was like a steel band and rather than engage in a ridiculous struggle in which she had a suspicion he might well be the victor, she gave in. She said spiritedly, 'What does it matter to you?'

'I'm a better judge of that than you—don't bother answering that question—I can tell by your voice that you haven't heard a word from him, that he hasn't contacted you all this time—and a damn good thing too!'

Fleur said very low, 'It's no use telling you, is it? We've had all this out before. You're wasting your time!'

Logan didn't appear to be listening, his voice all at once forceful, curt with anger. 'You still haven't come to your senses, then? You refuse to face facts. You're a stubborn little fool, Fox,' he ground out. 'If you'd only see things the way they are!'

Wildly she struggled to wrench herself free of his grip, but his arm held her an unwilling prisoner. 'If I'd known,' she cried breathlessly, 'that you were going to go on about Bart all over again I wouldn't have come with you!' All at once the dark cloud of frustration and resentment that was building up inside her exploded. 'That's the reason why you waited for me at the hospital tonight, I suppose? So you could have another dig at me about Bart!' At last she found herself freed of his clutch and, flushed and angry, she flung around to face him. 'Waiting all those hours so that you could get me on my own,' she flung at him, 'just so that you can say that you're right and I'm wrong about Bart! Just for your own satisfaction, so you can score a victory over me. Well, you won't!' she cried, 'because you'll never change my mind, never, never, never! What does it matter to you, for heaven's sake, what I think about Bart? It couldn't possibly mean anything to you!'

'It matters a lot.' The words were so low they were snatched away in the roaring of the wind, rising in intensity, the clap of thunder and the drumming of rain on the roof of the car, and afterwards she wondered if she had merely imagined them.

All at once a dreadful thought shot through her mind. What if she had been wrong in taxing Logan with waiting for her for the purpose of making his own point, scoring a victory over her? He must have spent long hours waiting until she was ready to leave the hospital. He would have to arrange for his own horse to be taken back to the station as well as find himself a car in which to drive back with her. To ease her conscience in the matter she said in a milder tone, 'It was your idea to wait for me, I suppose?'

'That's right.' The gravelly voice sounded entirely unperturbed. 'Your dad seemed to go along with the suggestion,' he added smoothly. Yes, of course, her thoughts ran, had Logan not volunteered to take her back to the station, her father would have had to put in the long hours of waiting. Aloud she asked, 'How about the horses, the float?' She forced her voice to a light careless note. 'I suppose Christina would take them back?'

'Oh, she'd be okay. She's used to handling stock and

she's a fantastic driver. I gave her a hand to load the horses into the float and she took off in the Land Rover.' His voice rang with confidence, and Fleur could have kicked herself for once again dragging the other girl's name into the conversation.

The miles slipped away as they sped on through the stormy night, ragged outlines of hills rising against a dark sky, and there was nothing in all the world, Fleur mused, but Logan and herself, enclosed in their own private world. A silence had fallen between them, but it wasn't an angry silence, she mused. She was all too aware of his arm that had slipped around her shoulders, his nearness that was lulling her into a dreamy state of forbidden happiness. Was he too, she wondered, aware of the life force, powerful and inescapable, throbbing between them?

All at once, with a shock of surprise, she glimpsed a weathered signpost 'Te Haruru Station' looming out of driving rain, and soon they were swinging into the track winding down to the homestead with its lighted windows beaming out into the darkness. A lantern formed a pool of light on the verandah and Logan drew up at the foot of the steps. He switched off the engine, then swung around to face her. Still caught in a spell, she tried for lightness. 'Haven't you forgotten something?' She put her hand over his, still resting on her shoulder. The next moment he was smoothing the copper hair back from her temples. For a strange silent moment they stared at each other in the dim light of the dashboard. His hands slid down to cup her smooth cheeks and, unprepared for the tenderness of his touch, a tremor went through her and she clasped her hands in her lap to hide the shaking. Her heart was beating unevenly and wildly she clutched at all those resolves about resisting him she had so conveniently shelved just when she most needed them. She tried to pull his hands away from her face, but it was already too late for anything but the waves of wild sweet content that were submerging her senses. The next moment he drew her close in his arms and fire coursed through her veins as his lips moved gently over her mouth.

The next moment a door was flung open and voices called above the noise of wind and rain. 'Here they are!' Feeling as though she was in a dream, Fleur was dazedly aware of a group hurrying out on to the verandah. Then she was getting out of the car and Logan, who had taken off his jacket, was throwing it around her shoulders. Then they were running up the rain-slashed steps, to be immediately engulfed in a torrent of questions as everyone talked at once. Fleur heard it all with only a part of her mind—Logan's explanation of the long delay, giving them the latest news of Tom's state of health.

'We've been ringing through to the hospital every hour on the hour,' said Rusty as the party moved down the hall and into the lounge room. 'Now that we've got the latest bulletin we can relax a bit. The doctors think he'll be okay?'

'Sure as they can be!' said Logan. 'They're expecting him to come around some time in the next forty-eight hours, but that's not unusual with concussion—Well, that's it, folks, gotta go!' For a moment his warm glance went to Fleur. 'Fleur will fill you in with the details.' He had gone, running down the verandah steps and out into the rainswept night. Of course he would be visiting Christina, Fleur thought, over an aching sense of loss and a dull sense of let-down. The clamour of voices echoing around her reached her as from a distance. 'Didn't she do well! How's our Rodeo Queen?' The laughter and teasing comments that were partly a relief from tension scarcely registered with her.

'Are you all right, Fox?' All at once she became aware of her father's voice, tinged with concern.

'Of course I am!' With an effort she pulled herself together. She forced a bright smile to her lips and was grateful at that moment to Daphne, who unexpectedly came to her rescue.

'There's nothing wrong with the girl,' said Daphne in her forceful manner, 'that hot coffee and a bite to eat won't put right!'

Fleur sent her a wobbly grin. If only life were that simple!

A little later, finding herself alone for a few minutes, her sense of confusion fell away and instead came the familiar sense of vexation and conflict. How could she have abandoned so swiftly all her plans for ignoring Logan, of demonstrating to him in no uncertain fashion how she *really* felt about him? Blindly she stared down into the steaming mug of coffee Daphne was handing to her. Next time she wouldn't weaken so easily. Next time it would be different!

CHAPTER TEN

THROUGH the long hours of darkness Fleur tossed and turned endlessly, unable to banish Logan's face from her mind. She knew that his caresses tonight had affected her more than she cared to admit. The sweetness and excitement of his lips on hers stayed with her, she couldn't seem to make herself forget. The truth came with shattering impact. She didn't want to forget, she longed to stay in the closeness of his arms for ever. She loved him. Why hadn't she recognised the truth before? His strong masculine face rose before her mental vision—the hazel eyes with their inscrutable expression. Or was that only when he looked at her? The deep rumbling tones that were so attractive yet said such devastating things to her! She was deeply, irrevocably in love with Logan, of all men. All the time I thought I hated him, and now . . . A cold hand seemed to close around her heart. Was there ever such a fool? It's no use wanting him, loving him, no use at all. Tears squeezed from behind her eyelids and trickled down her cheeks. Forget him, he's not for you. If it hadn't been for Christina . . .

Her thoughts flew off at a tangent. Why did the other woman have to be so appealing? And why did Christina resent her? For plainly she regarded Fleur as a possible rival where Logan's affections were concerned. If the older woman imagined he could possibly be attracted to herself, Fleur thought wryly, Christina must indeed have a jealous nature. Once again the tiny voice of truth spoke up. 'If Logan were your man, your own love, wouldn't you feel jealous of any attractive woman of his acquaintance?' She knew only too well the answer to that query.

That week she made certain she came down to breakfast long after Logan had left the house. It wasn't hard to arrange, seeing that he was up and about very early, giving the men their working programme for the day. The difficult thing, she told herself on a sigh, was to resist the urge to seek him out, for the longing to be with him was all but unsurmountable.

In the evenings Logan drove away in his car, returning late at night. She should be glad, Fleur told herself bitterly, that his desire to be with Christina on every possible occasion gave her no worries about avoiding him. She *should* be glad, yet the ache of longing persisted, the anguish that no amount of commonsense advice given to herself could banish.

I'll have to take myself in hand, she scolded herself, organise myself into getting hospital work somewhere far away from here, up North maybe. While her determination was high she sat down and wrote out an application to a country hospital, then stamped the envelope and slipped it into the blue canvas mail bag. There, it was done! Before long she would be away from here and never see Logan again—a sick feeling shot through her—or hear his voice calling her 'Fox'. If only things had worked out differently, the familiar thoughts returned to her mind, the regrets she couldn't seem to banish for long.

You've got to get over your feelings for him, she chided herself, and while you stay here, seeing him every day, just being in his presence is enough to undo all those resolutions about not caring for him. It's too late, I do care—terribly—I always will. And so long as he doesn't guess how I feel about him, and no one here suspects the truth ... At the end of the day, however, even that consolation was denied her, for it was clear that others had noticed her listlessness, the dark shadows under her eyes. And trust Daphne, she thought, to comment on the fact at the dining table. She might have known those shrewd darting eyes would miss nothing.

'I don't know what's wrong with you lately, Fleur,' Daphne said in her no-nonsense way. 'You've been picking at your meals all week. If you're not heading for this anorexia nervosa I've been hearing so much about lately with young girls, it's my cooking——'

'I can tell you what's wrong,' Rusty's twinkling eyes swept Fleur's wan face as he attempted one of his heavy-handed jokes. 'She's in love, of course—look at that!'

To her horror Fleur felt a vivid tide of pink sweep up her creamy cheeks. 'That proves it,' grinned Rusty, and Fleur was thankful that Logan wasn't at the table to join in the goodnatured laughter.

Only when she was out riding up in the hill paddocks could she forget for a short time the anguish that possessed her. And even then there was the shame-making knowledge that all the time she longed to meet up with him on the lonely slopes, even though she knew that Logan would merely take the opportunity of provoking her into saying things she would later bitterly regret. And suppose her emotional response should betray her real feelings for him?

One day she was following a track high above the sea, reining in her mount for a moment as she gazed over the tossing expanse of ocean and the restless waves pounding in over glinting black sands. A white line of foam zipped across the surface of the rippling waves and on the cliff face gnarled pohutukawa trees snaked a precarious hold on the rocky surface, their blossoms staining the sand below with fallen crimson tassels. All the blazing beauty of Te Haruru, she mused on a sigh, the Maori name signifying 'the resting place of the wind', and in her present state of mind it meant exactly nothing to her.

A long time later, as she took the path leading to the homestead, she came in sight of a blue ute drawn up outside Tom's neatly painted bungalow. As she neared the vehicle the thought came to her that if her world had fallen apart, for Jane the wheel of fortune had spun in a different direction. For the other girl, seated at the wheel of the ute, looked radiant, pinpointing Fleur's own heaviness of heart.

It was mean of her to feel this way, she thought remorsefully. She was glad, she really was, for the other girl's happiness.

'Hi, Fleur, I'm home! They kept me a bit longer because of the old leg.' Tom waved a crutch at her from the open window.

'Welcome back!' Fleur's gaze moved to Jane's smiling face. 'Don't forget that if you want any nursing done, I'm available!'

'Thanks, Fleur,' called Tom, 'but I happen to have my own private one.' As she caught the intimate glance that passed between husband and wife, Fleur felt her heart contract with an ache of longing.

'Maybe you're right at that!' she called back. 'See you!' She watched as Jane guided the ute through the entrance and into their own spot of paradise. It was ridiculous, Fleur told herself as she urged Sally forward, to feel this jealousy for those two. Everyone couldn't be lucky enough to find their own perfect mate, but if they were, unconsciously she sighed, it would be like stumbling on the gold at the foot of the rainbow and the pot as well!

'Wait, Fox!' Her heart plunged and glancing over her shoulder, she found Logan riding towards her.

Pulling her mount to a stop, she found herself gazing towards him as if she had never seen him before. His face, browned by the hot New Zealand summer sun, his thick, crisply curling dark hair falling over his forehead, catching lights in the sunshine. His hazel eyes veiled by those ridiculously long lashes, eyeing her with an expression that was unreadable. She loved everything about him. He was very striking and his voice, rich and deep, caught you unawares and did things to your emotions.

'Where have you been hiding lately?' he demanded. 'Not avoiding me, by any chance, are you, Fox?'

'What an idea!' Everything else forgotten in the sheer delight of being with him once again, she turned to face him, the long vertical dimple flickering in her cheek, laugther sparkling her eyes.

'Missed you.' Of course he didn't mean the light words, but somehow the sheer happiness persisted.

They rode side by side, the horses keeping in step, talking of nothing things. The thought went through Fleur's mind that to anyone passing they would give an impression of a man and a girl enjoying a ride together, but it wasn't like that, not really, not for her. Being with him was a delicate balance of pleasure and pain, and all the time the insistent thoughts beat a refrain in her mind. If only . . . if only . . . It was too good to last, of course, because all too soon they neared the homestead and Logan left her to ride down to the stockyards.

The following day Fleur found, for the first time in her life, that time hung heavily on her hands. She found too that in spite of her feverish efforts to fill each moment with activity, the thoughts and hopeless dreams of Logan came crowding back to mind. Logan, in love with her, loving her as she loved him, wanting her. In an effort to banish the ache of longing, she pushed straying tendrils of bright copper-coloured hair back from her forehead. Get busy, girl; thoughts of Logan will get you nowhere! A long ride over the hills was the best antidote to anguish, hadn't she found that out?

Much later in the day, she had brushed Sally down and back in the house she was going along the hall on her way to her own room when the telephone bell pealed and Daphne, who happened to be nearby at the time, lifted the receiver. 'Oh, there you are, Fleur! It's for you—a man's voice.'

'Oh!' Instinctively she slowed. That would be Bruce calling her, for sure, something that happened almost daily. She knew exactly what he would say. How much he missed her. He was counting the days until his crop-dusting assignment in another district came to an end and he could come to Te Haruru and be with her once again. The awful part of it was, the thought ran through her mind as she picked up the receiver, was that as usual, she had forgotten all about him.

'Bart here. Are you alone? Can we talk, sweet, without the whole world being in on it?' Over the sudden pounding of her heart she caught the urgency and tenseness of his tone.

'Yes, I can talk, but——'

Swiftly he cut across her astonished voice. 'Listen, love, I've got to tell you, get things straightened out between us——'

'It's okay,' now it was her turn to interrupt. 'Where are you? Where are you calling from?'

'Never mind all that now! I've only got time for the important stuff like my getting the idea that you'd let me down that day in Auckland. I waited for you at the ferry wharf until the last minute. I had to catch the Sydney plane that day, you know that——'

'I understand!'

'But you don't, sweetheart! Just yesterday I came across an old Kiwi newspaper and there was this account of a plane crash down your way, photos of the burnt out plane and all! I nearly passed out when I read it! Then I got to the bit where you walked out of the bush the next day, safe and sound! Wow-ee—was that the best bit of news I ever had in my life! You could have heard my sigh of relief all the way across the Tasman! So now, my sweet,' all at once the laughter had died away from his voice, but now his low persuasive tones no longer had power to stir her, 'it's back to square one for both of us, right?'

'No! Listen,' said Fleur breathlessly, 'you don't understand, things have changed——'

'You haven't a thing to worry about!' Was he deliberately ignoring her protests? she wondered, as the seductive tones that once could have sent her world spinning around her ran on. 'Look, honey, I've got it all figured out. You catch the plane to Sydney day after tomorrow and I'll be right here at the airport to meet you, and from then on—Man! Will I ever be sure of meeting that Auckland plane!'

She played for time. 'Where are you staying in Sydney?'

'Oh, that,' all at once the low tones were evasive, 'I get around a fair bit, here and there. Not to worry, I'll be at the airport bang on time, and this time there won't be any hold-ups!'

'No!' At last Fleur had come to her senses. 'I'm not coming, Bart.'

'What's that?'

'It's all over between us. I'm sorry, but that's the way it is.'

'Changed your mind, have you?' All at once his voice was low and ugly, barbed with resentment. 'I might have known I couldn't trust you! Found someone else, is that it?' came the sneering tones. And before she could speak, 'That Logan character—the guy you spent the night with in the bush after the plane crash. What did you talk about all those hours together, eh? Me? Maybe you didn't talk too much, not after he'd let you in on a few things. Maybe you had better things to do out there in the bush together, like——'

'Stop it!' The hot blood rushed to her cheeks and her voice rang with anger. 'If you think I'm going to stay here listening to you——'

'But you didn't mind listening to the Logan guy!' came the sneering tones, 'when he told you about missing sheep when it came to the count-down and account books that didn't add up because someone had put their signature to the odd cheque for a thousand bucks or so last year.'

Fleur drew in her breath sharply. 'It was you——'

'Who else? You little fool! Anyone could pull the wool over your eyes! Did you really think I didn't have my own little methods of making a bit of extra income on the side? You and your dad—trusting fools, both of you. You were asking for it. It was like taking candy from a baby. No one even suspected anything was wrong until that Logan character started poking his nose in. And now he's got my girl as well!' The sneering tones mimicked her soft accents. '"Where are you living, Bart?"' As if I'd tell you, knowing what you do now. Do you think I want you around?'

Before she realised what she was doing Fleur had crashed the receiver violently into its cradle.

She stood motionless, the colour draining away from her face as the conflicting emotions chased one another through her mind. Logan! He had told her the truth again and again, but she had refused to believe him. Words he had said to her during their long night under the stars returned to prick at her consciousness. 'I have no need to make up to the boss's daughter!' Was that the way in which Bart had regarded her? The answer was all too plain. It was the oddest thing, she marvelled, that she felt no real pain at the break with Bart. Even his shattering disclosures of guilt left her with a sense of relief. Maybe deep down she had always suspected the truth. All that mattered to her was Logan, and one consuming thought filled her mind. 'I've got to let him know that I know the truth at last, that he was right about Bart all the time.' He'll be hateful and sardonic about it, he won't let me off easily, I know, but all the same ... The thought was imprinted in letters of fire on her mind. 'I've got to tell him.' It mattered to her more than anything else in the world.

'You feeling all right, Fox?' She brought her heavy gaze to meet her father's concerned glance.

'It's just—I've had a bit of a shock,' she told him. 'That was a call from Australia, from Bart. You were right,' she went on slowly, 'when you told me about Bart having been downright dishonest. He admitted the whole thing to me. He—thought I knew!'

'That's great news!' Could it be her imagination, she wondered, that made the lined face look suddenly younger, more carefree. 'You just about made me forget what I came to see you about,' he was saying. 'A letter for you, Fox. It just came in the mail.'

She raised dull eyes, her voice apathetic. 'That will be the answer to my application for a nursing position in a hospital up North.'

'A job?' His tone was sharp with alarm. 'I was hoping you might stay put here for a month or so yet.'

'No,' she said on a sigh, 'not now.'

'I see, Fox. This news you got today has made a difference to you?'

She let it go at that, thankful that no one would suspect the real reason for her stress of mind. Something at last, she thought wryly, for which she could be thankful to Bart. Her father's anxious voice roused her from her musing. 'Open it, then, and let me know the worst!'

Like a girl in a dream, Fleur ripped open the typed envelope. Would her father put the shaking of her fingers down to the shock of Bart's disclosure? Her eyes ran over the contents of the letter. 'That's it,' she crushed the page into the pocket of her denim jeans. 'They want me to start right away. I've got to go, Dad. There's something awfully important I've got to see to!'

His concerned gaze rested on her strained young face. 'Where are you going?'

She eyed him with her blank, unseeing stare. 'I'm off for a ride, Dad.'

'But you've only just come in!' Unheeding his puzzled glance, she was hurrying from the room, all her thoughts with Logan. Now that she would be leaving here so soon it was very important that she explain matters to him. She owed him that much! First, though, she would have to find him. He could be working somewhere up in the hills. Or could be he was with Christina at Red Gums. A tide of anguish washed over her. He spent a lot of time with Christina. She tried to push aside the heartache. Yes, she would try Red Gums first of all.

Sally was still tethered where she had left her, and she swung herself up into the saddle. As she rode up a winding track Colin shouted a greeting from sun-dried slopes above. 'Hi, Fleur, where are you bound for?'

She raised a dazed white face. 'Do you know where Logan is right now?'

He shrugged muscular shoulders beneath the thin cotton shirt. 'Search me! He was going to work up at number three block some time today, but I haven't seen him around. What do you want him for?'

But she had ridden on, her set glance taking in

nothing but the track ahead. Presently she had opened and closed a gate and was out on the coast road, stones spinning up from the mare's hooves as she cantered on down the metalled track. Soon Fleur was in sight of the entrance to Red Gums, scarcely aware in the tumult of her thoughts that a newly painted signboard, 'Equestrian Centre' swung from ornamental chains. As she rode on down the cleared, tree-shaded driveway, she noticed on some other level of her mind the changes that had been made to the neglected property. Long lines of dividing fences, jumps already set up and the shining roofs of newly erected stables and outbuildings. Well groomed horses and ponies grazed in paddocks and the old colonial homestead, although not repainted, was no doubt renovated and modernised throughout. It just went to show, she thought hollowly, what could be achieved in a short time with Logan's expertise and no doubt his financial backing as well.

'Looking for me?' A husky voice cut across her bitter thoughts and she glanced up to see Christina approaching her. In work-stained jeans, a white blouse open at the throat revealing a suntanned V, Christina seemed more appealing than ever, but there was no welcome in the starry blue eyes with their spiky black lashes. 'Oh, it's the little girl from Te Haruru! What brings you here?'

The patronising words sparked a hot resentment in Fleur's distraught mind. Why must Christina insist on treating her as a somewhat irritating child? The other girl must know, Logan would have told her, that Fleur happened to be a trained nurse and twenty-one years of age. Just because she happened to be a mere five feet and a bit to Christina's willowy height ... With an effort she bit back the angry words that trembled on her lips, because she knew that to argue the matter would be to stamp her as childlike indeed! Wildly she searched her mind for a suitable explanation for visiting Christina's home, and in her confusion, she gave voice to the last thing she wanted to say. 'I was looking for Logan——'

'Oh yes?' Christina's lovely mouth twisted contemptuously and her glance raked Fleur's vulnerable young face.

'Just to give him a message,' Fleur said hurriedly. 'But it's not really important.'

'I didn't think it would be.' The implication was plain.

'But if he's not about——'

'He's not, actually.' Christina's cool tones were tinged with a long-suffering inflection. Her disparaging glance said quite plainly, You can't help yourself, can you? You just can't keep away from him! The husky voice ran on, 'But if you're so interested I'm expecting him to call at some time today—some business stuff I want him to go through with me. He knows that I'm a total loss when it comes to getting a good deal.' Her tone said, why should I bother myself with boring business problems when Logan's always available to help me out of difficulties with the Centre? 'Shall I tell him you were looking for him?' The cool tones cut deep.

Fleur could feel the pink colour rising in her cheeks. 'It doesn't matter.'

'No, I didn't think you'd want to leave a message for him.' But Fleur had heard enough. Swiftly she pulled on the rein, turning her mount in the driveway, and shot away. As she galloped up the winding coast road the pounding of hooves on the rough metal kept time with her angry thoughts. Damn! Damn! Damn! If only she hadn't gone there today! Now Logan would think— he'd think exactly what Christina had intimated with her cool two-edged glance. That Fleur was so madly in love with him that she couldn't help herself chasing after him, even to Red Gums. She had a swift humiliating mental picture of the other two laughing together, amused at the antics of a silly girl who was too much in love to hide her feelings for her father's partner. The seething thoughts remained with her as she turned into the hill paddocks of Te Haruru and followed a sheep trail up a slope. She was scarcely aware of the sheep that fled from the onslaught of the mare's hooves or the black steers that eyed her progress

with curious velvety brown eyes. With another part of
her mind, however, she must have known where she
was bound for, for all at once she caught sight of
Logan, a lone horseman set against a backdrop of
empty hills. He was quite a distance away and appeared
to be heading off a few sheep moving in the direction of
a winding track up a bush-covered hillside. Acting
instinctively, Fleur prodded Sally to a canter, heading
her mount towards the stragglers. The next moment she
realised that Logan had caught sight of her as his ear-
splitting whistle echoed in her ears. A swift glance over
her shoulder showed him galloping after her, his shouts
of 'Fox! Fox!' carried on the wind.

He's telling me I'm not riding fast enough, she
thought, and dug her heels into the mare's warm flanks.
If he wanted a race with her, he could have it! Crouched
low in the saddle, she was flying over sun-dried grass,
her hair streaming behind her in a copper-coloured
cloud and the air singing in her ears. She had reached
the start of the track when the thudding of hooves
behind her was loud, and the next minute Logan had
caught up with her and the two mounts were galloping
abreast. Then in a swift movement that took her utterly
by surprise he leaned towards her and a strong
muscular arm plucked her from the saddle and placed
her in front of him. The next moment he had pulled his
stockhorse to a violent stop and Sally halted too, the
reins trailing on the ground.

Fleur, breathless, all too aware of the heart-knocking
sheer joy of finding herself caught close to his hard
chest, pushed the damp tendrils of hair from her eyes
and twisted around to gaze up at him. 'Why,' she asked
bewilderedly, 'did you do that?' Vaguely she was aware
of the grey pallor around his mouth.

'You crazy little fool, Fox!' He was grasping her so
tightly she could scarcely breathe. He was all but
shouting at her. 'Didn't you hear me yelling at you?
Why in hell didn't you stop when I told you?'

'I don't know what you're getting so het up about,'
she flung back at him. 'It was only a race! I was looking
for you——'

'A race!' His voice was hoarse with emotion. 'Is that what you thought? Take a look ahead of you,' he blazed, 'there, between those two high trees!'

She could scarcely think straight for the heady rapture of his touch, his arms around her. It was a moment before she could concentrate on what he was saying for the wild excitement pulsing through her senses. Then she saw it. 'Oh God, that fallen telephone wire,' she exclaimed on a horrified breath, 'stretched taut between the trees farther up the track——'

'At just the right height to catch the neck of anyone on horseback tearing straight ahead, unable to stop! I got word of the line being down a while ago and I was on my way to see to it when you came along——' His low tones broke. 'You, Fox, that you should be the one—*you*——' Suddenly his hold around her waist loosened and he dropped to the ground, holding out his arms. 'Come, my darling! This is where you belong!' She made to jump to the grass, but he caught her close before her feet had touched the ground, swinging her round and round in an excess of excitement. 'That's how I feel about you!' At last he set her down, then dropped down on the warm grass at her side. 'Love you . . .' He turned her to face him, raining kisses on her forehead, her small nose, her dust-stained cheeks and, at last, her soft lips. His seeking lips on hers set flames running through her, and the wild sweet happiness of all her improbable dreams took over.

'You're trembling, Fox. You're safe with me, my darling!'

She raised a face, flushed with happiness, from his warm chest. 'It's not fear—it's *you*——'

'That's all I want to know, my love.' His deep exultant laugh filled her ears. 'I've loved you from the start,' he said huskily, 'that day when I picked you up at the airport . . . you must have guessed.'

The long vertical dimple flickered in her cheek. 'How could I when you were so beastly to me? I thought you hated me.'

Very gently Logan traced with his finger the soft line of her lips. His hazel eyes were no longer veiled but deep and intent. 'I had to defend myself somehow against that appealing little face of yours! There was something about you. From that first moment I saw you I couldn't seem to get you out of my mind.' He raised her tanned fingers to his lips. 'And then there was Bart right there in the picture! You seemed to have some kind of loyalty complex about him——'

She nestled close to him. 'Call it pigheadedness! I was on my way to tell you. I don't know how I could have been so blind as not to believe what you told me about him.'

'So long as you believe me now when I say I love you.' Once again he caught her close in his arms, and now his kisses were no longer gentle but urgent and demanding. In the hot sunshine the only sound was a bellbird's chime falling on the clear air, but Fleur, fathoms deep in a newly-found happiness, was unaware of the silvery notes.

At last she drew herself free, looking up at him misty-eyed. 'Logan——'

He cupped her flushed face in lean tanned hands. 'You look lovelier than ever when you've just been kissed!'

There were things that must be said, questions that must be answered. 'Logan, what about Christina? You did seem to think a lot of that woman!'

He grinned, twisting a strand of coppery-coloured hair around his finger. 'Still do. She's quite special, Christina.'

'You—think so?' For the life of her Fleur couldn't keep the betraying wobble from her voice.

'So that's it!' He tilted her small chin and looked into her face. 'That's what you've been holding against me all this time? You got the idea that Christina and I——'

She said very low, 'What else could I think?'

'Guess I can't altogether blame you for getting the wrong idea.' All at once the glint was back in his hazel eyes. 'She means a lot to me, that sister of mine!'

'What—did you say?' She eyed him incredulously. 'Are you telling me——?'

'That's right. Christina's been through a tough time

these past two years, just about went under completely once or twice. Then she got an idea that if she could start a new life in a place where no one had ever heard of her, she could make a go of things, pick up the pieces and get herself straightened out. It was a chance I couldn't afford to miss, not after all that she'd been through, and I was only too glad to go along with the scheme. I needed a larger acreage for sheep and cattle farming anyway, so I bought a share of Te Haruru from your father and I was lucky enough to find land not too far away where Christina could set up her riding school. She had always been a show-jumper in the old days at home, she knew all about dressage, it seemed to be the answer to her problem.'

'So that,' Fleur was still trying to fit the pieces of the puzzle into place, 'was why you wanted her to win the barrel race?'

'Just as a sort of confidence-booster for her.' He sent her a quizzical grin. 'But I didn't count on a top girl rider turning up at the rodeo!'

From the shelter of his arms she glanced up at him, a dimple flickering in her cheek. 'Sorry about that.'

He dropped a kiss on her short nose. 'Don't be. I've got a feeling that Christina is well on the way to recovery already.'

'If only you'd let me in on it, told me who she was!'

Logan shook his head. 'That's just what I couldn't do, my sweet. It was all part of the deal. I gave Christina my solemn promise that I wouldn't let on to anyone at all who she was, although,' his voice deepened, 'I came close to it once or twice. Luckily you took it I was going on about Bart's two-faced trickery and you wouldn't listen.'

She said softly, 'If only I had!' She brought her mind back to the deep masculine voice.

'Fate's handed Christina some fairly hard knocks and she just wasn't there when the luck was being handed out—ever heard of Fiona Page? That was her professional name.'

'But of course!' Fleur looked up at him in amazement. 'The New Zealand fashion model who

became famous overnight! I've seen pictures of her lots
of times in high class fashion magazines, photographs
showing her modelling in salons in Paris and London
and New York. No wonder I had a strange feeling all
the time that I'd seen her before somewhere. Only she
looked different in those pictures——'

'All that was a long while ago. She gave it all away
when she fell in love with a man she met in England, a
no-hoper who went through all the money she made in
the salons and finished up by killing himself in a car
smash. No great loss,' the deep tones were steely,
'except that he happened to have their small boy in the
car at the time and he was killed too in the crash.
Christina had always been a highly strung type and
after that she went completely to pieces. She spent a
year in nerve hospitals overseas, and finally I brought
her back here and managed to talk her into trying out
an entirely different way of life, out in the open air.
And it's working already! She's been frozen into herself
for so long, but up here she's showing all sorts of
emotional reactions——'

Fleur threw him a teasing glance. 'Like being jealous
of me?'

'Great! She's coming around to feeling emotionally
involved with other people. She'll be able to stand on
her own feet from now on, I'm certain of it. Besides,'
his kisses feathered her forehead, her cheeks, her small
chin, 'no one could help liking you, loving you . . .'

A long time afterwards he murmured, 'What was it
you wanted to see me about?'

'Oh, that.' Fleur smiled up into the strong masculine
face she loved. 'It was about Bart. You were right about
him all along. He rang me from Sydney and admitted
the whole thing. To think,' she raised a flushed and
radiant face to his soft deep gaze, 'that I came looking
for you to let you know that I'd be leaving in the
morning to take up a nursing job at a hospital up
North!' She said very low, 'It was the hardest decision I
ever had to make, leaving you. I didn't dream that you
cared——'

'I care.' Logan's deep voice was husky with emotion.

You'll never know how much, my darling. I'll tell you something else,' he murmured against her ear, 'don't you think it's about time the old homestead put on a wedding, a very special wedding?'

'Oh, I do! I do! Just as soon as——' Fleur never completed the words she had been about to say, for Logan's mouth came down on hers in a kiss that sent her world spinning out of orbit, and there was nothing but the sweet and heady rapture of his caress.